Waves Of Recovery

The Life Of An Advocate Of Latino Civil Rights

Maurice Jourdane

To the doctors and nurses who saved my life, the friends and family who gave me no choice but to recover, and the campesinos toiling in the fields to put fruits and vegetables on their family's table.

Contents

Author's Note

"About a year after I was nearly killed in the fields near Delano, I was in the Imperial Valley representing farm workers who had been fired for supporting Cesar Chavez. One of the Union's volunteers asked how I managed to be back trying cases so soon after sustaining serious injuries when I collided with an 80-ton oil rig. With little to do in the evenings in El Centro, I began writing the story that eventually became this book. My goal is to tell how I managed to come back from a trauma, hoping it may help others do the same, whether it is after a serious vehicle collision, a divorce, death of a loved one, or financial disaster.

Some of the names have been changed to protect the right to privacy and the attorney-client privilege. The events presented all occurred. The views expressed are my views as an advocate for farm workers in rural California from 1968 until 1980. I have recently joined California's former governor Jerry Brown in his effort to eliminate the widespread mistreatment of workers.

Because I was unaware of what was going on around me during my recovery much of the time, the book is based in large part on what others told me. Fortunately, my brother saved notes I wrote while hospitalized. The dialog is based on the best of my recollection. Because the events happened a number of years ago, the words are not precisely what was said."

One

Pulling out of the Santa Maria Fairground parking lot at 12:08 AM., I wished I could have stayed. What a fool I am to set up a meeting with a witness early Saturday morning after Diecisčis de Septiembre, I thought.

I drove north a few miles on Highway 101 until taking the off-ramp onto two-lane Highway 166 heading east. During the day, travelers on the remote road carved through golden hills speckled with wind-twisted black oaks. The road gradually climbs through the Los Padres National Forest, skirts California's Coast Range, and suddenly drops into the San Joaquin Valley. The passing landscape remains nearly barren, cacti replacing the oak. Bleak hush-flood-scarred arroyos replacing the gentle valleys. It is the desert. At night it is sheer blackness. With the exception of several flickering bulbs in the desolate area of Coyama, a lonely driver rarely sees a light between Highway 101 and Maricopa. Over the winding road I listened to country music as my thoughts rambled. This Plymouth is a pretty good car. I wonder what Kathy's doing in Kauai right now. Maybe I'll go see her at Christmas. I haven't been to Hawaii for a long time.

Maricopa is 65 miles east of Highway 101, the link between Los Angeles to the South and San Jose and San Francisco to the north, and 19 miles west of highway 99, the link between Los Angeles to the south and Bakersfield, Fresno and Sacramento to the north. From Maricopa to Bakersfield stretches an irrigated desert that yields hundreds of thousands of tons of cotton, carrots, melons, and grapes. Passing through Maricopa. I had a choice, stay on Highway 166 to Highway 99 then north to Bakersfield or go left to Taft and take Bear Mountain Road to Highway 99 then north to Bakersfield. Both are straight and flat. I chose to stay on Highway 166. At 2:20 in the morning, I drove the only vehicle on the road.

My thoughts drifted back to the day before. I started El Dieciséis de Septiembre, Mexico's Independence Day, in the Delano Agricultural Labor Relations Board office reviewing farm workers statements given to board agent Shirley Treviño. While reading, I felt someone's silent presence. I looked up to see Shirley watching me. "Hi, love," she said smiling. "Don't forget we have a meeting at 3:00 with the grape company president. Maybe we can settle the numerous unfair labor-practice charges, but I agree with what he told us a couple days ago, we're wasting our time."

Since Shirley and I had met with the president of one of the world's largest grape growers a few days earlier, the corporation had laid off additional harvesters who supported the United Farm Workers.

*   *   *

A couple miles out of Maricopa, I saw lights approaching the road through the field off to my left. What a weird time for a produce truck to be working, I thought. As the lights neared the highway, they began to accelerate and angle to their left, the direction I was headed. No Panic. I assumed the truck would enter the highway after I passed. Suddenly, I realized my expectation was wrong.

When I grasped that the black oil rig heading directly into my path was not going to stop—before pulling from the dirt access road onto narrow highway 166—instant terror flushed through my veins. I felt like when I was a 17-year old surfer on a calm afternoon at Sunset Beach on Oahu suddenly became horror when a rogue twenty-foot wave abruptly climbed on the horizon outside the take off point where I waited with a handful of other surfers.

Now, fifteen-years later, I instinctively slammed on the brakes. The Plymouth was 201 feet or thirteen car lengths from collision. It was 2:26 AM. Sleep deprivation made my reaction time slower than twelve-hours earlier. Eight-tenths of a second passed

2

before my right boot sole touched the brake pedal. I was five car lengths closer to collision. The side of the black oil rig was 126-feet away. Like a puck sliding down a shuffleboard table in an empty bar, the Plymouth skidded down the isolated desert road. Each tenth-of-a-second, the fully loaded seventy-ton oil rig was nine-feet closer. A half-second after my foot hit the brake pedal, 81 feet or less than six car lengths remained for the beige four-door to stop skidding into annihilation. By the time the Plymouth traveled those 81 feet, the black dinosaur loaded with raw oil was an irresistible and inexorable wall across the road.

Just as there is no way to avoid the shock of a giant-rogue wave that suddenly soars on the horizon, one-hundred-and- twenty-six feet is not far enough to stop a car traveling sixty- two miles an hour. The front end slammed into the oil rig's underside. The Plymouth's frame twisted like a paper clip. Like a church key opening a can of beer, the hood shattered the windshield and pierced the car's interior. Bleeding profusely, I lay unconscious pinned between the twisted steering wheel and the ruptured car seat. No matter how badly I wanted to avoid hitting that truck, I had placed myself in a position where the collision was unavoidable. The questions became, why the oil rig didn't stop before entering the highway, and could I avoid the almost inevitable result.

The rig driver apparently didn't think I could. Expecting the 70 tons of oil he carried to explode, he jumped from the diesel cab and ran down the black desert highway.

Two

I grew up like millions of other kids. What our parents lacked in dollars, they gave in trust and freedom. Since I had freedom, I had choices. Freedom and choices can lead to limitless adventure and pleasure or to misadventure and tragedy. They can also enable a child to develop the self-confidence critical to making it through the wrong choices and inevitable hard times.

I made the first important choice I recall when I was eight years old. We were camping at Lake Arrowhead in the Angeles Crest National Forest, only an hour east of Los Angeles. My younger brother John and I were fishing from shore, wishing we had money to rent a rowboat. After sitting for several hours without a bite, I suggested we go swimming. John reminded me that Mom told us we shouldn't go in the water. Pointing to the light-green muck covering the normally dark water, he said it was too dirty to swim in. I laughed saying it was only moss.

I chose to disregard our mother's admonishment and took a chance. John chose to stay safe on the rock with his fishing line hanging in the water. He has always been the more sensible one. Pulling in his line, John put a fresh ball of Velveeta cheese on his hook and told me to go in if I wanted, but he was going to stay there and catch the big brown trout he knew lived near the big boulder. Half-hour later, I shivered onto the granite rock, trying to dry in the sun. I told John I got out because it smelled bad.

"I told you," John bragged in his I'm-smarter-than-you tone.

The fall semester began a week later. Within a couple days of the start of school, I asked mom if I could stay home because my back hurt.

After examining me, our family doctor sent me to Los Angeles County General Hospital. There, the doctor told my mom; "If you can return at four we can do a spinal tap today."

"Can't it wait a few days. Mom?" I begged in front of the doctor who looked to me like a withered ogre. I probably looked to him like a spoiled brat. "Like maybe Saturday?" I asked. "That way I won't miss school...."

Mom looked at the doctor. "I think we better do it today," the doctor said firmly.

Just after three that afternoon, my parents and I pulled away from our modest Huntington Park home in the family year-old, green, 1950 four-door Plymouth. I sat in the rear seat, alone. Scared, I saw my brothers, my sister, and Everett who was my best friend kneeling on our front lawn. They were praying.

I had polio, the plague of the 1950s.

Not much was feared more. Almost daily in Los Angeles the newspaper reported a story like, "Eleven more Long Beach youths placed in iron lungs, or "Only one in three who has polio will walk again." The radio reported stories like, "Today the Department of Health reports two hundred new polio cases diagnosed this week."

The doctor told my mom and dad that I could spend the rest of my life in an iron lung or crippled, but my mother continued to believe that I would be completely cured if I kept my faith and looked at the good side—not the worst possible side of ordeals we all undergo in life. That night and for the weeks to follow, I was interned in Queen of Angels Hospital.

Each day I underwent the Sister Kenney treatment, an experimental method to alleviate the devastating effect of polio on the muscles. The nuns kept me wrapped in steaming towels, and, when I was awake, kept me constantly moving.

My choice to swim in the cool water at Lake Arrowhead caused me to miss the third grade. Even though I missed school, I learned before I reached my teens that with persistence, hard work, support of my family and friends coupled with faith, a positive view of life and a reason to recover-we may surpass the worst disasters and come out ahead.

When I entered the hospital, I was able to read very little. I can't blame television, since it was a new discovery, and there were no Ninja Turtles to occupy my evenings, but at home I had constantly played games with my brothers and sister. In the Los Angeles hospital I was a lonely eight-year old. It was before the days when parents could stay overnight with their sick children or when children could visit their sick brother or sister at the hospital. Having no one to play with, and no cartoons to watch, I read Huckleberry Finn word by word. Reading was slow and difficult when I entered the hospital, but with persistence and hard work, I soon felt reading was as comfortable as lying in a bathtub of warm water on a cool evening. Before I left the hospital, I was exploring the river and building a raft with Huck and our friend Tom Sawyer. With the hours spent reading, and my imagination running wild at night, the days passed, quickly in retrospect, but very slowly at the time. After I returned home, once a week I met with a home teacher who left lessons, which I completed for her review the following week. Fortunately, my mother was a natural teacher. Between the individual attention given by the home teacher and my mother's support, I returned to school far ahead of my classmates in reading, writing and arithmetic. I had changed from an average second grader into the brightest kid in the fourth grade. From then on, school was easy and I received A's without ever really trying.

Another beneficial consequence of experiencing polio was spending the entire year playing with my three-year old brother, Tom. The confidence that Tom showed in me-as his older brother-silently enabled me to restore my self-assurance. Daily, Tom and I walked to Salt Lake Park where I hit the ball and he chased it. He would chase 1,000 balls in an afternoon. I became a pretty good hitter and Tom became a good runner. Tom and I develop a closeness, which most brothers don't have time to harvest-reassuring me that I would again be a normal kid. Years later, after spending the final years of his teens in Vietnam, like many Vietnam veterans, Tom went through some hard times. I was silently at his side.

Another result of polio was that I had to attend twice-weekly physical therapy. Doctors feared I would suffer permanent muscle damage. What started out as hot towels wrapped around my weakened muscles evolved before long into swimming. When the therapy started, I could barely float on my back and swim a little under water. Before the year was over, through determination and effort, I conquered laps like an age-group competitive swimmer. By the time I reached high school, what I learned in those bi-weekly visits helped me win my high school league championship swimming the individual medley and the butterfly leg of the medley relay. Most important, it meant a ticket to summer jobs lifeguarding, which enabled me to afford college. I learned that with resolve and toil I could accomplish any goal

Finally, pollo turned out to encourage a rewarding change in the way I saw myself. Growing up as one of four children in a lower-middle class home, I did not exude self-confidence when I entered the third grade. Not long after returning to school, I ran home one day and excitedly told my mother, "My teacher told the kids I'm a hero for surviving polio. It's neat." A week later, I came home and proudly told my parents, "The kids elected me president of our class today. Everyone wants to be my friend." For the first time in my life, I was the focus of a spotlight. I learned quickly that doing well at whatever I did meant the spotlight shines. From that time on, I always tried to give 120 percent to be the best at whatever I do. It became a character trait I always pursued.

As a child my parents told me about two great American athletes who won Olympics gold medals, an Oklahoma born Native American Jim Thorpe—- winner of the pentathlon and decathlon in Stockholm in 1912, and Jesse Owens—- an African American from Alabama who won four gold medals in Hitler's Berlin in

1936 in the 200 meters, 400 meters, broad jump and 400-meter relay. Subconsciously, I formed the goal of following in their footsteps and becoming an Olympic athlete. Then came the disease many Americas feared most, polio, but with the goal of one day being an Olympic athlete I came out of it a stronger eight-year-old.

Years later, a collision with an oil rig would test my belief that things will probably get worse if you expect them to, or that you'll recover if you have a positive attitude, work hard, are persistent, have support, and self-confidence. I also learned that to recuperate we have to have something to live for, something more important than just getting better. Through the fear I felt in the general hospital when they stuck a two-inch needle into my spine to learn I had polio; the pain I felt when my weak leg muscles were wrapped in scalding towels; the frustration I felt in my effort to walk again; and the distress I endured swimming the thousands of laps, I had an unyielding resolve to walk and run like a normal youngster. I would never make it to the Olympics, but I would someday ride giant waves at Makaha and Sunset Beach on Oahu's North Shore and run more than 75 marathons through the streets of Honolulu, Los Angeles, San Francisco, San Diego, and many other areas. I learned that even when I make the wrong choice, it is not so bad if I don't give up.

Three

At 3:06 AM., a California Highway Patrol officer pulled up in the dark night behind a car embedded into the side of a black oil rig stretched across the narrow two-lane country road. The front end of the car was a jagged mass of metal; the shattered windshield was flush against the truck's side frame below the oil tanks. The officer raised his flashlight to look into the car's interior. The metal post between the windshield and door thrust through my lace like a spear through a fish head. Blood covered my clothing and what was left of my face. The officer checked for pulse. To his surprise, there was a slight murmur.

An ambulance pulled up.

For several hours, paramedics used a pry bar and a hammer trying to remove me from the demolished car. Unable to force the car doors open, the rescuers sent for an acetylene torch. The officer walked the moonless asphalt to the oil rig driver who had remained down the road, while the paramedics tried to extricate me from the wreckage. The rig driver told the officer that before pulling onto the highway from the dirt access road to the oil tanks, he stopped and looked in both directions.

"You didn't see the headlights before you pulled onto the highway?" the officer asked,

"There weren't no headlights. That's what I'm tellin' you," slurred the rig driver. "That guy was on drugs or plain drunk. He was drivin' with no lights."

The officer looked off into the blackness and thought, a driver couldn't make it fifty feet without headlights tonight.

Several hours after the paramedics began, they were able to free me from the destroyed car, and orderlies wheeled the stretcher on which I laid into a plush Bakersfield's hospital. Seeing my bloody face and shirt, the emergency room resident on duty could have thought to himself. Jesus! They should be taking that guy to a morgue, not to a hospital at 5:40 in the morning when I'm here alone and about to get off my 18-hour shift. The resident probably walked over to the stretcher as a nurse was taking my pulse and asked if the patient was alive, half expecting a negative response.

In any case, the nurse told the resident that I had a pulse. although it was very faint.

For the next three hours, the doctor and two nurses cleaned the extensive lacerations, most likely expecting me, a stranger, to die any second. By 8 AM., hospital staff had scoured my wallet for information on insurance coverage. "We can't afford to do welfare cases," the doctor apparently said when they told him they found nothing. The private hospital transferred me to the County General. By law, it had to treat the destitute.

For the next 36 hours, no one in my family or any of my friends heard I was lying unconscious, teetering on the edge of death at the Kern County General Hospital intensive care unit. Finally, Sunday evening just after five, a hospital orderly contacted Ellen Sward whose phone number he had found in my blood-soaked wallet. Not knowing what to do, Ellen called Byron Georgiou, a graduate of Stanford University and Harvard Law School who had become my close friend over the previous several years. Byron will know what to do, Ellen thought.

Around 4 PM., Hawaii time, the phone rang in Kathy's wooden one-bedroom home in Kapaa, Kauai.

Four

When César Chavez heard about the wreck, he posted a guard at my hospital room door. The union leader was sure it had been no accident. For too long, I had been a pebble in the growers' boot. César knew that because of my reputation as a vigorous advocate to improve farm workers' working conditions, many considered me a Chavista. He did not want me killed in The Bakersfield General Hospital where—he recalled—Dolores Huerta had been fed pesticide-poisoned grapes when she went there to give birth to her daughter. Too many Chavistas had become martyrs.

*   *   *

I first met César Chávez ten years before when I spent the summer working for California Rural Legal Assistance in Delano after my second year of law school. I left the Valley feeling anger and frustration having seen no drinking water or toilets in the field and workers stooped from dawn to dusk with no breaks. I had learned the stooped field laborers worked without complaining because they had families to feed. The agony I felt seeing the poverty of those who put tomatoes and melons on our tables, and the anger I felt seeing field laborers work stooped over in a shadeless 120-degree fields was overcome by contentment. I felt joy sharing laughter and meals with farm worker families. In September, 1967, watching Delano fade behind me filtered through the pesticide dust engulfing the green grape vines, I knew I would be back in the San Joaquin Valley.

I finished law school at the University of California's Hasting College of Law in San Francisco, wrote a law review article on the constitutionality of the exclusion of farm workers from the National Labor Relations Act, and moved to Salinas, 100-miles south of San Francisco, to represent farm workers for California Rural Legal Assistance.

Kathy and I and our friend, former University of California quarterback Terry McDonell, who would go on to become managing editor of Sports Illustrated, bought a cabin on a couple acres in the Aptos redwoods, a community between Watsonville and Santa Cruz. It became our Aptos stronghold. I saw scores of clients daily in Salinas and one evening a week in the Catholic Church parish hall in Soledad 30-miles to the south. In Soledad, I worked with former farm worker Héctor De La Rosa. Héctor and I began our years working together when we represented nine and ten-year old children of farm workers labeled mentally retarded because they scored low on English-administered intelligence tests. We learned that Spanish-speaking children across the state were being labeled mentally retarded because they scored low on the English-administered tests.

We forced school districts from Oregon to Mexico, from the Pacific Ocean to Arizona and Nevada, to stop testing the intelligence of children in a language they did not understand and to remove them from classes for the mentally retarded around 55,000 Spanish-speaking children who had been wrongly labeled mentally retarded, just in California. The case won by the nine brave Soledad children who fought their false label as mentally retarded would become the basis for the federal law Individuals with Disabilities Educational Act, an act that prohibits placing children in classes for the mentally retarded because they score low on IQ tests administered in a language they do not speak, provides for due process before a child can be labeled in need of special education, and requires parental consent before a child is deported from the normal classroom.

During my second summer in Soledad, I met Sebastian Carmona. His sun-worn face made him look far older than his 40 years. He told me of his back injury. He asked me to get rid of the tool that forces him to do stoop labor, the cortito. The cortito is a hoe with a normal size metal blade but an eight-inch wooden handle. A group of Carmona's friends told of their grueling experiences working with the cortito.

At Héctor's insistence I worked stooped over in a sugar beet field
with a short hoe. By eight in the morning, before the sun broke
through the early morning overcast, I was ready to quit. My
lower back ached and my right shoulder throbbed. I had been
there less than two hours and I hurt all over. By nine, the thick-
mustached contractor was yelling at me when I stood upright
rubbing my lower spine, "If you can't keep up you can quit,
lawyer."

I could see the rest of the crew a quarter mile ahead, their bent
bodies briskly moving down the half-mile long rows, thinning
the small green plants. As the sun set just before dark. I walked
wearily from the field. I had survived one long day, but learned
after returning to the office that night that I had to refer
Carmona's case to a private attorney who would seek workers
compensation for Carmona. Hurt that I had to abandon my
dream of stopping growers from callously disabling hundreds of
thousands of farm workers by forcing them to weed and thin
long rows of lettuce and celery with a short-handled hoe, I was
silently content there was no longer a reason for me to spend
another day suffering in the field, raising and lowering a tool
farm workers in the east called El Brazo del Diablo, the Arm of
the Devil.

Not long after my day of stoop labor, César Chávez came to
town. For years the growers had refused to talk with Chávez
even though the workers in the Salinas Valley lettuce fields
wanted his union. After Delano grape growers signed contracts
with Cesar's union, the powerful Teamsters and the Salinas
Valley lettuce growers entered into contracts. Many workers
belonged to César's union and refused to work under a contract
signed by a union that did not represent them. César knew that
the contracts kept his union out of the Salinas fields and that the
workers were losing the benefits he had reaped in Delano after
the international grape boycott. When Chávez refused to turn his
back on the Salinas Valley farm workers and asked America to
boycott lettuce, the Monterey County sheriff's deputies arrested

him. César fasted in jail until just before Christmas when the Supreme Court ordered the labor leader released. After he was free of the jail bars, Chávez asked me to help workers obtain unemployment insurance benefits, workers who were afraid to work in the fields controlled by growers who treated them like slaves and Teamster goons whose only interest in farm workers were their dues. Chávez also asked me to find Sebastian Carmona and get the short-handled hoe outlawed.

Soon, I learned that the agribusiness industry had reason for keeping the workers bent over with their faces in the dust. If you keep control by forcing your workers to bend over, what happens to your control if they stand up? Workers can bend over and do what they're told or they can stand tall. If you're denying your workers decent working conditions, decent pay, toilets in the field, vacations, pensions and time-and-a-half when they work long hours, you'd better have something to keep them in line. "Just like the Southern plantation owners had whips to keep the black slaves in line," Héctor reminded me, "the corporations have short-handled hoes to keep control over their brown-skinned slaves. It's their symbol of power."

For over a year, Héctor and I gathered evidence. We obtained farm workers' sworn statements telling of the pain and permanent disability caused by the short hoe and physicians" statements telling of the physical effect on the body of bending over all day. Finally, we filed a petition to ban the short-handled hoe.

Hearings on the short-handled hoe lasted all summer. In San Diego, a grower pushed me deeper into the farm workers' struggle when he knocked me into a wall. After hearing doctors after doctor testify that using the short- handled hoe causes workers to become permanently crippled, and hearing numerous farm workers tell of the severe pain they suffered bending every day from sunrise to sunset chopping weeds with the short-handled hoe, the Reagan-appointed Industrial Safety Board denied our petition. It felt that the cost to growers of replacing the short- handled hoe outweighed the harm to farm workers.

Several years later, I argued the case before the Supreme Court. Almost five years after I met Sebastian Carmona in Soledad, the Supreme Court decided the short-handle hoe was a harmful tool used by farm workers. Within months, around 300,000 short-handled hoes were no longer used in California's fields.

In retrospect, I could have quit while I was ahead, but instead I moved to California's new Agricultural Labor Relations Board where I was fighting the growers' effort to stop enforcement of a new law that allowed farm workers to join unions like other Americans. Growers across the state were firing workers who supported César Chávez. Seeing the firings as cruel and illegal, I left the central office in Sacramento and went to the Imperial Valley where I joined hot San Jose trial litigator Sam Cohen and his task force stars Shirley Treviño and Carlos Bowker fighting for workers in the field.

By January, 1976, the United Farm Workers was filing an election petition almost every day. When an election was conducted a week after the petition was filed, César's union won. In the middle of the month, the Board's general counsel called to tell me that the agriculture industry was putting on a massive press effort to convince California's public that the Agricultural Labor Relations Board was biased in favor of the United Farm Workers.

"Can't we tell the people the truth? The law merely lets farm workers freely choose for themselves if they want a union. If the farm workers want the United Farm Workers as their union, that union wins the elections. The workers vote in secret in ballot booths and each worker puts their ballot together with all the others in a ballot box. There's no way a worker who marked any ballot can be identified. We're merely doing the job they were hired to do, to enforce the law. To say they're biased in favor of unions is like saying cops are biased in favor of victims."

"The public knows that, Jourdane, but the agribusiness industry has lobbyists scurrying all over this town to tell its story to the legislators. We don't. It has been able to badger enough legislators to get them to cut-off the funds we need to enforce the law."

"How much industry money went into the campaign coffers of the Sacramento Legislators on that one?" I asked.

On February 6, 1976, the Legislature cut-off the Farm Labor Board's money. I called a staff meeting to discuss the uncertain future. "Well, that's it for now. We've run out of money so it's time to go home," sighed a Sacramento field examiner who was happy to return to his wife and baby in the Capitol who he had to leave behind when he was transferred by the Board to the Imperial Valley.

"You should go back to your family, Frank. But I think I have a job to finish here, with or without funds," I responded.

"Jourdane," Frank persisted. "I've been working for the State for years. When the money runs out, we collect unemployment insurance 'til we get another job in a different agency."

"All of you are free to take off if you want," I responded. "I hope some of you stay and help finish the unfair labor practice cases we're working on. I'm a lawyer and the rules of ethics for lawyers require us not to abandon a single case. For you, what you do depends on what you feel is right. If we finish the investigations, when the agency someday reopens, the farm workers won't have lost everything. Their cases can be picked up and taken to trial. Farm workers were fired because they exercised the rights we told them they enjoyed. Can we just abandon them?"

The Imperial Valley staff voted overwhelmingly to finish without pay the cases they had been working on. When the General Counsel in Sacramento learned what we were doing, he sent in the State Police who locked the office and confiscated the files. However, the El Centro Farm Labor Board staff was warned by an anonymous source of the planned police invasion. It rapidly copied the files and took the copies to Carlos Bowker's home in Heber.

The Farm Labor Board employees who had been living in motels while paid moved into a labor camp run by a friend of Bowker in Brawley. We slept there free and used the common kitchen.

*   *   *

By midnight on the Sunday after my wreck, farm workers began arriving at the hospital. Shortly after noon on Monday, my parents pulled into the hospital parking lot, which was packed with farm workers. The waiting room was full of family members or friends of injured or sick patients. Almost all were Mexican or African American. It didn't surprise my parents that this was where he would find me.

At the end of the gray hallway, a bulky Latino guard outside the intensive care unit doorway asked for the visitors' identification. A gray-haired doctor walked up. "Good morning, or I guess it's afternoon now. Can I help you?"

"We're Maurice Jourdane's family," indicated my older sister Barbara Jean. "We're here to see him."

After my family had donned lime-green gowns, the hospital required intensive-care-unit visitors to wear— the doctor asked them to have the nurse page him before they left. He wanted to talk with them.

After several unsuccessful tries to awaken me, the three walked from the intensive care ward. Tom went outside to get our mom who waited outside the hospital, unwilling or unable to see her son so destroyed.

Ten minutes later. Mom, and Tom slowly walked into the doctor's office.

The lanky doctor introduced himself. "I wanted to talk with the four of you here because I think you'd rather be alone after you hear what I have to say."

"Go for it," said Tom bravely, "We're tough." Tom later admitted that at the moment none of my family looked very tough.

"Your son, Mr. and Mrs. Jourdane, has several fractures in the frontal portion of his cranium and many in the zygomatic bones and mandible."

"That means he has breaks in his forehead, checks and jaw, right doctor?" asked Barbara Jean.

"Yes," continued the doctor, appearing mildly bothered by an inquisitive young lady interrupting him. Simplifying his words so they would all understand, he continued. "The numerous gashes on his face, from his forehead to his chin, have been closed with hundreds of stitches. However, he has far more serious problems. The right orbit, pardon me, eyeball, is punctured and has to be removed. The left is lacerated and may have to be removed as well. Most of the patient's teeth are broken or were knocked out. The nasal area is depressed. The nasal passage is very constricted. He is alive now and if he survives he will need a tracheotomy."

"What's a tracheotomy?" Barbara Jean asked in a fearful voice.

"A tube will be inserted into the patient's trachea or windpipe, to enable oxygen to travel to his lungs...."

"In lay language, doctor, you will have to cut his throat, right?" asked Barbara Jean bitterly.

"I guess you could put it that way, if you must," the doctor replied, sighing in growing displeasure with the interruptions. "In any case," he continued, "because he is still comatose, we can't estimate brain damage, but given the severe injuries, it's serious."

"So brain damage is likely," mused Tom.

"The brain is protected by a skull. Your brother's skull is broken apart. Blood may have invaded most of the cranium bringing the patient close to brain death."

"It sounds serious, doctor?" said Tom, his usually strong voice now breaking.

"Is it serious when an egg shell breaks?" The four starred. Tears trickled down Mom's cheek.

"The brain has four primary functions, "continued the doctor after handing Mom a Kleenex. "It controls movement-walking, talking, things like that. It controls senses-sight, hearing, touch, smell, and feeling. It remembers things, and finally, it enables us to reason and inspires creative thought. Right now, the patient's brain injury causes him to be unable to perform any of those four tasks. With time, we may find out how many, if any, he is able to handle, but speculating on that is a waste of our time today."

"You don't expect him to live, do you, Doctor?" asked Dad.

"Your son, Mr. Jourdane, is in very serious condition. Traveling about 60-miles an hour, his head hit unyielding metal on the oilrig. . If he survives he will no doubt have severe brain damage,"

"Doctor, you can't be so sure," interrupted my older sister, who cared for, fought for and baby-sat me for years. "You don't know that guy lying in there like I do. My brother has gone through a lot in his life that most people don't make it through. If it was his time to die, he'd be dead now."

"You're a loving sister. Is it Barbara?" asked the gentle doctor.

"Barbara Jean."

"It's surprising your brother has lived this long. If he doesn't die today, he will tomorrow or the next day. If somehow he makes it to the weekend, he'll die of an infection. If by some miracle he lives through the injuries and survives an infection, he'll be a vegetable the rest of his life."

"We'll see, doctor. I know my brother a little better than you do. He might have suffered some brain damage. You might know more about that than me. The important thing is he's alive. Just don't blow that. I'll thank you when I walk out of this hospital with Mo at my side."

Angrily, Barbara Jean stood and stormed out.

Five

While Tom and Mom slowly shuffled toward the hospital entrance and slowly descended the hospital steps, Carlos Bowker and Shirley Treviño talked with Dad and Barbara Jean.

I had become a friend of Carlos and Shirley two years earlier after I moved from the Agricultural Labor Relations Board's central office in Sacramento to the Imperial Valley. Each morning at 4 AM., the three of us were at the border passing out leaflets stating the new rights guaranteed by the Agricultural Labor Relations Act to thousands of farm workers crossing from Mexicali to board company buses to carry them to California's fields. Many mornings by seven, Shirley, Carlos, and I were in a field conducting an election to enable the farm workers to decide secretly whether they wanted a union and if so whether it was the Teamsters or United Farm Workers.

*　　　*　　　*

On my first morning in the Imperial Valley during the fall of 1975, I pulled into the parking lot beside the farm labor board office, a rundown one-story building on a bleak side street in the desert town. When I walked into the office, I heard a strongly accented male voice behind me, "Ey Ese (Hey, man). What you doing in the valle (valley)?"

I turned. The light-complected Mexican who approached with a broad grin across his face, his hand outstretched was Carlos Bowker. "I heard you was coming to help us out. A lot of shit's been coming down here. The UFW and the Teamsters are preparing for battle. The cops do whatever the growers say."

Like so many of the farm workers I was committed to join in their struggle to improve life, Carlos Bowker was born in the pueblo in central Mexico. When he was four-years old, his mother left for the United States to earn money so her family could survive in an area of Mexico where there were no jobs available for a twenty-five-year old single mother. Carlos remained with his grandmother in a tiny home in the less-than-1000 population village. He longed for his mother, but cherished his grandmother and did well in school.

When Carlos was eleven, his mother married and Carlos moved to live with her and his new stepfather in El Centro, California, ten miles north of Mexicali and the border. He spoke only Spanish and had no immigration papers.

Not understanding the language all his teachers spoke, and having no one at home to help him with homework, Carlos immediately fell behind the other students in his classes. Year by year, while Carlos was learning English, the academic gap between him and his classmates grew. In junior high, he began getting in fights, mostly with White classmates who made fun of his strong Spanish accent and the burritos instead of sandwiches he carried to school in his lunch bag. After he reached high school, his teachers who were frustrated with their inability to teach him, subjected Carlos to an intelligence test in a language he did not understand, and announced they had found the problem. Carlos was declared mentally retarded. Carlos dropped out of school.

When summer came, 16-year old Carlos and his buddy Tiger headed north to find work in the fields. They arrived in Firebaugh about 45 miles west of Fresno, and began cutting lettuce. He and Tiger moved into a concrete labor camp, joined eight other lettuce cutters in a sleeping dorm, and ate meals in the large communal dining area. When the harvest was over in Firebaugh, Carlos and Tiger moved into a similar camp in nearby Mendota, the sleeping dorm was like an oven and many of the workers spent the night gambling. This led to fights and stabbings. Having to be in the field before dawn but unable to get the sleep he so desperately needed to carry him through the day stooped in the lettuce rows wielding his lettuce knife, Carlos moved from the dorms into his Volkswagen bus parked outside.

He continued to eat his meals with the workers in the common dining facility, but slept in the bus.

Many Friday nights, after the workers were paid they would line up to pay $5 each to visit a White prostitute imported from Fresno who would take on 30 or 40 sexually hungry farm laborers in a single night. Having left their loved ones behind in the Imperial Valley, Carlos and Tiger did not join the line.

The summer before Carlos turned nineteen, he was in Calexico playing pool one evening with a companion Joe Rodríguez. Rodriguez told Carlos about beginning to work for a program under President Johnson's War on Poverty. Rodriguez convinced Carlos to take the lettuce season off and attend Imperial Valley College. Carlos did and soon found himself living in San Diego attending San Diego State University. He was active in MECHA and decided to return to the Imperial Valley and work for California Rural Legal Assistance.

One day in 1973 when I was in San Diego for a hearing in our effort to ban the short-handled hoe, Carlos arrived with a busload of Imperial Valley farm workers who told the board about the horror of stooping all summer rhythmically raising and lowering a cortito in the 105 degree Imperial Valley heat. Within a couple years of that San Diego hearing, after I had begun working for the Agricultural Labor Relations Board in Sacramento, Carlos called from the Imperial Valley. He had heard about the new board and wanted to start with it as a field examiner. I told him I would call him back.

Several days later, after I failed to return Carlos's call, he took off for Salinas. He called me from a pay phone after he arrived in the town over 500 miles northwest of the Imperial Valley. I told him to stay where he was while I checked on the possibility of him obtaining a job with the farm labor board. Half-hour later, I returned his call. "Go to the new farm labor board office in the shopping center at Main und Laurel. Ask for Paula," I told him. When the Agricultural Labor Relations Board opened in August,

1975, the General Counsel hired experienced National Labor Relations Board agents, but none spoke Spanish. Since the only language spoken by almost all farm workers is Spanish, we desperately needed bilingual agents. Carlos's persistence to reach a goal paid off.

While Carlos and I talked at the Agricultural Labor Relations Board office in late October, 1975, a slender Latina walked through the door to a back room. Carlos introduced me to Shirley Treviño. Shirley, whose straight black hair hung to her lower back, had grown up in Bakersfield, attended the University of Santa Clara, and was a paralegal for San Jose's Legal Aid when recruited to come to the Imperial Valley. Each night throughout that winter, I joined Carlos and Shirley at the Agricultural Labor Relations Board office printing leaflets to advise farm workers of the rights guaranteed by the new farm labor law.

*   *   *

On that hot September afternoon in Bakersfield almost two years later, Dad asked why all the people were gathered on the lawn.

"It's a vigil for your son, Mr. Jourdane," replied Shirley.

"All these people knew Mo?" Dad asked.

"Not long after your son came to this area, the word was out the cortito lawyer was here working with the Labor Board, Mo went to homes and labor camps telling farm workers about the new farm labor law and how it would protect them if they wanted to join a union. He stood up to the companies they work for when they were fired because they supported the union."

"I'd like to thank them for being here to pray for my son," said Mom, joining my father.

"Every one of them would love to meet you," said Shirley.

Seeing a makeshift altar, Dad remarked on the strong influence the church has in Mexico. "We'll be in church tonight praying for Mo," Shirley said, "and we'll be there every night until he's better."

Dad, Mom, Tom and Barbara Jean, each lost in thought, melded into the dark-haired men, women, und children on the grass.

Seeing all the people praying. Dad walked silently. How ironic, he thought. I tried so hard to get that kid to go to church, to be a good Catholic, I saw myself as a failure when he and his brothers quit going to mass, choosing to surf instead. I guess even though we failed in getting him to attend mass, we did something right. All these people are praying for him. Who would have believed someone who chose the ocean over the church would get a sea of people out to pray? He'd better make it or a whole lot of people will think prayers don't help. If he does make it, I hope each one of these people knows their prayers made the difference.

I know he'll make it, thought my mother. He always does. It seems like his whole life I've been worried about him recovering from something. When he was a child he never missed school, except when he had polio. But he's the worst of all the kids when it comes to getting hurt. A hundred times I've told him to be careful, not to be such a risk-taker. And when he does go down, he goes down hard. But he always gets up like nothing happened. Mo has always known he has too much to live for to let anything get in his way, even an oil truck.

Tom was thinking, I wish Mo would hurry up and get better so we can get out of this desert and go surfing.

While my family stood lost in thought on the hot September afternoon, Shirley approached my mother accompanied by an older man and a young woman. "Mrs. Jourdane, this is Maria Hernández and her father Tomás. They'd like to meet you."

"Buenas tardes." Mom said, smiling as she wished the Hernández father and daughter good afternoon in her fluent Spanish with a strong American accent. Mom had spent a year in South America learning to speak the home language of the children she taught at an East Los Angeles junior high. In Bakersfield, her face lifted from sadness to pride as she spoke the language of those who wished to meet her.

"Buenas tardes, Senora," replied María, the teenage grape picker.

"Do you live nearby?" Mom asked.

"We live in a small house in Arvin," replied 90-pound Maria "You know Arvin?"

"I haven't been there, but Mo has talked about it." Mom smiled. "He has many friends there. Arvin isn't far, is it?" she asked.

"About 10 miles over there," replied the black-haired youth in Spanish, pointing to the east. "It is not far. This summer your son helped my father and I get our jobs back at Tejón Ranch after it fired us for supporting César Chávez."

Maria paused, took a deep breath, and continued. "Señor Jourdane came to our home and took dinner with us. We do not have a lot of money but my mother she cooks very good. We were proud when your son came."

Again Maria paused. Again she took a deep breath, her voice breaking. She continued.

"I never thanked Señor Jourdane. Will you thank him for me when he is better?"

"Claro," responded Mom. "I'm glad my son could help you"

Tears flowed from Maria's almond eyes.

Around four that afternoon, Mom and Dad were still among the massed farm workers outside the hospital when John and his lithe Polynesian wife, Muffett, pulled into the Bakersfield hospital parking lot. Flying Pan Am from Honolulu to San Francisco, they drove a rented Toyota Corolla for the next five hours through the stifling valley heat.

The word having spread that Cesar Chávez was convinced that my collision with the oil tanker could not have been an accident, the guard at the intensive-care unit door was suspicious of every huero (white person) who wanted to enter the ward. He was ready to ask John for identification when he heard his voice. The guard and I had spoken many times over the previous several years. The familiarity in John's voice struck him. He found the list of family members Tom had given him that morning. "What'd you say your name was?" he asked.

John and Muffett entered the antiseptic-reeking room. In the darkness John discerned Barbara and Tom. If John hadn't surmised who was in the bed, he wouldn't have recognized me.

"Hi, Tom. Hi, Barb," he said softly. "Why am I whispering? The best thing we could do is shout and wake him up. "MO," he yelled, "WAKE UP." I didn't respond. "He still hasn't changed; always wants to sleep," John said, trying desperately to raise the spirits of those in the room.

"He's always been shy in front of groups," Barbara said, feeling slightly uplifted with John there.

"Knowing Mo, I know he's pretending to be asleep, "kidded John. "He did that all the time on the top bunk when we were kids and I tried to talk story with him from the lower bunk."

Six

The phone in Kathy's Kapaa cottage rang once, twice, three times, four, five. Byron was about to set the receiver down when an out of breath female voice answered. "This is Kathy."

"Hi, Kathy, I don't know if you know who I am. I'm Byron Georgiou, I work with Mo in California."

"Hi. What's happening?"

"I'm sorry to bother you, but Mo was in a wreck…"

"He….what?"

"He was in a wreck yesterday early morning. The hospital didn't have the number of anyone in his family so to make a long story short, I got involved..."

"Is he all right?"

"I'm not sure. He's in a coma…"

"God. What should I do? I'll come over. I have to get a flight. Where is he?"

*   *   *

The end of spring semester my junior year of college more than a dozen years earlier. I was at a college street party celebrating no more finals. I noticed a slender brunette in a short white blouse and faded cut-off Levi's sparkle among friends. She looked my way.

I smiled.

She smiled back.

Although I grew up around my older sister and all her friends, and had female friends most of my life, I was still shy around strange girls. I walked to the beer keg on the curb in the driveway of the SAE fraternity house, tilted a paper cup mostly with foam, took a deep breath—hoping it would make me courageous—and walked toward the girl who had captured my emotions, as "Surfin' USA" blasted from the stereo speaker on the fraternity house porch.

"Hi," I said.

"Hi," she responded in her friendly manner.

"Wanna dance?"

"Sure"

Two minutes later, the Beach Boys had finished telling the world what was happening all-over-La-Jolla and down Doheny way. The girl with gray-blue eyes and I walked slowly back to the curb.

"I'm Mo Jourdane. I don't think we've met."

"I'm Kathy Flynn. They call me Flynn. Glad to meet you, Mo Jourdane."

Flynn smiled, extending her hand. I gently held the long slender fingers. "This is about to end. Wanna go get something to eat?" I asked, my heart skipping like a high-speed printing press.

"I'm leaving for Fresno. Maybe, I'll see you when I get back."

One late June evening, ten days later, my surfing buddy Terry McDonell and I sat on the red porch steps of the Surfrider, our dirty-white, wood-frame home surrounded by modem fraternity and sorority houses. Flynn crossed Eleventh Street and waved. Climbing the Surfrider's steps, her rough-out cowboy boots thundered through the wooden porch. She nodded to McDonell, who she did not know, and asked if I still wanted to go out, as she accepted a bottle of Millers and the opener from McDonell.

Raising the brown bottle to her full lips, Flynn apparently noticed the surf boards lying on the porch. She glanced at me and nodded, smiling. "Figures. 'Wanta' go to Gilroy?" she asked

"Gilroy? What for? There are no waves in Gilroy."

"There's a corral. On Friday nights they have a bull-riding contest. Everyone puts in ten bucks. They put all the money in a pot and it goes to the rider who scores the highest. You ride and they grade those who stay on for eight seconds."

"You ride bulls?" I asked eagerly, imagining the lithe cowgirl on the back of a powerful Black Angus.

"No way. I barrel race. I figure if you can ride waves, you can ride a little bull. I'm just going along to cheer you on."

"Yeah, right! I'm going to ride a bull. Flynn, you're from the country, not me. I'm from the heart of LA. The only bulls I ever saw were the few brave ones that escaped from the stockyards in Vernon—on their way to becoming hamburgers—which ran through Huntington Park's pepper tree lined streets chased by urban cowboys. I ain't riding no bull."

An hour later Flynn, Terry, and I pulled onto a dirt road in Gilroy—a cluster of farms 300 miles south of San Jose. McDonell parked his aging MG convertible amidst dusty old pick-up trucks owned by the rodeo regulars. When Flynn offered to put up my $10 entry fee, being four beers less sober than when I arrived! laughed. "I will if McDonell will. All we can do is die. We can try anything, once."

After half-hour sitting on the corral fence, carefully watching the other riders, I swung my Levi clad legs into the chute, lowered slowly onto the bull's hindquarter and carefully tightened around my fist the rope encircling the bull's underside. Flynn and Terry stood on the lower rail of the fence across the corral. "I can't believe I got him to do it," Flynn giggled. "Does he know what he's doing?"

Terry chuckled. "No. You're seeing the real Mo Jourdane. He makes a choice to do something, and he does it. He thinks he can do anything."

Flynn chuckled, "He doesn't have any idea what he's getting into."

Before the gate swung open, the bull jerked violently into the railing. My hand slipped from the rope around the bull's midsection and I fell to the dirt inside the narrow chute. Just as the bull's metal-hard hoofs beneath its two thousand pounds kicked, apparently hoping to crush my skull, I grabbed for the railing. The fingers of my left hand touched but slipped from the weathered oak.

Luckily, my left hand caught a wire hanging across the chute gate. My frayed tennis shoe caught the railing. I managed to scramble out of the chute. When I climbed back onto the bull, a real bull rider leaned over the railing and showed me how to wrap my right hand firmly under the rope that tightly girdled the bull. With a Texas drawl the older wrangler told me I could only use one hand, but as long as I held on tight and leaned forward on the animal, I could stay on his back. I took a deep breath in uncertain anticipation waiting for the buzzer to sound. I was certain my self confidence would enable me to conquer the brutal black beast. Suddenly, the chute gate swung open. The black bull dropped its head, horns like scimitars ready to sink into my diaphragm, snapped to the right, raised its head abruptly, spun left, and my 130-pound body was on the ground.

I rode for four seconds. The bull's right rear hoof missed my naked left ear by inches. Self confidence did not enable me to stay on the bull's back until the buzzer sounded.

On the ride back to San Jose, Terry was bragging. He had stayed on the bull two seconds longer than me.

*   *   *

That fall, Flynn and I were having a coke in the school cafeteria when one of her friends joined us. She told Flynn the school was laying off one of the few women professors on campus.

"What do you expect?" Kathy sneered angrily. "This fucking school is no different than the rest of the country. A woman's place is in the home changing baby diapers. Let the men be the legislators, professors, run the corporations, the doctors and dentists; everything except housekeepers, maids, secretaries and elementary school teachers."

Having never been the victim of racial or sex discrimination, I couldn't understand Kathy's concern over a professor being laid off. She stared in disbelief at my naiveté when I said, "Probably, there are not enough students to keep all the teachers we have."

Flynn patiently began to explain life in America from a woman's perspective, I listened and learned.

The next day, I discovered more about the woman who was embezzling my heart. While walking with Flynn to her Greek-Philosopher's class, a scraggly long-haired youth handed me a leaflet. I read aloud the large red print, "GET OUT OF VIETNAM NOW."

Flynn looked at the young anti-war activists and said calmly "Right on, Brother." She turned to me and continued, "We met last night and decided to pass out those leaflets today. "Wanna help me. I have to be here at two."

I came from a family of veterans that stretched from a brother in Vietnam back to a drummer boy in the Revolutionary War. I rose for the Star-Spangled Banner and held my hand over my heart when reciting the Pledge of Allegiance, but I was with Flynn at two, while she handed out leaflets.

Throughout the fall, Kathy and I were almost inseparable; studying, eating, playing, and laughing together. She taught me about women and questioned why the United States was fighting a war on the other side of the world. She understood why we fought the Nazis in Europe in World War II, even though Hitler's storm troopers killed her father, but she would never understand why young Americans were dying in another country's civil war in a Southeast Asia jungle. Every weekend, she went with me to Santa Cruz surfing, and by Thanksgiving, I was sharing turkey with her family in Fresno.

In January, Flynn and I and my surfboard went to Mexico. We drove her Impala to Mexicali where we caught the ancient Mexican train to Mazatlan. For thirty-six hours we bounced with Mexico's underclass on wooden seats. Somewhere, between Hermosillo and Guaymas Bay, the train stopped at a trail crossing the desert to an arid pueblo. A lone Indian wandered off and the train started to move, again.

When the locomotive stopped several hours later in Obregon, I heard Flynn talk with a Mexican child selling oranges at the train window. I remarked that I didn't know she spoke Spanish so well.

She reminded me that previous Thanksgiving I had learned that her step-father's family were growers. "They hire lots of workers from Mexico," she said, "especially in the summer. Every season since I was little, I packed peaches where almost everyone spoke only Spanish."

When we arrived in Mazatlan, Flynn and I moved into a rusty teardrop trailer in a run-down mobile home park on the beach just north of town. That night I learned that Flynn was a woman I hardly knew. She was not only a warrior fighting for women's equality and a nonviolent world, but she was not afraid to move around in our tiny trailer in her bikini panties, with her inviting small breasts.

For two days Flynn lay on the beach while I surfed. By the third day she told me she was bored. She suggested we hitchhike to Guadalajara.

The next morning at six, after leaving my surfboard with the manager of the mobile home park, Flynn and I stood alongside Highway 2, space just south of Mazatlan. After thinking an hour seemed like three, I felt elated when I saw a 1949 Chevy stop "A dónde va?" I asked the driver.

"A Guadalajara."

"Super," I cried. Flynn and I jumped into the rear seat.

Four-hours later, the sputtering Chevy approached Tepic. In the hills just outside the pueblo, it stopped running. With the old sedan blocking the narrow two-lane road through the jungle, the driver and I tried to blow debris out of the carburetor filter. Kathy sat shaded by an over-grown banana tree reading John Bamford Parkes A History al Mexico. Finally the old car started and sputtered its way into town.

After talking with the first mechanic we encountered, the driver returned to the car. Leaning through the driver's side window, he told Flynn and me. "I'm sorry but we can go no further today. Carburetor needs a part. I have to go back to Mazatlan on bus tomorrow to buy."

"How far is Guadalajara?" asked Flynn.

"Four hours," responded the driver dejectedly.

Flynn and I grabbed our bags and walked a couple miles through the steaming rain forest to a small, run-down bus station. "Late tomorrow," responded the elderly clerk when Flynn asked when a bus was leaving for Guadalajara. "The only bus leaving town today is not a real bus. There is a truck going to Puerto Vallarta, tonight."

Kathy turned and asked, "Wanna go to the beach?"

"Why not?"

At six that evening we climbed into the back of a diesel flatbed. A canvas tent covered wooden benches. Not long before dark we began the eleven-hour 120-mile ride to Puerto Vallarta. All night through dense cocoa trees, the old ton-and-a-half truck wove on a one-lane dirt road; wild banana tree leaves erasing the thick dust from its fenders.

Around midnight my head rested on Kathy's shoulder; my eyes were closed. "Are you awake?" she whispered.

"Uh, huh! Every time I start to fall asleep we hit a bump and I'm jolted back to life. I wish we were there."

"I was just thinking about our future. What are you gonna do with your life?"

"Lifeguard and surf." I managed to grin, raising my head and rubbing my eyes and forehead.

"Come on," said Kathy, looking serious. "I mean really do. Like a career. You know. I might want to hang with you if you make the right choice"

"Is that a proposal?"

"No! First tell me what you're going to do when you grow up. Then, I might think about proposing."

"What if I told you I've been thinking about going to law school?"

"I'd rather see you fighting for clients here at home than killing children in a far away jungle. What goes through a 17 year old American's mind as he pulls the trigger to kill someone he's never seen before?"

At a loss for words, I sat silently, Kathy brushed her soft lips to mine.

When we managed to part, I fixed my eyes on hers and confessed, "Kath, the problem is I'm not willing to give up surfing for law school and end up having to live away from the ocean somewhere representing clients."

"Well, think about it, Jourdane. I don't much like lawyers, but I would attend court to watch you fight for justice for poor people who are getting screwed over by a greedy collection agency or denied a home by a racist landlord. But if surfing is more important to you than fighting for the poor, well that's up to you."

We fell asleep, our lips together.

Seven

The morning my family and friends arrived in Bakersfield, 3,000 miles to the west, storm clouds blocked the sunrise. Kathy left her Kapaa cottage. Carol was driving her to the airport in Lihue. Kathy's Aloha Air flight to Honolulu was scheduled to depart at 6:40. "This is the earliest I've been up since we moved here," confessed Kathy.

"I know." The small Italian grinned, concentrating through heavy rain on the narrow sugar-cane-framed road.

Half-hour later, they stood in the drizzle at the Lihue terminal. "I thought you were kidding when I got home last night and you said you were going to the mainland," said Carol.

"I never thought about not going," replied Kathy, trying to smile. "When Mo's friend called and told me about the wreck, I knew I had to be there."

Fifty minutes later, as Kathy finished her third cup of coffee, she heard the pilot of the eight-passenger plane announce. "We'll be down in five minutes. I apologize for the bouncy ride, Aloha Airlines hopes to see you again. Mahalo!"

While waiting in Honolulu for her 9:30 flight to San Francisco, Kathy bought the latest copy of Esquire, unaware that her friend Terry McDonell was about to become its editor on his path to Sports Illustrated, a copy of Vogue, and wished she could have had a couple hours more sleep.

During her flight over the Pacific, she thought about her arrival in Bakersfield that lay ahead. I know Mo's family will be like my own. But what if they're angry because we split up? Do they have any idea what happened? And what about Mo's friends?

*　　　*　　　*

Kathy pulled into the hospital parking lot shortly before sunset. She slid out of her rented green Pinto not knowing what to expect. I might be dead. She walked toward the hospital entrance. Suddenly she heard someone calling. She turned. She ran toward Tom.

After Tom had returned from Vietnam seven-years earlier he moved into the barn on our Aptos three acres. For several years, while I was fighting for farm workers, Kathy and Tom maintained the property. Together, they planted, irrigated and harvested vegetables. They drank coffee and talked about everything from why a 17-year-old goes to war in Asia to who would win the World Series. Now, after Kathy had been gone for two years, it was like she saw him last weekend. It was like she had never left. The two embraced. "Is he all right, Tom?" She whispered.

Tom sadly shook his head. "It was bound to happen, Kathy. If not in a car in the Kem County fields, on a surfboard in Hawaii, on skis at Heavenly Valley, or riding a motorcycle through the ocean breeze on the narrow road between Carmel and Big Sur. He's always lived very close to the edge."

"I think all of the Jourdanes do," Kathy said weakly, "How is he?"

Pretty banged up. He's still unconscious. We can go see him, but let me warn ya, it's pretty bad."

"I'd suggest we go get some wine first to make it easier," Kathy half-seriously, "but I might as well face the hard part first, then we can go get some wine." She took Tom's hand and walked toward the hospital entrance.

Eight

Walking to the hospital entrance, Kathy and Tom passed a group of Chicanas sitting silently on the grass; Kathy felt the stares of distrust. After she and Tom entered the hospital, the Latinas were no longer silent. "Who's the chick Tom's with?" asked Norma.

Angie, Norma's friend, shrugged her shoulders.

"I bet she's Mo's ex who lives in Hawaii," Norma said casually running her fingers through her short black hair. "I wonder what she's doing here."

"Who knows," said Angie, a valley homegirl with whom I had become a friend that summer. "I wondered what she looked like. Mo told me about her one time. He said they split up and she took off for Hawaii because he spent too much time away from home fighting farm workers' problems. It surprises me she'd come back now. We'll see how long she stays around. Bakersfield isn't Waikiki. I thought she'd look different. Mo said she was a grower's kid from Fresno or some place, so I guess I thought she'd be blond and whiter."

Norma chuckled. "She's so dark that she looks like one of us. No wonder Mo hung with her."

As Tom and Kathy approached the intensive care unit, Chicanas on the grass outside were rolling in laughter. Walking down the hall, Tom whispered, "There's a guy at the door protecting Mo. He controls who gets in."

A guard at his door concerned Kathy. Same old shit, she thought. His life is still in danger. I hope his commitment to improving the life of farm workers turns out to be worth it. Before she commented, Tom was talking with the guard. "This is Kathy. She's okay."

"I'm Pancho Sánchez. Mucho gusto (much pleasure)." The guard stared admiringly at the slender brunette standing before him.

Kathy and Tom entered the darkened room. Like those before her, Kathy tried to awaken me, to get me to acknowledge her being there. I didn't. Like a lover or small child's mother, she carefully traced my cut face with her soft finger. She tried to remain calm but suddenly broke into tears. Tom put an arm around her shoulder as they walked away from the ominously silent room into the hallway. When the Chicanas saw the stranger walk from the hospital entrance crying while held by Tom, they felt sadness for the sobbing-dark woman, whoever she was.

While Kathy und Tom crossed the grass, she began to tell him why she left Aptos. He interrupted her. "Kathy. You don't have to explain anything to me. I was surprised when it happened, because I'd seen you and Mo together for so long. I asked Mo about it once while we were surfing at Pleasure Point, but he just took off on a wave. He wasn't going to tell me nothing."

When my family saw Kathy in Bakersfield that Monday afternoon, each felt inner warmth. The expression of love caused Kathy to flash back on the morning she decided to leave Santa Cruz. Kathy awoke to whimpering outside the door. She raised her head from the soft pillow on the king-size bed in our dark redwood bedroom. She lay silently, listening as the ivy rustled against the window. She heard the whimpering again. It wasn't the ivy. She wasn't dreaming.

She jumped from bed and ran to the front door wearing only the bikini panties she slept in. She glanced at the clock hanging on the kitchen wall. It was 9:23 AM. I had left for the office three hours earlier. Pulling the front door open, she screamed. Lying in the dust at her feet was our six-year-old brown and white dog, Timber, his white chest covered with fresh oozing blood. It streamed into a pool beneath him. Rushing through the open door, she bent down and cradled his head. The phone rang. She frantically ran back into the living room and picked up the receiver. Staring in fear through the open front door at her dying companion, she whispered, "Hello."

"Is the lawyer there?" mumbled an unseen voice into Kathy's ear.

Who is this?

"Is Jourdane there?"

"Who is this?"

"Listen bitch. This ain't 20 questions. I wanna talk to Jourdane."

"He's at work. Who is this?"

"When he gets home, you tell your old man if he don't back off, you're next." The phone went dead.

Kathy stood as motionless as the table lamp. Finally, she forced her hand to dial my office.

"Rural Legal Assistance," answered Angie when Kathy finally got through after she shakily misdialed twice.

"Hi Angie," she managed to say coherently. "Is Mo there?"

"He's in court, Kathy. Would you like me to have him call you when he gets back?"

After telling Angie yes, Kathy hung up and ran outside. She kneeled beside Timber touching his blood soaked chest. She could feel breathing. Thank God, she thought. He's still alive. I have to get him to the vet. She ran to the bedroom, slid into sweatshirt and Levis and managed to lift her 60-pound dog into her Firebird. Moments later, she was speeding alongside Aptos Creek as it slowly meandered down the hill to the ocean. "Do you know how it happened?" the veterinarian asked after doing surgery on the sedated sheep dog.

"No. I just heard him outside and then found him lying there."

"Well, I can't say for certain but it looks like someone slashed him open with a butcher knife. He has a three-inch-long wound that's over an inch deep. He's lucky to be alive. The weapon missed his heart and lungs or you'd have a dead dog in there."

Ten minutes later, Kathy pulled in behind the Triad, a small clothing store on Pacific mall in downtown Santa Cruz. When she saw her partner, Carol, the woman she bought the store with several years earlier, she broke into tears.

"What's the matter, Sister?" asked Carol.

Kathy told Carol about Timber and the phone call. Holding her best friend as she sobbed, Carol asked what Kathy intended to do.

"I have to talk to Mo. We gotta get out of here. They've been threatening him since he started working on that damned short-hoe case. If we don't leave for a while, I know they're going to kill him."

"Will he go?"

"Maybe if I have the tickets when he gets home and he sees what happened to Timber"

Just before seven, my yellow Volkswagen bug pulled up the dirt drive. Kathy ran to meet me before I was out of the car. "Oh, Mo, you're finally here. I tried to call you. The worst thing happened." Taking my hand, she led the way toward the front door.

A half-hour later, Kathy finished telling me everything that happened that day. She pulled out the tickets to Hawaii and wrapped her slender arms around my neck. She pressed her lips to mine urgently, "So we'll go tomorrow. We can come back when it's safe. Timber will be okay at the vet for a week and Carol will let him stay at her house if we need to be away longer. Come on. We have to pack."

I sat silently, deep in thought. Kathy continued. "Mo. It's gotten too vicious for me. When you were still a law student and we lived in Bakersfield, life was so mellow. We visited your clients in their homes and went wherever we wanted and nothing bad happened. Now it's different. I think it all started a couple years ago when the farm workers were on strike in the San Joaquin Valley. First, that young union supporter from Yemen was killed by the cop and then a week later Juan de la Cruz was shot to death in the field."

Slowly I sat up, staring blankly. I shook my head. "Kath, you've always been braver than me. I learned that when you talked me into going to Gilroy and riding bulls when I barely knew you. I saw the guard point the gun at you when we were trying to talk with farm workers on the Giumarra picket line near Bakersfield—when I was still a law student and your refusal to be scared off. I know you don't run unless there is something real to run from. I agree, you have to go. It pisses me off that Timber got stabbed. It would kill me if something happened to you. But I can't go with you right now. Our effort to ban the short-handled hoe is almost over. I have an oral argument before the Supreme Court next week. Then we can go anywhere you want. But if I leave now, what I've been doing for the past five years is all for nothing. I owe it to the farm workers who are bent over all day in the fields not to walk away now. Together we chose to do what I'm doing. I'm too deep into the farm workers struggle to leave in the middle. You've always supported my belief that when we see something wrong, we can't just walk away and forget it. I want you to go to the Islands and I'll be there as soon as I can. I love you too much to let you stay around here now. You gotta go. We'll be together someday."

"Mo, I'm so afraid. Not just for me but for you and Timber. Don't make me go alone. Please come with me."

"I can't. Kath."

Kathy cried, pushing my arm away when I tried to put it around her shoulder. "For years the farm workers have been taking you away from me," she sobbed. "It's time for me to live my own life. Carol and I talked about it this morning. We decided if you weren't coming with me, she is. I'll come back when you're ready to care as much about me as you do about your job."

I tried to talk with her, but she demanded that I leave her alone. Over the weekend after Kathy was gone, I couldn't do anything. On Saturday I got up and tried to make breakfast but when my eggs were cooked I gave them to Timber. I went surfing with Tom but sat in the water without even paddling for waves. On Saturday night I went to bed just after dark. I missed Kathy. She filled my thoughts all day and my dreams all night.

The next Wednesday I argued the short hoe case in the Supreme Court. I left the courtroom depressed. I don't care if we win or lose, I thought, while I drove back to Salinas, If only Kathy would come back. Why didn't I ever listen to her?

I wanted to talk with her but didn't know where she was. A week later I received a postcard. "Hawaii is as good as ever. Good sun. Warm water. Good people. I might stay for a while. Love, Flynn."

I stood confused. I believed she was coming back. I immediately called Carol's husband. Mike told him he had talked with Carol the night before. "I'm surprised Kathy hasn't called you. Carol said she and Kathy are going to Kauai to live for a while. I think they're going to rent a house there. I thought you knew they aren't coming back for a while."

I sat on the edge of the double bed in the bedroom Kathy and I had shared. I tried to respond to Mike but nothing came out. She's not coming back? 1 thought. She never said that. Maybe Mike is mistaken. I'll just wait until she calls.

By the following Saturday, Kathy still had not called. I went to her store hoping someone there could tell me something. As I walked in I saw Blake, a tall-slender single mother of three, behind the counter. "Hi Mo," she smiled, "How you doing?""

"Okay, I guess. Have you heard from Kathy?"

I got a letter from her last week. She and Carol are renting a cottage in Kapaa, Kauai. How's it feel being a bachelor again?"

Blake and Kathy were close friends. Blake worked in the store whenever Carol or Kathy had to be elsewhere. "Blake, did Kathy tell you she isn't coming back? I know she was scared when she left but I thought she'd be back in Santa Cruz in a week or so."

Blake walked from behind the counter and put her arm around my shoulder. "Yeah, I knew," she slowly admitted, looking into my sad eyes. "It wasn't just the threat and Timber. She felt she had lost you to the farm workers. For a few years she's been trying to tell you that. I hope I'm not being a fink on my friend, but Kathy has fallen for a Filipino guy she met on the plane going to Hawaii. I guess she wants to stay and be with him for a while."

I walked out of the store feeling as though I had been hit in the stomach, the wind knocked out of me. I walked to the corner of Pacific and Soquel and sat on the curb sipping lemonade. "Okay, Jourdane," I said to myself, "you should have known this day was coming, You had to help farm workers and it cost you Kathy. What are you gonna do?"

I walked down the block to a travel agent and bought a ticket to Hawaii, leaving the following morning. At noon the next day, my United Airlines flight from San Francisco touched down in Honolulu. I walked through the Boeing 707 door into a terminal hallway without ever touching the tarmac. I flashed back to the moment I disembarked from the Standard Air flight 15 years earlier. Then, I walked down narrow stairs from the propeller driven plane to the burning pavement. The Honolulu terminal, located on the same piece of land abutting Pearl Harbor had no walls. Deep brown Koa poles held up a thatched roof covering several open booths. All around were smiling Asian faces. Now, except for the mumu-clad young woman placing leis around the neck of Midwest elders on holiday. I could have been in Dallas or Chicago. Most of the faces were no longer Asian, and there were walls. It was so much nicer, I thought, when the Honolulu terminal was open. Why do we always build walls?

At the Aloha Airlines I bought a ticket to Kauai. An hour later, I stood in the Lihue terminal. Unlike Honolulu, the Lihue terminal was open and Asian faces surrounded the arriving passengers. This is a whole lot more like the Hawaii I remember, I thought. I rented a Toyota Corolla and headed ten miles north to Kapaa. Having imagined my destination as a couple of old huts sitting on wooden poles, and unable to shake the thought of Kathy possibly leaving for good, I had not considered how 1 would find her. The Kapua city limits sign abruptly appeared, and I drove into a town with perhaps a thousand small wooden buildings

"Jourdane," I silently reminded myself as I parked the rented car. "You haven't had any food since a taco in Aptos 22 hours ago. It's time for nourishment."

Minutes later I walked out of a corner grocery store with a plate lunch of Spam, potato salad and rice and Pepsi. I sat on a tree stump in the long grass beside the road, scooped plain white rice from the once-used paper plate to my waiting mouth, and popped open the cola. Okay, Man, I thought. Now you're here. How're ya gonna find her and what're ya gonna say to her when you do?

Suddenly, about 50 yards away, Kathy walked up from the beach in her bikini. Her slender body was tanner than ever, her long brown hair streaked with blonde. She and a dark young man walked up the hill holding hands. I didn't know whether to yell greetings or sit silently hoping she would pass without seeing me. She saw me. "Mo. What the fuck are you doing here?" She dropped the young man's hand.

"Hi, Kath." I rose, timidly approached and then hugged my wife of almost seven years. "I came to see you. Can we talk, alone?"

"Sure, Mo. This is Kimo," she said, a blush on her face as she turned to the young Asian.

"My pleasure," I said politely, offering my hand to the man who, at that moment, I wanted to punch.

"See you lata', Sista," said her friend, walking back toward the beach.

"It's good to see you." Kathy smiled. "Even if it does surprise the shit out of me. I can't believe you're here. How've you been?"

"Okay, I guess."

Boldly, Kathy took my hand and focused her blue eyes on mine. She spoke softly. "I'm sorry it turned out this way. Mo. I still love you and I will always love you, but I got lonely. I know you are helping people who need your help, but I need someone who spends time with me."

"So you didn't leave because Timber was stabbed? And the threat?"

"Sure I did. It scared the shit out of me. But once I was away and met Kimo, I realized that I needed to be with someone who thinks I'm more important than his job. You can't do that. Mo, and it hurts."

"But I love you, Kath."

"I know, Mo. I've always known you loved me, but I needed more. I needed someone to talk with when I got home from work, but you were always somewhere else. When we were first together, when you were still in law school, we used to go to the horse races on Saturday, even though we had little money. Now we can afford to do that, but you don't have time. We used to sit on the sand holding hands and after the sun went down we'd kiss. Now, the only time I even see you is between your cases. I need more, Mo, I once wrote an article called 'A Kiss in Time Saves Nine. You didn't have time to read it. You ought to."

"Are you gone forever?" I asked, my normally cheerful lips turning downward.

"Cheer up, Mo. Of course I'm not gone forever. Forever's a long, long time. I will always be your friend. But right now I need to have my own life. I've decided to try to live here for a while and see if I can have it."

I stood without words by the side of the road. My head throbbing with the pain of failure, my heart sprinting with the fear of loneliness, my stomach hollow. So much I wanted to say remained trapped inside me like puzzle pieces in a locked wooden box. But nothing came out. Finally, looking down at my hands I mumbled, "I thought you always knew how much I love you and that was enough. I guess I was wrong."

"Are you going to stay here, I mean on Kauai, for a while? There are lots of neat places here we could see together."

"No, I think I'll stay over tonight and split in the morning."

"Will you at least go out and get drunk with me tonight? I know where they have super Mai Tais."

"Uh, huh," I said weakly, feeling my spirit slightly rise for the first time in a week.

That night Kathy and I drank beer, then wine then tequila from the bottle. We never got to Mai Tais.

After I dropped Kathy off at her cottage in Kappa, I drove to find a motel room near the airport in Lihue. As I passed through the dark rain forest that hugged the road like a python, I wondered how I could live without her. But for her, I thought, I'd be a beach bum in Laguna or dead in a Southeast Asia jungle. She worked as a receptionist at the medical society in San Jose to pay the rent while I sat in law school classes. She went with me to Delano and always encouraged me to represent farm workers. She taught me more about the real world and war; and women and justice than most people ever have the chance to learn.

For one of the few times in my life I felt alone. I should be mad, I thought, her walking out on me, but I don't feel anger. If I had given her the time she needed I would have cheated my clients out of adequate representation in the most critical moments in their lives. The fucking war in poverty. Not only do soldiers die in battle but war causes too many casualties on the home front.

Kathy and my relationship as the near-perfect portrait of young lovers had ended like the near-perfect, but overripe, purple plum dropping from the tree to the ground and decaying in the earth. I had chosen to join the struggle to improve farm workers' living conditions and let slip away my first love. Kathy and I would remain close friends, but our years of adventurous young lovers had become history.

Nine

Around 10 PM., Angie Carmona slipped away from her Chicana friends and called Tom. "Come with me to try to see your brother." she pleaded when he walked over. "I know I'm not supposed to visit him since I'm not family, and it's after visiting hours, but you can get us in."

"Now I know why you and Mo are friends," grinned Tom. "You're as much of an outlaw as he was at his outlaw peak. Come on. Let's give it a try. All they can do is throw us out."

Silently, Angie and Tom entered the hospital. Halfway down the dark hallway, Tom whispered. "Wait here for a minute. I have a plan." Angie stopped. Tom continued down the hall toward the intensive-care unit.

"Pancho, I don't have anything to do," he told the guard sitting outside the closed door. "If you want to go get a coffee or something, I'll stay here and watch the door for you."

"Thanks, guy. I could use a break." Sánchez slowly stood, stretched and walked toward the cafeteria.

When the guard was around the comer, Tom waved to Angie. She ran down the hall, looking over her shoulder. No one was watching. Without saying a word, Tom signaled her to enter the small room.

The room was dark; the only light flickered from life-monitoring screens reflecting my heartbeat, blood pressure, and brain waves. Angie could see the bed. She talked quietly to me. "Mo. Mo. It's Angie," she whispered in my ear. " It's Angie. Can you hear me?"

I didn't visibly respond.

The persistent Latina kept trying. Angie blamed herself for my wreck. On the way to Santa Maria I had stopped at a pay phone and called asking her to go by my apartment and unlock it. I had left my key inside. She had forgotten. Now she had to find out if I went to the apartment on the night of the wreck and was in the accident after leaving because I could not get in.

After repeatedly failing to get a response, she thought, maybe I could hear her, but couldn't talk because of my injuries. She whispered, "Babe, I'm gonna hold your hand. When you hear me squeeze mine. Okay?"

She took my seemingly lifeless hand and whispered "Okay Mo. If you hear me, squeeze my hand."

I didn't respond.

"Please. Show me you can hear me. It's Angie. I need to talk to you."

Then it happened. Feeling a squeeze. Angie ran out the door, "Tom. Tom. He heard me. He heard me. He's gonna be alright. Oh, thank God. Thank God."

Tom didn't know if I squeezed Angie's hand, or she had hallucinated her wishful thoughts. He raced into the room with her at his side. "Mo. It's Tom, squeeze my hand if you can hear me."

I did not respond.

Come on man. Just squeeze it a little. I know you're gonna make it. Just try to squeeze."

Tom felt nothing but a limp hand. Finally, he turned to Angie. Disappointed, but glad to have someone around who had the spirit to believe I would make it, he smiled. "I think he likes you better than me. Let's get outta' here before the guard returns and catches us."

Tom grabbed Angie's hand and the two ran through the door. They had just left the room when they saw Pancho walk around the corner. "Thanks," he called to Tom. "I needed that break. César doesn't realize how hard it is to stand in the same spot for eight hours. It's like being back in the field without toilets."

Once outside, Tom and Angie found John and Muffett. "He's coming out of it," Angie cried. "I told him to squeeze my hand, and he did."

"Are you sure?" asked Muffett hopefully.

"Unless I was dreaming, it happened. I promise."

Muffett and John ran to the intensive-care unit. Sánchez would not let them enter.

While the four melted into the massed of farm workers on the grass outside the hospital, Angie begged John and Muffett to believe she felt me respond.

Standing in the moonless night, Tom asked John how long he was staying over on the mainland.

"I haven't even thought about that. I came thinking Mo might be dead when I got here. It looks like he's gonna be here for a long time, but we have to get back in a few days. What about you?"

"Til it's over. There ain't no way I can sit in a class knowing he's in the hospital in intensive care."

*   *   *

Around the same time, Mom arrived home from Bakersfield and spoke with my cousin who told her about a friend who was a lawyer in Santa Ana. "I don't need a lawyer, Bob, I have two in my family, you and Mo," Mom responded.

"Well, Ruth, I do estate planning, and Mo can't represent himself. My friend is one of the best personal injury lawyers in California. He could send someone up there right away and start talking with witnesses."

Within hours, attorney Wylie Aitkin's investigator was on his way to the road between Bakersfield and Maricopa to take pictures of an access road and lots.

Meanwhile, hundreds of farm workers holding candles stood in small groups on the grass surrounding the hospital. The workers had erected a makeshift altar and were there to pray for the huero lawyer who had wandered into their valley and trespassed into their hearts. By 2 AM., the area around the hospital was vacant except for the farm workers praying before the Virgin of Guadalupe. They would stay until I recovered.

Ten

The next morning, Tom pulled into Coco's parking lot near Highway 99. He saw Kathy's rented Pinto. Tom, John and Byron Georgiou entered and joined her at a table. "Hi, sista'. How ya 'doin'?" asked Tom as he slid in and gave her a hug.

"A lot better than last night."

"You sound ready to go back to the Islands," said John, yawning.

"I couldn't sleep last night thinking about the guard at Mo's door, and how the doctor says he's going to die."

"He probably will if he stays here?" said Tom.

"Maybe we should see if we can transfer him to a hospital in the Bay Area," Kathy suggested.

"We were talking about that," said John.

"You know any doctors up there?"

"When Mo was going to law school, I worked for the Santa Clara County Medical Society," Kathy replied. "The president of the society was a friend. What's his name? Doctor Besson. Jerry Besson. I think he was a surgeon. Maybe I should call him"

"Why don't we go see how Mo is?" suggested Tom. "He needs to be alive to go to a different hospital."

Kathy went to my apartment to call information for San Jose hospital. Ten minutes later she was asking the doctor if he remembered her boyfriend when she worked for the medical society. She explained to Dr Besson that I had been in a serious wreck and was in the hospital in Bakersfield. She told him that the doctors in Bakersfield said I was going to die. Plus, the UFW had posted a guard at the door because César Chávez felt someone was trying to kill me Kathy asked if Dr. Besson could get me to a hospital in the Bay Area.

"If he's seriously injured or someone's trying to kill him, changing hospitals isn't going to help." Dr. Besson replied.

"I know, doctor, but can you try?"

"Normally, to get a patient admitted into a hospital other than to the emergency room, the patient's doctor requests admission…"

"Can you do that?

"Kathy, I'm an internist, I can't help Mo..."

"Don't you know people at Stanford?"

Half-hour later, the phone rang. Tom and John heard one side of Kathy's conversation with Dr. Besson. "You talked with a doctor at Stanford? It's a lot more serious than a broken arm, Doctor. His face is all torn up. His skull is fractured, and they say he'll probably have brain damage."

Doctor Besson put Kathy on hold. She explained to John and Tom that Stanford Hospital might take me, but it was a teaching hospital and would admit me only if I needed treatment that would be useful in teaching students to mend unusual injuries.

Doctor Besson came back on the line.

"Super," exclaimed Kathy.

Eleven

At 8 AM., the next morning, I was in the ambulance on my way to the Bakersfield airport with Kathy at my side. While hospital aides pushed my stretcher to an awaiting Cessna for the flight to the Bay area, John and Muffett waited at the airport for their flight to San Francisco en route to Honolulu.

Several hours later, a white and blue ambulance pulled to the curb behind Stanford Hospital in the northwest corner of the ten-thousand acre university campus. The emergency room's double doors swung open. Two attendants rushed out to push me in. Waiting inside was youthful Doctor Kaplan. At his side were a resident and three medical students attending one of the best medical schools in the world. As they wheeled me in, a nurse walking by my side rattled, "pulse, 78. heartbeat, normal. Blood pressure, 110 over 70. breathing, very erratic."

Doctor Kaplan noticed Kathy standing off to the side, silently watching. "Are you with the patient?" he asked.

"Yes, sir." she responded, not taking her eyes off me.

"I'm Ernie Kaplan. I know you'd like to stay, but I'd appreciate it if you waited in the cafeteria. I'll come down after we examine the patient." The sandy brown haired reconstructive surgeon offered Kathy a friendly smile backed by serious eyes.

* * *

"He has a lot of severe injuries," said the resident. "Where do you want to start?"

"How about at the top," said Kaplan. "Let me pull this bandage off and get a better look at the upper frontal portion of …Uh oh, someone put gauze over a fracture of the frontal cranium."

"Wow," whispered one of the students to another. "You never put gauze on a skull fracture. It causes a high risk of bacterial meningitis."

After removing the gauze, Kaplan said, "Let's get X-rays of the cranium. He appears to have several fractures in the frontal portion and I'd say many in the zygomatic bones and mandible."

While Dr. Kaplan examined my face more carefully, he rambled. Every medical student in the room scribbled the doctor's words. He continued. "I don't see any other obvious injuries. His breathing worries me. All the injuries become irrelevant if he suffocates." Kaplan asked the nurse for an incisor. He deftly cut through my trachea, saying very little as he proceeded. "Clamps. Tube. Sutures."

Within minutes, I had a tube attached to a respirator protruding from the front of my neck. The medical students stared at Doctor Kaplan with admiration.

*   *   *

Entering the hospital cafeteria, Kaplan saw the dark young lady sitting alone against the wall in a short blouse that revealed her slender tan stomach and faded Levi's. He introduced himself.

Reaching for a Winston cigarette, Kathy, mildly angry at having been thrown out of the emergency room, nodded, thinking, another doctor. Here we go again.

As if he read thoughts emanating from her skeptical blue eyes, Kaplan cautiously revealed, "If you're close to Mr. Jourdane, I think we're going to talk a lot over the next few months. I'll feel better if you know something about me. I'm the reconstructive surgeon who is going to rebuild your friend. I grew up in Central LA, attended Hamilton High School, and UCLA on scholarship. I majored in sculpting until my third year at the University. Then my tiny but persistent mother talked me into applying to medical school. I think she feared I'd become a North Beach beatnik. During my third year of medical school, I had to choose a specialty. I chose reconstructive surgery because it's a field where I could meld my art interest with my medical training."

"Reconstructive surgery is just the fancy name for a plastic surgeon, isn't it?" asked Kathy, showing slightly more interest, but still skeptical.

"Plastic surgery is one branch of reconstructive surgery. I could return to Hollywood and make millions lifting want-to-be-starlets breasts and eliminating wish-I-still-was-a-starlet's wrinkles, but I choose to rebuild broken faces for wages of little more than a gas station attendant." Kaplan smiled.

Kathy smiled.

"So now that you know me so well, what's your name?" smiled the doctor.

"I'm sorry," said Kathy offering her hand to hide her embarrassment. "I'm Kathy."

"Were you with Mr. Jourdane when the wreck occurred?"

"No. I was in Hawaii. We split up a couple years ago, but we're still good friends. What can you tell me about his condition?" asked Kathy, feeling closer to the young doctor by the second.

"I just took a brief look at him. They're taking X-rays now and I'll know more when they're completed."

"Can you tell me anything?"

"A little. To begin with, there's no medical reason why your friend is alive. He's very lucky."

"And he has thousands of farm workers praying for him. César Chávez has encouraged workers not to give up anything important without a fight."

"Keep saying your prayers," said the doctor. "And keep your hope, but try not to develop any expectations. You may be very disappointed. We can't promise anything."

Suddenly, Kathy heard the beeper in Kaplan's shirt pocket. "I have to go, Kathy. We'll talk more later. You don't live near the hospital do you?"

"No, I live in Hawaii."

"Have you thought about where you're going to stay?"

"Mo's brother is driving up from Bakersfield right now. Once he's here, we'll find a place."

"Until you get a more permanent place, I suggest the Riviera which is within walking distance, down on El Camino next to the Stanford Shopping Center. It's close and it's reasonable."

"I'll wait here 'til Tom arrives," replied Kathy.

*   *   *

Kathy was still in the cafeteria reading when Tom and Jesse walked in several hours later. "So tell us what you learned." said Tom as he slid in beside her on the narrow bench.

Kathy summarized what Doctor Kaplan had told her. "Last I heard they were taking X-rays, but I haven't talked to anyone for a couple hours. Mo's doctor is young and full of spirit. Plus he's handsome. I think we made a good move in having your brother brought here."

Before Tom could respond. Doctor Kaplan came in.

"Doctor, I just started to tell Mo's brother Tom and his wife Jesse what you told me, but I should let you do it, if you don't mind."

"I don't mind telling what I know, but I do mind being called doctor by a young woman who's not my patient. It's Ernie."

"When we spoke earlier, Kathy, I hadn't seen the X- rays. I have now, and they confirm what we believed. Your husband has several major cranial or skull fractures and a multitude of fractures to his jaw. He has two breaks in the frontal...excuse me, in the forehead. One of the breaks, the one over his right eye, is quite serious. The other, more in the middle of his forehead, isn't as serious, but it could have resulted in his death, for reasons I don't need to go into…"

58

"Ernie, with us, it's better to go into everything, "interrupted Kathy. "Plus, now I'm curious. How could it have caused his death?"

"It's no big deal because we caught it. But it could have been."

When Kaplan finished explaining what he found. Tom shook his head, "No wonder the Bakersfield doctor expected Mo to die from an infection by the week-end."

"Well," said Kaplan, "we caught the mistake and have corrected it. We'll know in a day or two if we're too late. In addition to the two forehead breaks, he has 27 breaks in cheekbones and jaw."

"Twenty seven?" exclaimed Tom

"Most of the breaks are remediable," said Kaplan "The problem is his left cheek bone. It's been destroyed. It'll be our job to reconstruct it. Also serious is Mo's right eye. It's punctured"

"Can you fix it?" Kathy asked.

"It's like a popped water balloon. We could suture and refill it, but that might cause blindness in the left eye, too. The left eye is already in serious trouble. Mo may be blind in that eye regardless of the contagious effect the right eye can have on it."

"It'll kill Mo if he's blind," Tom said in a defeated tone. "Everything he lives for requires vision. Adios surfing. Adios being a lawyer. Adios reading. Adios almost everything he lives for."

Hearing Tom reminded Kaplan that the most serious emotional victims of a severe trauma are the victim's family and friends. The doctor decided this wasn't the time to talk about probable brain damage and the likelihood I would never surf or be a lawyer again regardless of my sight. "Because he's in a coma now, it's risky to anesthetize Mo now," continued the doctor. "Hopefully, he'll come out of the coma soon, and we'll set the breaks. After he's recovered from that, we'll begin to rebuild the cheek bone and transplant cartilage, muscle, and tissue,"

"Sounds like it's going to take a long time," sighed Tom.

"I'd say your brother is looking at ten years of surgery." The doctor thought, but did not say, assuming he comes out of the coma.

As if Kathy had read his mind, she asked Kaplan, "What are his chances, Ernie? I mean him coming out of the coma."

"It's hard to say. Right after the wreck, I'd have given a hundred-to-one against him. Now, four days later and with the gauze removed, it's probably fifty-fifty. But who knows when. Every day from here on that he doesn't come around, the odds get longer, but I don't like to bet. Especially in people's lives."

After talking with Kaplan, Tom and Kathy walked to the intensive care unit to see how I was doing in my new surroundings. Like the hospital in Bakersfield there was an intense odor of disinfectant and television monitors above the bed. When Tom saw me, he bolted in shock, "What's that coming out of his throat?"

"I don't know." responded Kathy. "On the plane he was having trouble breathing."

Twelve

Tom, Kathy and Jesse rented a dingy apartment on El Camino Real a mile from Stanford Hospital. The next day at dawn, five days after the wreck, Tom was at my bedside. When he walked past the nurses' station late in the afternoon, a nurse called out, "Mr. Jourdane?"

Tom stopped.

"You won't believe this. Sir, but there's a woman on the phone who says she works with Governor Brown. She asked to speak with Mo Jourdane. When I told her he was comatose, a guy came on the line and said he wanted to talk with whoever's around. I don't know who it really is. You want to talk to him?"

*   *   *

On February 16, 1976, several days after the Legislature terminated the funds to administer the Agricultural Labor Relations Board, the five remaining investigators and I were working in Bowker's kitchen when the phone rang. Carlos answered. "It's for you, Jourdane. The lady says it's the Governor's office." "Chale! Such important people you hang around with Carlos," kidded Shirley. "You know the governor, Mo?"

"Nope," I responded, blushing as I walked across the room to take the phone from Carlos. "I've seen him on TV but that's about it."

"Hello." I said curiously into the receiver.

"One moment," replied the female voice at the other end.

"Hello, Jourdane?"

"Good morning, Governor."

"What the hell are you guys doing down there? Have you seceded from the State? Haven't you heard the Farm labor Board's shut down?"

"No Sir. We aren't seceding. We heard the Board ran out of money but we feel we have an ethical duty not to abandon cases."

"Jourdane, I appreciate you and your companions' strong feelings regarding ethical duties. But as state employees, what about your duty to comply with the Legislature's will?"

"I don't think we're showing disrespect for the Legislature, Governor. All the Legislature did was cut-off the money to pay us. It didn't terminate our employment or repeal the farm labor law. Under the Agricultural Labor Relations Act you managed to get passed, farm workers have rights. We've told them since the law was enacted they have the right to join and support a union. Some have been fired because they listened to us and relied on the rights we said they had. We can't just walk away."

"The Legislature will again fund the farm labor board if we let the situation cool down for a while. What you guys are doing may seem best for farm workers from your limited perspective but if the Legislature decides it has to repeal the law to stop you, the farm workers you're trying to help will lose all their rights under the Farm Labor Law. If that happens the cases you're so diligently investigating aren't going to be worth the paper your reports are written on. If you guys close down and go home, the farm labor board will have money a lot sooner than if the Legislature sees you as rebels who are challenging its authority."

"If you tell us to shut down, we'll do what you say. You've shown your support for the farm workers and I believe you'd only tell us to cool it if our doing so is in their best interest."

"I'm telling you to cool it, Jourdane. Why don't you come up to Sacramento and we can talk about where we go from here. Sam

Cohen tells me you're a good lawyer, and I shouldn't let you get away."

"Thank you Governor. To have an attorney who is as good as Cohen says that is truly an honor. Most of my clothes are still in my apartment near the Florin Road ALRB office in Sacramento so I have to come there anyway. I'll come by your office when I'm back up there."

When I sat down the receiver. Shirley screamed, "You chicken-shit Gabacho. 'Yes Sir." "No Sir. As soon as the establishment says jump, you ask, "How high, Sir? You're like all the rest, Jourdane. Screw it. See ya around." Shirley walked out slamming the front door and was gone. The remaining four investigators and I drafted reports on their partially completed investigations and I called the United Farm Workers. Paralegal Tom Dalzell agreed to talk to the workers and get information necessary to protect their cases. "And be sure to get a permanent address for them," I reminded him, "so we can get in touch with them when we're back."

*   *   *

When I returned to Sacramento, I stopped by the governor's office. After walking to the end of the carpeted hallway, I entered a small office and introduced myself to the young dark-haired secretary. "You're the Mo Jourdane that's been causing so much trouble in the Imperial Valley?"

Innocently, I shrugged my shoulders.

Nodding toward a closed door, she told me that the governor was waiting to see me. I entered. The Governor of California was sitting across the room on one of the sofas chatting with his chief executive, Gray Davis. Continuing his conversation, the governor waved me over to join them.

"We're discussing something you're familiar with, Jourdane." said the Governor. "We need to figure out what we're going to do to get your Farm Labor Board re-opened. Got any ideas?"

Before I responded, the governor smiled, "I hear if we fire some inside troublemakers, the appropriation bill will pass."

"Let me guess who," I remarked, slightly embarrassed.

"They say you and your accomplices are Chávez supporters."

"They want to get rid of us because we believe in the law you wrote, Governor, and we try to enforce it. Bias is a claim they have to make because they can't admit even to themselves that farm workers they employ support César Chávez and the United Farm Workers."

The Governor smiled, changing the subject. "I can probably get you a job until the Board reopens over at the attorney general's office helping with the farm labor cases that are on appeal."

"No thanks Governor. It wouldn't be fair to the people I work with that have no work now that the Board is shut down. I'll look around and find something."

I left the Governor's office not sure what I was going to do to survive until the Board was refunded. I had saved a little money but it would run out before long. That night, I had just walked into my apartment when the phone rang. It was Marshall Ganz, the Chief Organizer for the United Farm Workers. Marshall and I had become well acquainted during the previous fall and winter we both spent in the Imperial Valley.

"You have anything lined up? A job I mean," asked Marshall in his right-to-the-point manner.

"Not yet. But I'll find something."

"The Governor's running in the Oregon primary for president. Why don't you get some of the Board employees who are out of work and go to Portland and help him win?"

Two days later, Carlos Bowker and I drove to Portland in my battered Toyota with a surf rack permanently attached to the roof. We arrived having no idea what we were going to do. Within two days, Bowker was in charge of the Latino vote in the upcoming Oregon primary and I was in charge of advance for a three day tour the Governor was making before Election Day. Georgiou flew in from California and Shirley Treviño and some of her friends from San Jose came up to help with the campaign.

Brown won the Oregon primary, receiving more votes than both Jimmy Carter and Hubert Humphrey. After Oregon, the Governor's campaign sent Byron Georgiou and I to Rhode Island to oversee advance for trips to the state by the Governor, his mother and father, and the actress star of the hit movie Nashville, Ronnie Blakely.

 The night before the election, Ronnie Blakely, her assistant Mirandi Babitz, Byron and I rode in Joey Palerino's family limousine when he took the Governor to the airport to return to California. Rumor around the campaign was that Joey's father was a principal Democrat leader in Providence and some even claimed he was the Godfather of the Italian machine. After dropping the governor off on the tarmac, Joey, Ronnie, Mirandi, Byron, and I went to the hotel where Brown's campaign was staying and spent the night drinking California wine and talking story. Around dawn, Mirandi and I wandered down the hallway to her room where we finally stopped laughing.

 Over the following years, Mirandi would become one of my most loved friends. We were together at the beach, in the City, in the mountains and in the Islands. Both Mirandi and I were the descendants of Jews from Latvia, who came to America to escape the purges around the turn of the Twentieth Century. We were both children of the sixties. While I was marching behind the Jefferson Airplane to protest the war in Vietnam, Mirandi was in England with the Beatles. While I was raised in southeast Los Angeles, Mirandi was raised in Hollywood. While I was fighting for farm workers in the Salinas Valley, Mirandi was producing music concerts throughout California. While I was driving from Santa Maria to Bakersfield during the early hours of September 17, Mirandi was driving from Santa Monica to the Aptos stronghold. While I ended up in the hospital in

Bakersfield, Mirandi ended up in the hospital in Santa Cruz. Around the same time I collided with the oil tanker she went blind in one eye. We would remain friends for as long as we lived. Mirandi was my true friend and sister.

After winning the Rhode Island primary, Governor Brown decided to enter the race in New Jersey. There, both California and New Jersey volunteers handled the campaign, but the people who did most of the work were United Farm Worker members and supporters. It was incredible to see Arturo Rodriguez, president of the farm workers union since César Chávez death, an organizer at the time of the election in 1976 and Gretchen Laue, a boycotter from the east, setting up house meetings in Rhode Island and New Jersey. They did all the things in the political campaign that they did in union organizing campaigns. Again Governor Brown won the primary.

I returned to New York to help the Governor at the Democrats convention. Jimmy Carter was nominated.

I enjoyed the campaign, except when Carter's people who were ruthlessly running the convention tried to stop César Chávez from nominating Governor Brown for president. I was handling advance for the Governor at the convention. On the afternoon before nominations were made, I got a backstage pass for Chávez so he could have some time to go over his nominating speech. Chávez arrived at Madison Square Gardens about an hour before he was scheduled to nominate Brown for president. The Democrats' security guard wouldn't let him pass. The guard claimed César had to not only have the backstage pass but a pass to enter the building where the convention was being held. I explained to the guard who Chávez was and that he was going to nominate Brown. I told him the people running the convention had only given me the backstage pass and said that was all he needed. Like Mad Magazine's—What Me Worry, the guard grinned. "Not tonight it isn't. He laughed until I threatened to go tell Walter Cronkite, who was about thirty yards away, what the convention officials were doing to the most noteworthy labor leader in the country. That night my persistence to reach a goal paid off, but the next day I watched politics at its low tide. Many delegates Brown won in the primaries vanished when the Democrats' machine put on the pressure. Almost the only people who stuck with the governor were the California delegation and supporters of the United Farm Workers from all over the country. I guess the union supporters recognized that Governor Brown understands how important farm workers are to this country and that César Chávez respected him for that.

While at the Democratic convention, the Governor told me the Board had been refunded and I ought to get back to California quick. He said he appointed a new General Counsel for the agency. I expected Byron, Carlos and I would automatically have our jobs back.

The evening I arrived back in town, Carlos Bowker called from the Imperial Valley. "Welcome back to the oven, man. You'll never guess what's happening."

"I give up. Unless you're gonna tell me the sun exploded and that's why it's so hot. It must be 90 degrees outside and it's almost midnight."

"Stop bitching. It's a hundred here en la valle. Anyway, I guess you haven't heard. The word around is that because of our strong law enforcement approach to the Farm Labor Law, the growers see you and me as lurking piranhas. Why don't you check around and call me back."

The next morning, I stopped by Byron Georgiou's tiny wooden duplex in Oak Park, one of Sacramento's poorest neighborhoods. When I walked through the door, he asked if I had seen the morning paper. Byron told me that a member of the State Assembly from the San Joaquin Valley asked the Governor on behalf of the Central Valley growers to assure them the infamous Maurice Jourdane not be again thrusted upon California's agricultural industry. "You know," he continued, "yesterday the new general counsel refused to hire Ellen Lake because he thinks she's too pro-farm worker. Think we have a chance?"

"Who knows, but let me call the Governor's office and see what they say. I'm sure they'll tell me if they think there's a problem."

Ten minutes later, I was talking with the Governor's personal secretary. "The Governor's not available but let me check on Mr. Davis," she said. Moments later, the voice of Gray Davis, the Governor's Chief of Staff, was on the line. Davis told me that Byron and I did not need the Governor's input. We had our jobs. He suggested we go talk with the General Counsel.

The next morning, Byron and I were at work at the Farm Labor Board Sacramento office writing briefs in support of Board decisions which had been appealed to higher courts. Again, my persistence to reach a goal paid off. I relished being a lawyer again. I had no idea whether the Governor's office had told the General Counsel to hire us, but my satisfaction had a very short life.

Within the first few days the General Counsel buzzed into my office. "In a month we're reopening the farm labor board. I need a Chief of Operations. Will you take the job?" he asked. Like Jerry Cohen, Sam Cohen, and other good lawyers, the General Counsel used few words.

"What's the job involve?" I asked, surprised, but honored, by the request from the man I hardly knew.

"Help hire and train a new staff, for now. Once that's done, we'll talk,"

Reluctantly, I answered, "Okay, for now. I'd rather keep working on the appeals but I'll help hire and train the staff if you need someone to do that."

"Good. We have two months. We need 35 lawyers, 45 field examiners, 15 clerical and four office managers. I think it'll be possible only if we split up the task. I'll interview the applicants for office director and I'll find someone to interview the clericals. You interview the attorney applicants and I'll talk with Byron about interviewing applicants for field examiner positions. By mid-October, we had hired and trained the staff and sent them to offices in Salinas, El Centro, San Diego, Oxnard and Delano. I asked the General Counsel to let me go to the field and be a trial lawyer. He told me to wait. Two days before Halloween, the general counsel reluctantly allowed me to leave Sacramento to handle an unfair labor practice trial in Santa Maria. At the hearing, three fired lettuce cutters testified that one evening the previous summer they met to plan a campaign to petition for an election so the United Farm Workers could become their union. When they returned to work the following morning. the foreman fired them. After the three testified, the State rested. The company presented its case. The foreman testified he fired the three after they reported to work drunk. After the company rested and the judge sent the parties home until the following day, I sat in the United Farm Workers' office having a taco and a coke, talking with Peter Cohen. the younger brother of the UFW's General Counsel Jerry Cohen."... so this morning," said Peter. "I went to the field and talked with four guys who were there when the company fired De Lara, Gómez and Madril. They told me the three were not drunk the day the company fired them. They said that before your clients got to work, they heard the assistant foreman tell the foreman about the three meetings with others to seek an Agricultural Labor Relations Board election. The four guys I talked to say they could tell from how mad the foreman got that the three were in trouble."

That evening Peter and I drove to a labor camp where I talked with the four witnesses. "I am sorry, Señor Abogado," said the most outspoken of the four. "We tell you what we hear because no one from the company is here to know what we say. But we can't tell it in court. If we do, we will be fired and no one in the Valley will hire us. We will be, como se dice, black-listed."

For hours, Peter and I tried to urge the workers to appear at the hearing and just tell the truth. "The State will protect you," I promised.

The workers laughed at my naive remark.

At midnight Peter and I were walking out the door when I suddenly stopped. "Wait," I asserted in Spanish to the four tired workers. "I have an idea. There might be a way you can help us enforce the farm labor law and not fear being fired. How many workers were there the morning you heard the informer tell the foreman about the meeting the night before?"

"All of us. Two crews. Maybe 70 in all."

"Super. Let me tell you my idea."

The following morning at nine, I called the State's first rebuttal witness. "The State calls Juan Doe." As the judge and company attorney sat with their mouths agape, Juan Doe was led into the courtroom with a brown paper sack over his head.

"Objection," screamed the company lawyer. "Objection. Objection."

The judge held up a hand to silence the company lawyer. He looked at me with a questioning expression.

"Your honor," I began, slightly embarrassed. "I understand this may seem unusual but the only way we can protect Mr. Doe and his three companions who are here to tell the court what they heard the day the company fired Juan Gómez, Neo Madril and Julian De Lara is to permit these witnesses to appear in court with their heads covered to conceal their identity. The General Counsel feels that to protect these witnesses from retaliation it is necessary to withhold their identity from the company. If the court wishes to meet with them in private, we will be happy to arrange that."

I knew this proposed solution was questionable in light of a party's constitutional right to confront witnesses but I was an advocate for the farm workers. They were my clients who I had an ethical duty to diligently represent. I also was deeply committed to do whatever necessary to improve the lives of farm workers.

When I returned to Sacramento, the General Counsel and I struggled over my desire to return to the field and try cases. Finally, in February, my college fraternity brother and law school classmate John Moore called. Moore was the Directing Attorney in the Fresno ALRB office. He reminded me I was an attorney not a middle level bureaucrat. He had an important case he wanted me to try. I told the General Counsel I was quitting as Chief of Operations and was off to Delano to be a lawyer. Shirley arrived in Delano shortly after me. The United Farm Workers continued to win almost all elections. Again growers blamed Shirley and me because our relentless advocacy reflected our unfailing belief in enforcing the labor law.

A couple weeks before I was lying comatose in Stanford Hospital, the Governor's Legal Affairs Secretary, Tony Kline, called. The Governor wanted to talk with me.

"Me?" I asked, responding to the governor's secretary of legal affairs. "What for?"

"I'm about ready to move on. The Governor's thinking about bringing you in."

"I don't know anything about what happens in the governor's office."

A couple days later, after talking with the governor's secretary of legal affairs, I drove to Sacramento to talk with the Governor's chief of staff about working in the Governor's office. I told him that there were still bitter fights going on between the United Farm Workers and the corporations in the San Joaquin Valley and we were trying to guarantee fair elections. I assured him that I'd be honored to work in the Governor's office but not if it meant abandoning the farm workers.

"Finish the grape season in Delano," said Davis. "Call me when you're free, but stay out of trouble this time."

 The grape season had not ended by September 17.

*   *   *

Tom walked over and picked up the phone. He recognized the voice on the other end of the line. "This is Tom Jourdane, Mo's brother."

"Hi, Tom. This is Jerry Brown. How's Mo doing? I called hoping I could speak with him," the Governor said, "but they say he's in a coma."

Tom told the Governor that I got hurt pretty bad, I had lots of broken bones, what Kaplan said about the odds of coming out of the coma, but added that I had always bet on long shots.

The Governor told Tom he was sure I would pull through, I was a fighter who didn't give up easily, and that he would check with Tom again in a few days. When Tom later told me about the Governor's call, the support in Sacramento moved me a step nearer recovery. A wave.

The nurse who told Tom about the phone call watched in awe. "Was that really the governor's office?" she asked.

"Yeah," replied Tom.

The nurse who talked to Tom bubbled to another, "I was speaking with the Governor and I almost said, "Come on, buster, don't pull my leg.""

72

Thirteen

During the week after the collision, Tom, Jesse and Kathy spent many hours in the intensive care unit talking to my comatose body. My condition did not change.

On Saturday, when Tom walked down the hall toward the intensive care ward, he saw Shirley and Carlos standing outside the nurse's station. He could hear Shirley pleading with a stone-faced nurse, "... I know we're not family and I know you have rules but no one is here from his family, and we've driven all the way from Calexico."

Tom interrupted. "Hi, Shirley. Hi, Carlos. Having trouble?"

"Tom. Am I glad to see you," responded the middle-aged morning nurse in-charge. "These people say they are friends of Mr. Jourdane, but we don't have a list of approved visitors. We can't just let anyone in."

"Thanks. I appreciate your caution." Tom smiled. "These two desperados are both good friends of Mo. He's hung around with the wild side most of his life."

Fourteen

Sunday was the same as the day before. Carlos and Shirley were followed by a parade of friends including those from the Farm Labor Board, Rural Legal Assistance, Santa Cruz surfing partners, and even my childhood friend Jerry Perez who drove up from Southern California.

On Monday, it was back to normal for Tom, Jesse and Kathy. They spent most of the day next to the bed talking to me. I did not respond on Tuesday, Wednesday, Thursday or Friday. The weekend again brought friends.

Around eleven the following Friday morning. Tom and Jesse sat by the bed talking when I moved for the first time in over two weeks. Startled, Jesse and Tom stared at the lump under the blanket and the protruding swollen head. I moved again. A wave.

"Nurse, Nurse, get the doctor, I think Mo's coming out of it," shouted adrenaline-charged Tom. Within minutes, Doctor Kaplan was in the room.

"What's up? Tom"

"Ernie, he moved. We both saw him. It was like he was coming out of a deep sleep. Like he moved his neck back and forth and his shoulders, trying to fall back asleep."

Doctor Kaplan went to the side of the bed. He checked the monitors. All were normal. "Keep your hope, Tom, but don't expect miracles. Movement doesn't mean he's coming out of the coma. Sometimes movement is a good sign, but it's no guarantee. Take his hand and see if you can get a reaction,"

Tom did. "Mo. It's Tom, squeeze if you can hear me." Tom felt a slight squeeze.

"He is, doctor. He is," shouted Tom, more excited than when he was a ten-year old watching his first home run clear the fence in Little League baseball.

The three watched in awe. I lifted my right arm, placing the palm of my hand against my lips. I put the arm down. Seconds later I repeated the movement, spreading my index and middle finger as I put them to my mouth.

"Is he trying to say something?" asked Tom.

"I don't know," replied Kaplan, "maybe."

I made the motion a third time.

"I think he is trying to tell us something," speculated Kaplan with a puzzled look on his face, "but I can't figure out what."

When I did it again, Tom broke into laughter. "I got it. He wants a cigarette. I don't fucking believe it. Almost dead, unable to see, talk or breathe and he wants a cigarette." "Mo. I'm Tom, your brother. I know you want a cigarette but they're putting oxygen into your throat, and if you lit a cigarette in this room, we'd all be blown to Santa Cruz."

Without moving any part of my body except the hand I had been raising to my lips. I lifted my right fist, the middle finger protruding.

"He's going to make it," cried Tom. "The motherfucker's going to make it." My younger brother who didn't register for his final year at San Jose State that fall so he could stay with me hugged his cowgirl wife. They cried in each other's arms.

Kaplan was elated. He knew his work was about to begin. Before leaving to find the doctors with whom he would begin to rebuild my face and save my vision, he turned to Tom and Jesse. Grinning, he nodded his head. "You know," he said, "moving his hand to his mouth might have been his way of saying he wanted a cigarette, but it told us a lot more. It means we can thank God your brother isn't quadriplegic. With the massive injuries he sustained he could have been easy."

"I guess if you want a cigarette bad enough you'll do anything for it." Tom grinned. "He'll probably spend the rest of his days thanking a cigarette for saving his life."

Tom told Kaplan about the doctor in Bakersfield who explained that the brain has four functions, senses, movement, memory and reasoning. "That's right," responded Kaplan. "Your brother just showed us he hasn't totally lost two of those functions"

"He's able to move muscles." Tom responded. "He showed us that by raising his arm. That's control of movement. What's the second, memory?"

"No, I don't think he remembers smoking. Smoking is an addiction just like heroin or alcohol can be. He wants a cigarette because his body craves it, like a reflex. It's subconscious."

"So what did he show us?" asked Jesse.

"Think about it. He isn't able to talk, so he used sign language. That is reasoning. It may be a very illogical and crazy use of reasoning, asking for a cigarette when he's in the intensive care unit and unable to breathe, but he had to reason to do it." A wave.

*   *   *

That afternoon, Dr. Visnus, the surgeon who specializes in vision, was studying the X-ray, in Kaplan's office. Kaplan was talking with several students who were sitting in on the discussion of the first step in my reconstruction.

"Let's start with a list of the injuries," began Kaplan, stopping to think and study his notes.

"He has two fractures in his frontal skull. Looking at the X- rays, I see a three-centimeter fracture in the central anterior cranium surrounded by many bone fragments. The fracture appears to be set, but we need to remove those fragments before one gets into his bloodstream and causes a stroke. Let's list that as the first procedure,"

A resident scribbled notes.

"There's a second fracture over the right eye," Kaplan continued. "We can set that at the same time. It appears to be L-shaped with each leg perhaps three centimeters in length. Again, there are bone fragments that need to be removed. The apes of the L appears to be in contact with the right socket."

"That eye's going to have to come out," said Visnus.

"Let's talk more about that in a moment," said Kaplan. "We'll have to wire the horizontal break which runs from the socket almost to his temple. There's a major artery in there we'll have to watch out for."

"How long do you think that'll take, Ernie?" asked Visnus.

"I'd estimate about four hours for the two surgeries. I don't want to keep him under anesthesia longer than that in his fragile condition."

Kaplan asked the resident to call the operating room and see if they could reserve it for four hours the next morning.

"Okay," said Dr. Visnus, "let's go to that damaged eye; if we don't remove it soon he might lose the other one. If we can get consent we can do it after you deal with the skull fractures."

"I understand, responded Kaplan, "why do you want to remove the orbit as soon as possible, but if we wait another several weeks to set the jaw, we're going to have to rebreak many of the fractures in order to set them. They're rejoining."

Doctor Visnus sat pensive for several minutes. "The eye is an immediate problem, Ernie. If he pulls out of this, blindness will likely be the most serious loss to the patient. It's a relatively simple operation."

"Let me talk with his Family," said Kaplan. "Maybe we can do both procedures at the same time."

As Dr. Kaplan walked out of the room, a third-year medical student could have said, "This is more real than anything we've learned in school so far." Doctor Kaplan could make any discussion a teaching session. He knew that within a few years the students would be deciding what to do. Hopefully they would be at a hospital with someone experienced around to work with. If they weren't, the new doctors would have to make the decisions themselves. The medical students had learned that Doctor Kaplan wanted them to have a memory bank to withdraw from when they were out there alone.

Fifteen

Dr. Kaplan returned to the intensive care unit to ask if anyone knew how to get hold of Kathy. When he walked in, she was there. Kathy hugged him. "Oh, Doctor Kaplan. I'm sorry. Ernie. Tom told me what happened. I'm all chills."

Kaplan grinned. Kathy continued. "Many times over the past several weeks, especially in Bakersfield, I thought this would never happen. The best part of all is to know that not only does his body work but his mind, too. The first thing he thinks of when he comes out of it is a cigarette. That's the old Mo. Now I know with your help, he'll be home soon, back in a courtroom by summer, and on the slopes at Lake Tahoe next winter."

"Whoa!" said Kaplan. "I agree this is a big step but a courtroom by summer and Tahoe by winter might be a little more than even I can do."

"Listen, Ernie," said Kathy firmly but grinning. "There's a guy in Delano who is starting a union for farm workers. Their slogan is Si Se Puede. You know what that means?"

"I know about César Chávez and I know anything is possible, but a courtroom by summer? At least give us until fall. And skiing. That's a lot to expect. Anyway, I need to talk with you about something important now. Why don't we go down to the cafeteria?"

*   *   *

Kathy sat at a table and lit a cigarette. Kaplan returned with two cups of coffee. "You know, Kathy, you look like an entirely different person today than you were yesterday. It's like someone lit a fire in your eyes. And I think it's the first time I've seen your shining teeth through your attractive smile since you got here a couple weeks ago. You look a whole lot better when you're happy."

"Thanks. I feel a lot better." Kathy blushed.

"Anyway, I have to ask you two very important questions," said Kaplan. "I want you to think about them. You don't have to answer now."

"If you're going to ask for my hand in marriage, the answer is I'll consider it if you get Mo out of here in one piece, divorce your pretty wife, and quit being a doctor 24 hours a day. If it's something else, I'll probably do it."

"Since Mo arrived at Stanford he's been on a respirator. He may be able to breathe through the trachea, the tube in his throat, without the respirator, but we didn't want to take the chance, especially when he was in the coma and could have just silently died. We have to decide now whether to continue using the respirator."

Kathy smiled. "That's easy, Ernie. I know Mo will be happy to be breathing on his own again."

"But, you understand the risk."

"I understand there may be a risk. But life is full of risks. If Mo wouldn't have taken the risk of asking me to dance ten years ago, we never would have met. If he hadn't taken the risk of riding bulls, we wouldn't have ended up going together. If he hadn't taken the risk of suing the agribusiness corporations, farm workers would still be bent over using the short-handled hoe..."

"And if he hadn't taken the risk of driving from Santa Maria to Bakersfield in the middle of the night, he wouldn't be here now," said Kaplan. "That brings us to the second question. You know Mo's right eye is damaged beyond salvation."

Kathy looked at the doctor but didn't respond. He continued. "We have to remove it before it causes him to lose the little sight he may have in the left eye."

Still Kathy did not respond.

"I don't think he's able to knowingly consent to the operation, but I think it may be a medical necessity that we perform the surgery with or without consent. Of course the hospital would like consent in case of future litigation"

"Come on, Ernie. You get Mo out of here alive and he won't sue Stanford, but if I say okay, take his eye out, he'll never forgive me for consenting without talking with him. It's his eye, not mine. I can't make a decision like that for him. Let's wait a few days and hopefully he'll be able to understand and give consent or say no."

"I wish we could do that, Kathy. But we run a serious risk if we wait. We have to act immediately. We're performing surgery in the morning to mend the skull fractures. We could handle the damaged eye at the same time. If we don't do it tomorrow, it might cause him to be blind in the one eye he has before we get around to it. We'll do what we have to, Kathy, but I'll feel better if those close to him agree. Why don't you talk with Tom and Jesse and we'll talk in a couple hours?"

Kathy walked around the hospital looking for Tom as if in a San Joaquin Valley winter fog. Unable to find him, she returned to the intensive care unit. When she entered, she saw him talking to me with my swollen head sticking out of the covers on the bed. "... so as soon as we heard, we took off for Bakersfield. Shit were we scared. Then we..."

"Oh, hi, Kath. He doesn't respond, but I know he can hear me," explained Tom defensively, apparently embarrassed at being caught talking to an unmoving body.

"Tom, they want us to consent to having Mo's right eye removed." Kathy explained the doctor's fear of contagious interference of the left eye by the damaged right eye. "They want consent right now. You know Mo better than anybody. What should we do?"

Tom sat without responding. Finally, shaking his head said, "A hard one."

Kathy sat down and stared at me lying in the bed.

"Part of me says," Tom mused, "that if he could talk he'd tell us he'll get better by himself. But he trusts doctors pretty much. He might listen to them. Let's try to talk to him."

Taking my hand, like the San Joaquin Valley homegirl Angie had done in Bakersfield, Kathy said, "Mo, this is Kathy. Squeeze my hand if you understand me." After feeling slight pressure on her palm, she continued. "Your right eye got wiped out in the wreck. If they don't take it out, you may lose your sight in the other eye. Do they have your consent to remove it?"

There was no response.

Kathy tried again. "Mo, if you understand what I said, squeeze my hand."

I did not react.

Kathy looked at Tom with a help-me plea on her face.

"Maybe he got bored and went to sleep. How long until you have to let them know?"

"Ernie wants to know in a couple hours."

While Kathy and Tom talked to my apparently comatose body, the nurse came by and told them a visitor, Byron Georgiou, was outside.

*   *   *

When the Agricultural Labor Relations Act went into effect in August 1975, Byron, Ron Greenberg, and I were the legal staff. We lacked experience in labor law, but tried to balance the experience of company and Teamster labor-law attorneys we opposed with working whatever hours necessary to represent the farm workers. The law was written to protect. We worked seven days a week, ten hours a day, preparing for the tempest of litigation expected to seize the valley when the new legislation went into effect.

The torrent hit. During the first 17 days of the Farm Labor Board's existence, Greenberg, Georgiou, and I defended the new

82

law in 29 different courts. One day I was in Monterey County, the next in Fresno. Like migrant workers we traveled from courthouse to courthouse in Solano, Kern, Sacramento. San Francisco, Tulare, Riverside, Imperial. King, Contra Costa, San Diego, Merced and Santa Barbara counties. We fought the agribusiness corporations in state courts, federal courts and the California Supreme Court. By early November, the whirlwind had passed. The growers' efforts to crush the farm labor board slowed to a dribble. Meanwhile, widespread violations of the Farm Labor Relations Act cemented many farm workers' belief that the new law would never be enforced. Across the State, companies fired workers who exercised their new right to join a union. Georgiou went to Salinas. I went to the Imperial Valley. We began representing farm workers in nearly nonstop trials.

*　　　*　　　*

Now, my brother Tom went into the hospital hallway and told Byron what was happening, about me wanting a cigarette that morning and how they wanted consent to remove my eye. "You're the lawyer, Byron. See if you can get a legal consent," asked Tom.

"I'll try," answered the Harvard lawyer, taking Tom seriously, "but I don't know if he can understand well enough to give a knowing and intelligent consent."

"You use all the right words to sound like a lawyer, Byron, but you don't really have to try." Tom smiled.

"I will." Byron smiled.

Tom returned to my room and told Kathy that Byron would try to get my consent.

"I'll be in the coffee shop," she responded tiredly. "Come tell me if it works."

Byron and Tom entered the room. "Mo, Byron's here," said Tom, taking my hand. "Squeeze my hand if you understand."

Believing he felt a slight squeeze, Tom continued. "Byron wants to talk with you about your eye. Do you understand?"

I did not respond.

"Let me try," said Byron, moving beside the bed and taking my hand. "Mo, this is your old buddy. Squeeze if you can hear me." Byron thought he felt a squeeze. He continued.

"You were in a bad wreck. If they take out your damaged eye you won't lose your vision. If they don't...."

Byron could not continue. I did not respond. Tom went to the cafeteria. "How'd it go?" asked Kathy with hopeful eyes,

"Not so good. I don't know if he doesn't understand or doesn't want to respond, or is thinking about it," said Tom.

"Maybe it'll help if we tell him something to sweeten the deal," said Kathy. "Like he can still surf with one eye. Let's talk to Ernie." Kathy got up from the table and led the way down the hall to the reconstructive surgery department.

Once inside Kaplan's office, Tom explained the problem. "He probably doesn't understand you," responded the doctor after hearing the story and listening to Tom's theories of what might be going on in my mind. "Will it help if I tell him it won't ruin his looks? I can do that. We have a new technique. I can tell him truthfully that removing an eye won't disfigure him."

Kaplan headed for the intensive care unit. "Mo, this is Ernie Kaplan. I'm your doctor. Do you understand you were in a serious wreck? Squeeze my hand if you understand." The doctor felt a slight squeeze. "Okay, you're doing fine. Now comes the hard one. Do you consent to having us remove your right eye to save your left eye?"

There was no response.

Kaplan looked at the other three present and shrugged his shoulders in frustration.

"Let me try something," said Tom. "Mo, this is Tom. I know you understand. Are you not responding because you're still thinking about how to respond? Squeeze my hand if you're thinking about it." Tom thought he felt a squeeze.

"Ernie, tell him," Tom said.

"Mo, this is Doctor Kaplan. I want you to know we can replace your injured eye with an artificial eye that moves, blinks, everything, so no one will even notice it's not the eye you were born with. It will look exactly like your real eye. If we do nothing, you may be totally blind. What you'll be able to do after you get out of here depends on a lot more than having two eyes. Squeeze my hand if we have consent. Please."

There was no response.

"Let me try," said Kathy. "Mo, this is Kathy. I know you don't give a shit about appearance but if they take the bad eye out, at least you'll have the other one and be able to do everything. Babe, it's like the horse races. Remember when you were in law school and we used to go to Bay Meadows. Remember Poona Kahn in the ninth at Bay Meadows that cold winter afternoon? We could have gone home with our last stinkin' two dollars and felt like losers, but we bet the $2. We ate steak on the way home with almost a hundred dollars left over. This can be the same, if you don't give up. You'll go home a winner. Squeeze my hand if you do."

There was no response.

Kathy continued. "Mo. If the bad eye makes the good eye go blind, you'll never ride a wave again. If you leave this place with one eye good, you'll be back on your surfboard soon. Let them do what they have to do, please. Just squeeze my hand if it's okay."

After a long pause, I squeezed Kathy's hand. "He did it. He did it. He said okay." she screamed.

"That was super, Kathy," said Kaplan, "but it would be better if we had his consent in writing."

"Why?"

"So Mo can't later sue and say he never consented." advised Doctor Kaplan in a voice so serious apprehension submerged Kathy's hopefulness.

"Fuck. You're just like all the other doctors, Kaplan. Just when I was beginning to be fooled enough to trust you, you turn on me. If you won't take Mo's word, get the written consent yourself."

Kathy stomped from the room, infuriated that after she had been able to get me to consent to having my eye taken out, they still were forcing her to sign a consent.

"Let me try to help, doctor," offered Byron. Removing a ballpoint pen from his pocket, he said, "Mo, this is Byron. I'm placing a pen in your hand; I'll help you hold it. If you consent to removal of your eye, try to make an X on this paper." Ever so slowly, the pen left a jagged scrambled mark. Over it, with Byron's guidance, I made another mark crossing the first. "Okay, Doctor; get your consent form. He'll make an X and I'll witness it and there is your signature."

Ten minutes later, Kaplan returned with a consent form. Byron and I again went through the legal formula to obtain the signature of one unable to write and the hospital had its written consent.

That night, Byron, Tom, Jesse, and Kathy were having drinks at the Chart House down El Camino Real from Stanford. They talked about little but what had happened that day. "I don't know if I helped Mo give his consent," Byron pondered, "or whether I just held a pen allowing him to make a mark, not knowing or understanding what he was doing. It would never stand up in court, but I guess Stanford Hospital is satisfied."

"I'm glad you, not me, did it, Byron," laughed Kathy. "I sure wouldn't want to take the stand in a courtroom and testify under penalty of perjury that his consent was knowing and voluntary, much less given with understanding. But I guess they taught you at Harvard Law School how to come as close to the line as possible and still stay legal."

That evening, the first of a herd of medical students arrived at my bedside. My eyes were swollen closed, my body unmoving. I appeared to be a very seriously injured young man asleep. "Hi, Mr. Jourdane, " chirped a happy female voice. "I'm Kate. We're here to ask you some questions."

There was no response.

Kate continued. "Are you aware of anything you are allergic to?

There was no response.

"Mr. Jourdane, can you hear me?"

No response.

"Maybe he lapsed back into the coma." suggested the male student who had accompanied Kate. When he tried to shake my arm, I jerked it away.

"He's not in a coma," remarked Kate. "Mr. Jourdane, I'm Kate and this is Jim. We have to ask you a few questions. Are you allergic to anything you know of?"

No response.

"Maybe he just doesn't want to talk with us," said Jim to a dismayed young lady who couldn't believe a man wouldn't want to talk to her.

After 15 minutes of trying to get me to respond, the two medical students left frustrated. They didn't stop to think maybe I couldn't talk, so they never thought to do what Angie, the Arvin homegirl, had done in Bakersfield: try to have me respond by squeezing my hand.

Sixteen

At 6:40 AM. the next morning, while the anesthesiologist was telling a nurse how many milligrams of ether to add to the IV, Doctors Kaplan and Visnus joined them in the surgery room. Forty minutes later, the removal of my right eye was complete. Doctor Visnus attached the optic muscles to an implant that would allow a prosthetic eye to move normally. "Someday soon," he said to Kaplan, "when we cut an optic nerve, we won't have to helplessly watch it spring to the back of the brain like a broken rubber band. We're very close to transplanting eyes. Once we do that we'll attach the optic nerve to the implant. We'll be able to remove an orbit, like now, and replace it with another."

While Dr. Visnus removed his surgery gloves. Kaplan requested a scalpel and made an L shaped incision into the skin covering the central fracture of my forehead. He lifted the skin like a peel from a Valencia orange and spent almost an hour carefully manipulating tweezers to remove pebble-like fragments of shattered bone. Studying the X-ray confirmed that the fracture had precisely reset itself. I wish the other fracture was going to be this simple, he thought as he stitched the central wound.

He made a similar L-shaped incision over the fracture on the right side of my face, slightly above my eye socket. He again removed nuggets of bone fragments. "There's an overlap where the side of the skull meets the forehead," he thought aloud. "Because of the curvature, we're going to have to hold the bone in place with wire, after we get the sides of the jagged fracture to mesh."

Doctor Kaplan tried unsuccessfully to gently move and massage the sides of the fracture. Finally, he used force. The broken bone snapped into place. A wave. Kaplan sewed up the incision, looked at his watch, and removed his gloves. "Almost exactly four hours. Pretty good guess. Now we wait a few days, see how he progresses and go to step two. Let's remove the respirator and see what happens."

Carefully. Kaplan disconnected the respirator from the tube protruding from my throat. Everyone in the surgery room stared at the monitor screen reflecting my breathing. The off-white graph line that had been shooting up and down against the dark background with every breath I took for the previous weeks lay flat.

"He's not breathing." screamed an aide. "Get the respirator back on. quick."

"Hold on," said Kaplan. "Give him a chance. We can go several minutes without breathing before we face brain damage. The muscles around his lungs have been out of use for several weeks." The group waited silently, staring at the screen.

Doctor Kaplan walked into the hospital cafeteria where Kathy. Tom, Jesse, and Byron waited. "Went like a charm," he smiled as he headed for the coffee dispenser. When he returned moments later, he explained to the anxious visitors what he had done. All the listeners stared in awe when he slowly told them about removing the respirator, about me not immediately breathing, and about the sighs of relief when the surgeons and students saw the monitor's graph line shoot up just over a minute after he disconnected the respirator. A wave.

"How long 'til we can see him?" asked Kathy.

"Kathy, you can visit him in the recovery room in a couple hours, but it'll be best if the rest of you wait until he's back in the ward."

*   *   *

The day after my first major operation, I was again moving and responding to questions through squeezes. Two days later when Kathy walked in, Tom was at the side of the bed. "Kath, I thought of a new way for us to communicate with Mo. It might

89

take some practice but it's gonna be better than questions and squeezes. Let me get a pencil." Tom walked across the monitor-cluttered room to the nurse's station.

When he returned, he tore a paper towel from the chrome dispenser over the sink. He placed the torn paper in my hand. He held the pencil between my fingers and said. "Mo. This is a pencil. Move it and try to make a mark on the paper. I'll tell you if it does."

With Tom's patience and help holding the pencil, I made wobbly lines on the paper.

"When you want to say something, try to write on the paper."

"Since he can't see what he's writing, that might be kinda hard, won't it, Tom?" asked Kathy.

"Maybe," replied Tom. "But hard doesn't stop Mo. It might be slow at first, but he can do it. I learned a long time ago that when Mo has a goal he will do anything to reach it."

Perhaps Tom's statement was based on the adventure we lived when we were pre-teens. Once, we were camping in Yosemite Valley when I was about eleven. After lunch, John and I left camp to go fishing. Mom told us to be back by four since we were going to have a picnic dinner up on Glacier Point. Glacier Point crests the granite wall behind Camp Curry rising 2,000 feet straight up from Yosemite Valley.

While John and I walked toward the river, he suggested we climb the cliff trail up Glacier Point and meet our parents for dinner. I reminded him that the cliff trail is pretty steep, rising about six inches with each step.

With my brothers and sister, I had climbed most of the trails in the park, Nevada Falls, Yosemite Falls, Half Dome, and more. John replied we could handle the cliff trail, unless I was chicken.

When we returned to camp a couple hours later, I told mom about our plan. Apparently not thinking of the notorious steepness of the cliff trail, and trusting our good judgment, she said, "Okay."

About three that afternoon, our parents, Tom, and our sister Barbara Jean left for Glacier Point in the family Plymouth. John and I walked to the head of a cliff trail behind Camp Curry. There we saw a sign, "Trail Closed,"

Our family had already left. John and I decided we had to go for it.

The first mile was steep but we were young teenagers. Problems started when we were about 1,500 feet above the valley floor. A rockslide had covered the two-foot wide trail. Sheer cliff ascended to our left and plunged to our right. For the next two hours John and I slid on our bottoms, inch by inch, across the loose gravel. Every few seconds our movement caused loose granite gravel to fall to the valley over a thousand feet below. I almost cried in ecstasy when we reached the other side of the loose rock. We continued on, not knowing what to expect ahead. Luckily, the trial had been closed because of the slide we had crossed. We had told our mother we would meet her at the top so we had to do it. To keep our word we had to reach our goal, we had to climb a cliffside trail the rangers said was not passable. But for our goal, we never would have experienced one of our greatest adventures of all. Besides, we believed we were invincible.

*   *   *

Holding the pencil to help with its movement, Tom said, "try to make an X."

I left several snake-like lines that didn't cross.

"Good try, Mo," said Tom. "let's try making another one."

After the third try I finally was able to draw a very wobbly X.

"Super, man. I wish you could see this. It's great. I'm gonna save it for you. Now let's draw circles."

91

I managed to draw some loops that were more wobbly worm-like lines. The heads and tails of most of the words didn't touch.

"Okay. Maybe we better try the letter S."

After half-a-dozen attempts, I left a curved line vaguely resembling an "S". Tom and I spent the next two hours practicing all the letters in the alphabet. For those who could see, the product didn't look much like the alphabet, but it was a start. A wave.

During the practice, Kaplan came in and stood near the door silently watching. Tom glanced toward him and continued. When Tom was done with letters Y and Z, the doctor let out a sigh. Tom looked startled. "What's that about?" he asked.

"You're not a neurologist, Tom, but you just tested how serious Mo's brain damage is, and he passed?"

"Whata ya talkin' about, Ernie?" asked Tom, looking at Kaplan with a wondering expression.

"Before I answer that in terms of you and Mo, let me tell you a little more about the brain. There's been a lot of research lately on what part of the brain controls what bodily functions. It's pretty much agreed that the left side of the brain controls the right side of the body and vice versa. The left side also controls most rational and conscious functioning. The right side controls intuition and the subconscious functions."

"All I know," responded Tom, "is that of the four functions of the brain, Mo has shown the ability to move muscles and reason."

"Keep learning, Dr. Jourdane. Although your brother lost his right eye, most of your brother's injuries are to the left side of his head. We've been far more concerned over loss of memory. Today, I saw you ask your brother to make an R and T and a W and about five other letters. The marks he made don't look much like your normal R or T or W, but his mind told his hand to make the letter you asked him to write, without you helping guide the pencil. He remembered what an R and a T and a W looked like, and his brain sent a message to his hand to write the letter. That's memory and thought transmission from his brain to his hand. It might be a minor step to you, Tom, but let me tell you, it's monumental. He's able to function on a conscious logical level based on memory. What I saw you and Mo do showed me that damage to the left side of the brain is minimal."

Before I fell asleep that afternoon, I scribbled some overlapping lines that Tom assumed was an attempt to write a word. After what seemed like hours of trying, he and Kathy were unable to determine what I was trying to write, "Where am I?"

While Tom walked that evening from the hospital to his VW, he saw the intensive-care ward nurse who had spoken with the Governor several weeks earlier. Like an old friend, he walked with her to her small sedan. "Starting today," he told her confidently, "Mo's on the road to recovery. Knowing him, he'll never look back and say 'what if.' or 'if only' or ask why?"

"He may never have enough mental capacity to ask why," said the nurse. "Your brother's recovery has been good so far but don't get your hopes up. I've been working here too long watching patients limp down the impossible road ahead of your brother."

For the remainder of the week, Kathy, Tom or Jesse sat at my bedside encouraging me to try to write letters of the alphabet. Although I do not remember how I felt during these days, knowing myself pretty well, I am sure it was emotional agony to have to relearn what I had so easily mastered as a child.

*   *   *

When Tom and Kathy returned Thursday evening, Doctor Kaplan and the resident were in the intensive-care unit with several students talking about the next day's surgery. Kaplan studied the X-rays. He then examined my jaw. "Lots of breaks," he mused. "Some serious. But even the most serious can be held in place with wire."

"Won't that cause bulges which are visible after the surgery?" asked a first-year medical student looking worried.

"Sure," responded Kaplan with a straight face. "We'll precisely set the fractures, but the patient will perpetually walk around looking like a swarm of mosquitoes attacking his jaw."

As the bewildered student stared at him, Kaplan grinned. "I'm just kidding, Sue. We'll use microwire. It's thinner than thread. It won't be visible. But," continued Kaplan, turning to a resident, "these X-rays reflect a major problem. The collision has misaligned the patient's entire face, including his jaw."

Kaplan held up to the light an X-ray showing my head in portrait. He traced the X-ray with his index finger, as he said, "When our view isn't obstructed by the swelling, we see the lower portion of Mo's face is concave. His cheeks and jaw are depressed over a centimeter."

"Is there something we can do to pull it out?" asked Sue, the most vocal of the students.

"I hope. We will attach wires to the jaw. The wires are attached tautly to a circular brace affixed a couple inches from the skull. The wires pull out the depressed facial bones."

"We ought to be able to finish the jaw in three hours," the resident calculated.

Kaplan nodded. "We should then take some cartilage. He paused as he felt my wrist, forearm, ribs and above my knee, and continued, "from his quadriceps. We'll use it to rebuild the nasal area. We can take bone from a rib and start rebuilding the left cheek. Why don't we get out of here now and let the patient get some sleep?"

The resident and students paraded out of the room. Kaplan stayed for a moment and spoke to Tom. "Unlike the last operation, this one won't have an unpleasant after effect like removing his eye," he said, seeing Tom's concern.

"Is it an important operation, doctor?" asked Tom.

"At this stage, they're all important, Tom. This one will be the key to rebuilding his face."

The following day, surgery number two went as planned. A wave. When Kathy, Tom and Jesse came to see me that evening, I lay with a stainless steel ring around my shaved head. My teeth were enmeshed in wire like a child undergoing massive orthodontic work. Wire strands from the dental bracket connected my mandible or jawbone to a metal brace circling my head. Tom couldn't help but chuckle, "I don't know what all that metal's for, or if the surgery was successful, but it sure looks like they turned Mo into a spaceman."

"They did," giggled Kathy, "or they're trying to get him ready for heaven by letting him practice wearing a halo here on earth." Because I was sound asleep, the three left the hospital laughing about getting me a role in "Star Trek" or maybe even "Star Wars II."

Seventeen

That evening, Tom called Mom to inform her about my improvement and most recent surgery. After telling her about how funny I looked, she replied, "Tom, I've hardly ever had to remind you how to act around your brothers or your sister, but this is too important for me to stay quiet."

"What do you mean, Mom?"

"Since you kids were born, your dad and I have tried to do what we could to build up your self-confidence. There were times we barely had enough money for food and didn't have money for new shoes you needed desperately, but there was never a time we did anything that would lower the trust you had in yourselves."

"I'm hip, mom. You'd always come to our ball games and told us how good our swing was when we struck out. You came to our swim meets and it didn't matter to you if we came in last. You still treated us like we were the best. Why are you reminding me of that now?"

Your brother's going to look different for a while. Maybe forever. He won't be able to see or talk. Losing the face he's lived with his whole life and losing his ability to speak like a courtroom barrister can cause him to lose far more. It's important that you not do anything to reduce his self-confidence"

"I know that, mom. If he feels people are laughing at him, he'll feel he no longer belongs. He'll be afraid and alone."

"You're the only one of us who's there with him, so even though he's always been your big brother now it's your turn to take care of him. I know you can do it."

When Tom laid down the phone, he remembered him and me walking with our baseball bat and glove to Salt Lake Park when he was hardly more than a toddler and I was his big brother. He felt proud. Mom had again placed her trust in him to be at my side when I needed his help. He did not yet realize how immense the challenge would be.

Eighteen

The next morning, Tom and Kathy were sitting beside my hospital bed. "You were a psychology major in college weren't you, Kath?" Tom asked absently.

"Uh huh. I guess it made me a better receptionist after I graduated from college, the job for women who aren't elementary school teachers or nurses."

"You learned much about depression?"

"Some. Like what?"

"Like what causes it?"

There's no single cause of depression. The most common causes are unpleasant experiences in life like a divorce or death of a loved one."

"All people go through traumas. Why do some get depressed and others don't?"

"That can be the result of a lot of factors: nutritional deficit, exposure to toxins, fear, threats, lack of love, lack of joy, bacteria, viruses, many things. Maybe the most important is lack of friends or family to give support."

"Sounds complicated."

"It's even worse. Everyone is looking for a quick fix. Too many mental health experts have aligned with pharmaceutical companies to give the patient instant relief. They've learned that when a patient is depressed the patient has a low level of neurotransmitters..."

What are neurotransmitters?"

"Chemicals that send messages across synapses in the brain.

"A synapse is a gap between nerves, like wires, that send a message from part of the nervous system to another, right?"

"Uh huh." Kathy went on to explain that neurotransmitters, norepinephrine and serotonin, for example, are released from an axon, that is a presynaptic cell, into the synapse. A receptor called a dendrite in the postsynaptic nerve receives the neurotransmitter and passes on the chemical message. A trauma causes one's supply of a neurotransmitter to be low and the person becomes depressed. Pharmaceutical companies have learned that instead of dealing with the problem that makes the patient depressed, all they have to do is increase the patient's norepinephrine or serotonin level with drugs. Kathy felt it unfortunate that we make millions of children addicts of prescription drugs rather than doing the harder job, finding out why they're depressed.

"Mo doesn't like drugs." Tom responded. "So, we have to prevent him from becoming depressed in the old-fashioned way, with love and support, and a reason to live."

* * *

During the following week. Tom, Kathy or Jesse daily asked me simple questions and helped me try to respond in writing. When I scribbled more than a couple letters, it was illegible. Not being able to see what I wrote, invariably I scribbled one letter on top of another. The letters were very wobbly and smaller than I normally wrote. On Thursday afternoon, a week after I burst from the coma, Tom looked at the scribbling and said to Kathy. "It really looks like he's in pain when he tries to write. Think we're pushing too hard?"

"I'll ask Ernie," responded Kathy. "But if he's in pain, I don't think it's because he's trying to write. I think pain's part of the deal. It hurts to see him grimace but I'd rather see him in pain than dead,"

* * *

One morning when Tom arrived at the hospital, I handed him a piece of paper with scribbles. After 20 minutes, with Kathy's

98

help, Tom decoded part of the note. "My face hurts high on the right side..." The remainder of the note was unintelligible circles and lines. Tom told Kathy that if they wanted to communicate with me they had to ask questions I could answer yes or no. Because I repeatedly wrote one letter on top of another, my writing could not be read even with Tom and Kathy's persistence.

"We can ask him to write the letter Y if he wants to say yes and N if he wants to say no," Kathy suggested.

After explaining to me the new system, Tom asked, "Do you know where you are?"

"N," I wrote.

"This is Stanford Hospital."

I scribbled markings that were illegible until Tom asked me, "Does it say, "Who are you?"

"Y"

"I'm Tom. Your brother. Don't you remember me?" Tom tried to force a smile, praying I hadn't suffered brain damage so severe I forgot my own brother. He knew I could not see, but didn't I recognize his voice?

"Oh Yeah," I wrote, "Was just kidding."

Tom grinned. He did not know whether I was regaining my sense of humor or trying to cover up a serious mental problem. "Do you remember being in a wreck?"

"N," I wrote. "I just lost where I am."

"Besides your face and head, does any part of your body hurt especially bad?" asked Kathy.

"Y"

"Your stomach?""

"N."

"Your chest?"

"N"

"Your legs?"

"N."

"Your arms?"

I wrote an illegible answer.

Kathy showed the answer to Tom and Jesse, asking, "Could it be hand or hands?"

"Does your hand hurt?" Kathy asked.

"Y." I wrote.

"I wonder why," queried Tom. "I'm sure they X-rayed his entire body."

"Who knows?" responded Kathy. "Maybe it's a torn ligament or soft tissue injury that doesn't show up on an x-ray."

"Mo, point to anything else that hurts," asked Tom. I did not respond.

"He went to sleep," said Kathy, chuckling.

The three went to the cafeteria.

When Tom and Jesse returned, I was awake with a painful look on my face. "Where do you hurt?" Tom asked.

My answer was illegible.

"Mo, I can't read this," Tom said finally after studying the scribbles. "Where do you hurt?"

Again I tried to write something. Again it was unintelligible. After guessing possibilities, Tom finally got a "Y" when he asked. "Does any other part of your head hurt?"

"There is pain plus nightmares about my head. What is this?"

I scribbled, reaching for the circle surrounding my head. It took Tom and Jesse a long time to decipher what I had written and try to tell me why I had the metal ring circling my head. When Tom finished talking, I wrote, "It's this metal on my head I have bad dreams about."

"Mo, it's just a metal ring, sort of like a brace. You broke a lot of bones in your face. The brace is necessary to heal the breaks. We know the pain is bad. Keep trying to write. It'll take your mind off the pain. My Y and N idea was dumb. You tell us so much more when you write." Jesse saved the notes and would one day give them to me. They are quoted verbatim in this writing.

"The problem is you never learned how to read too good," I wrote, letting Tom read the note and handing him another. "Just kidding. For some reason I am not being..."

After unsuccessfully studying the note, Tom finally handed it back to me, "Mo, can you re-write the last three words."

I rewrote the words. Tom looked at the note and said, "Okay, brother, we're making progress but I still can't read the last two words. Can you write them one more time?"

Finally, Tom and Jesse were able to decipher the note to read, "Just kidding. For some reason I am not being allowed to talk. I really want to talk to you about cut throat. Can you..." I lay back without completing the sentence.

"Mo, keep your spirit. Once they take the brace off your jaw you will be talking for sure."

I handed Tom another. "I know you are right. I trust the doctors. Have to sleep now."

Looking at the scribbled notes I had written, Tom shrugged his shoulders and said, "I guess we learned today that Mo's span of attention is about five minutes. Then he falls asleep."

Jesse looked at her watch and asked, "Tom, how long do you think we've been talking to him and having him write notes?"

"Maybe five or ten minutes," he replied, displaying a few notes.

"We've been here three hours."

Embarrassed, Tom sheepishly grinned, "I guess it takes a long time to figure out what he's writing, but maybe he's right, we can't read too good."

Jesse smiled.

*   *   *

The following evening. Tom and my friend Luis López were there when I awoke. Apparently seeing that I looked particularly distraught, Tom asked what was wrong.

I scribbled, "They tried to give me medicine for pain. It didn't go in right and is stuck in my mouth. Can you open my mouth part way? It's killing me, the pain."

After finally deciphering the lengthy note, Tom and Luis didn't know how to respond. My mouth was wired shut and I was receiving medicine through the IV. Before he said anything, I handed him a second note. "I'm fucked. I'm blind. I feel like shit. It's real dark in this room. Sort of...." There were a few unreadable lines followed by, "The darker it gets, the harder it is to see. I know you are sitting next to me, but I can't see you. I really wish I could see with all my eyes. It's very difficult to look and not see."

"It'll get better," responded Luis, praying inside what he said was true.

Tom walked to the sink and waved Luis over. "He's obviously confused. You think it's safe to tell him about losing his eye."

After Tom explained what had happened and why the hospital had to remove my eye, I responded, "I can see with both. It changes. Most of the time, I still don't feel normal. I can't see hardly anything. One eye I can hardly see out of. Plus I can't breathe any good. I'm tired of fighting losing. I want to die."

"Mo, you don't want to die," pleaded Luis. "You have too much to live for and the fight for farm workers isn't over."

"The breathing problem is caused by the trach, Mo." Tom anxiously replied. "It'll get better."

"So is my right eye gone, now?

"Yep," responded Tom, hoping to convince me it was not important.

Catching the positive tone of his voice, I asked Tom, "I guess loss of my right eye is no big deal, right?"

"Naw," said Tom, hearing our mother tell him how important it is to be positive.

"Do I get money for it?"

"Probably."

"If someone takes something from you they have to pay." I wrote.

As Tom started to respond, I scribbled, "Yesterday I kept seeing a pillow that was a bunch of stars put together. Weird. huh?"

"Mo, you should tell Doctor Kaplan when you see things like that," Luis managed to say.

"It's okay. Luis," I wrote, reading his thoughts. "I'm not crazy. They got so much dope in me it's like an acid trip. When they leave me alone, I'll be okay. What time is it?"

Just then, Kathy came in. Tom showed Kathy the notes about wanting to die over a missing eye. Shaking her head slowly, Kathy looked into Tom's eyes. "I knew it was going to be bad when he realized what happened. After he's made it this far, I'll die if he falls into a depression he never comes out."

Nineteen

A few days later when Tom arrived at the hospital, he sat silently after I handed him a note. "What kind of things can't I do with only one eye?". When Tom looked up from the note, I handed him another. "Where is my eye?"

While Tom pondered how to answer, María Leslie walked in. Maria had been coming to Stanford Hospital since I arrived. She was a true multicultural American: African-American ancestry; born in Philadelphia: reared in Guadalajara, Mexico; and graduated at the top of her class at Mills College, an Ivy-League like liberal arts school for women in San Francisco's Bay Area. With her energy, her cultural background and her Spanish fluency, she, along with appealing Santa Monica beach girl and University of California at Berkeley graduate Ellen Sward, Shirley Treviño, and Margarita Decierdo, a half Filipina, half-Mexicana graduate of the University of California Santa Barbara gave California's Agricultural Labor Relations Board a dream team conducting elections and investigating unfair labor practice charges.

"Hi, lover." Maria chirped. "Almost well, I see. It's time for a test. What's your name?"

"Mo."

"Who am I?"

"I can't see you so I don't know for sure, but you sound like Maria."

"Good guess." María giggled.

"Where are we?" I wrote.

María sketched a map showing where Stanford is located between San Francisco and San Jose.

Holding the sketch upside down, unable to see but staring with my only eye as if I was studying it like a law book preparing for the bar exam, I finally set it down and asked, "So, when do I get to go home?"

"As soon as the doctors believe you're able to live alone in the mountains in Aptos, far from a hospital," answered Maria.

"If they let me go, I know the fastest way to get help. All I have to do is call 911."

*   *   *

A couple days later, Tom came in and asked how I was feeling.

"Okay, I guess," I wrote. "Is it night?"

"Nope. It's afternoon."

"Good," I wrote. "Then we can go for a walk. I can't remember my name." Unintelligible scribbling followed.

"Your name is Mo and you can't walk yet. You're still hooked up to machines."

"I thought they removed the machines."

"Just the respirator. They still have monitors checking your pulse and stuff. Plus, there's an IV stuck in your arm."

"Maybe in a little while I might be able to walk," I wrote. "Would you tell the doctor I want off the machines so we can go for a walk?"

"I'll talk to Kaplan."

"Thanks." I wrote, "I need to feel the air. I want to go outside real bad," I emphasized. "They won't even let me walk inside. Since I can't go in the sun, the only good thing I do is see you with both eyes."

Tom looked perplexed. I wrote, "I'm just kidding. My right eye got punished way worse in the wreck so they took it away."

The next morning, my sister was at my bedside when I awoke. After kissing my swollen cheek, she asked how I felt.

"Why can't I talk now?" I wrote.

"You'll be talking soon, Mo. If you're already thinking about talking, you must be feeling better."

"Not really. My right eye hurts. My right eye hurts," I wrote. "Did you know friends stole it?"

As Barbara Jean read, I continued. "It's dark all day outside. Is that 'cuz' with one eye I only see half the light?"

"Don't worry, said Barbara. "Your vision will improve." Trying to be as encouraging as she could, she added, "I bet they're treating you good here."

"I'm not being abused," I wrote, "but I feel beat to shit. If my eyes stays same, I am blind. As a lawyer, I am through. And I hate not being able to talk. Please tell the nurse to take the tube that comes out of my throat so I can talk."

Barbara left the hospital unsure whether I had suffered severe brain damage. She was concerned about my blindness and doubted I would ever again be a trial lawyer.

Twenty

When I awoke the next morning, Shirley was next to the bed. The last time I remembered hearing her speak was in the fairground parking lot in Santa Maria shortly before the wreck. The last thing I recalled her saying was, "Drive careful, Vato."

Now, I heard Shirley say they all missed me.

"I'm glad you finally came," I wrote.

"Mo, I've been coming to see you for weeks; since you had the wreck. You look so much better than when I first saw you." Shirley could see there was a long way to go. "Now that we can talk, or I can talk and you can write, we have a lot to talk about," she said gently. "Do you remember the wreck?"

"I can remember the dance on my last night, but not afterwards." I waited while Shirley read. I handed her another note. "I really need to talk with you about what happened that night, Shirley."

"Sure, but first tell me how you're feeling?"

"Okay," I wrote, "but I want to start talking."

"You will be soon, Mo. Probably when they take the wire off your teeth. You look like you didn't get too hurt except for your face."

"Yeah, but my knee got scratched in a wreck," I wrote. "Plus, my teeth are wired together and I keep yawning and pulling the bound teeth so hard it hurts. I can't make any movement with my teeth. They will probably want to do another operation."

"I don't think they plan to do another surgery on your jaw," Shirley responded.

"I've gone over it very carefully in my mind I'm ... (unreadable)," I wrote. "The surgery made memory very difficult. I don't want any more operations."

"It wasn't the surgery, Mo," encouraged Shirley. "You have the best doctor around. It's the wreck that causes you not to remember things, right now. Plus, all the dope they're filling you with to alleviate your pain. The doctor's very careful to do nothing that could hurt your memory."

"I know you are right. But I feel too torn apart to believe they have helped."

Wanting to distract me from thinking about my physical condition, Shirley said she had so much to tell me. "After they got rid of you in Bakersfield," she said, "the General Counsel transferred me to Salinas. It's bad for the farm workers in Delano with both of us gone. Because of what happened to you, the board agents and lawyers are afraid to vigorously enforce the law like we did."

Slowly, I began to write. When I finished, I handed Shirley a note. "I think if we meet for a day and figure out how to chill the fear of the Farm Labor Board agents and lawyers we can do it. I know all our people want to enforce the farm labor law. All they need is some encouragement and coordination."

"You can't leave the hospital so can we have the meeting here?"

Just then, Tom walked in. "I don't think the hospital will let you have a group of people here in intensive care," he said.

"Maybe we can wait until he's out of intensive care," Shirley said. "Do you know when he's moving to a normal room?"

"Let me go ask Ernie," said Tom.

"While Tom's looking for your doctor, let me tell you about the union election at Giumarra Vineyards," said Shirley. "You won't believe what happened."

After Shirley talked for ten minutes about how farm workers felt they were deprived of a fair election, I asked, "Has it been hot in Bakersfield?"

Shirley looked shocked. "Is this the same Mo Jourdane I worked with side-by-side during the past few years, fighting for farm workers' rights?" she asked herself. "He cares more about the weather than what happened on the election at the company he was negotiating with over unfair labor practice charges when his wreck occurred. If he's lost his commitment to farm workers, he has nothing to live for." She nearly cried fearing her old ally had suffered brain damage and would no longer be a fighter.

Just as she was about to tell me how she felt, Tom walked in. Tom told her that Doctor Kaplan said how long I would remain in the intensive care unit depended on my condition. "If we can wait, Shirley" Tom said, "there should be no problem with holding it in a normal hospital room where Mo will be eventually."

Shirley told Tom what just happened with me. "I'm not sure I want him at a meeting, any longer," she ended sadly.

"I know he sometimes shocks you, Shirley. He does me too, but we better get used to it. The doctors say it might not be a temporary condition."

"It better be temporary," threatened Shirley as she brusquely turned and left. "Just tell your fucking brother lying in there that the farm workers need him in Delano fighting, not hanging around a hospital talking crazy."

Twenty-One

One Saturday Kathy was beside the bed when I awoke.

"Hi, Kathy," I wrote. "I'm sorry I can't see you good yet." "That's the last thing you should be sorry for. There are lots of other things, but not that. How're you doing?"

"To be honest, I hurt pretty bad, right now. There's sharp metal causing pain in the right side of my head."

"Did it just start?"

I had the pain all night."

"Did you tell anyone?"

"Yeah. They gave me medicine that worked, but it made me feel weird. Now the pain's back. Most pain you have to beat alone. Medicine might help, but you have to beat it alone."

"I wish it could be me instead of you for a little while," whispered Kathy, "You know, when you first came out of the coma, you hardly ever mentioned pain. Now it seems like it's almost all you ever write about. Does it hurt all the time?"

"From the time I get up. It made me cry yesterday. Sometimes, there is a big part of me that feels it would be better to die than take this. I've had pain, and pain is pain, but I've had it."

When Kathy finished reading I wrote, "I know complaining doesn't make pain go away. I know I can't just cry over it and it will be okay. I have to look ahead. I'm sorry I bitch so much. They almost got me a couple weeks ago, but I will beat them."

"Is anything especially bad?" Kathy asked.

"My biggest problem now is my eyes. I hope they get better so I can see."

"You'll get better. I promise." "The only thing is the sooner the better. My vision is real bad."

After Kathy and I shared several hours alone together, she asked, "Do you think a lot about the wreck?"

"I guess I haven't really thought about it," I wrote. "I'm thinking too much about survival."

"Are you worrying about going back to work?"

"Not really. I hope I have enough of a head start on new lawyers to keep doing okay. But I am worried about not being able to see. It doesn't seem to be getting better." Trying to smile, I wrote, "but having you here makes me OK,"

"You bullshitter." Kathy smiled. "You sounded down, but now you're all happy, Mo."

"I am happy because you are here," I don't know why you came back from Hawaii, but I'm glad you're here. It's fun talking to you."

"Come on. When you get serious, you start talking bullshit."

"I'm serious," I wrote. "I'm okay now but I'll be way happier when I'm back all the way me. I think they're going to finish with my jaw completely this month. They are going to do final work to teeth next. Within a month I'm going to Mexico. Want to go with me? We didn't go for a long time, since a few years with David and Susan and Terry and Marcia and Rusev. Remember pulling over and riding waves with them at every break we saw between Manzanillo and Puerta Vallarta?"

Kathy smiled. "Who knows when that'll be?"

"A trip to Mexico would be fun for us. We can run. I can fall. You can laugh. Why are you here?"

Kathy laughed anxiously. "We have too many years together for me just to let you lie in a hospital across the ocean. We've gone our separate ways, but I still love you."

"Then you'll go to Mexico with me? We can go surfing. But maybe the wreck made me forget how to surf."

"You forgetting how to surf is like forgetting your name."

"One is hearsay, one is memory. My name is hearsay."

"Hearsay?"

"Hearsay is what someone else tells you. Like gossip. Someone else told me my name. Surfing is memory."

"You're still a lawyer. Soon you'll be back surfing again."

"I'm not a lawyer or a surfer anymore. Before I could see. I've been a whole lot of years winning with only minor defeats. This is the first big one, but I have enough family and friends like your saying it will be okay that I believe it."

While Kathy talked and I wrote, Byron Georgiou arrived. Byron was one of my most frequent visitors. He would drive the 650 miles from the Imperial Valley to Stanford Hospital. Sitting down, he nonchalantly asked how I felt.

"I undergo more pain each day than I ever had. It feels like a lot of pressure on my face."

"Does it hurt now?" he asked.

"Yes. It hurt this whole day since early this morning. "

"Can you describe it?"

"Constant pressure. Last night it hurt so bad and I'm not able to talk to ask for morphine or something to help."

"Is your face what hurts the most?"

"It hurts bad but not as bad as my throat, "

"Have you told your doctor about it?"

"I tried to but I don't think he understood. He thought I wanted the tube in my trachea removed. I know without the tube I cannot breathe and I need it, but is that what's causing my throat to hurt?"

"I'm not sure, Mo. I'll talk with Doctor Kaplan before I leave."

Just then Kaplan walked in. After examining me, he said he thought I had a simple sore throat aggravated by the tube.

I nodded my head as the doctor spoke. When Kaplan finished, I wrote, "Is the tube getting clogged?

After checking my throat, Kaplan replied, "looks okay."

"When I'm breathing now, I'm really breathing. Right?"

"Yes," replied Kaplan, smiling,

"Then, I don't need to breathe with the tube since I can do it myself. Right?"

"Wrong. The trach helps you breathe. Without it you wouldn't get enough air."

"But if I'm not breathing, I'm dead. I'm not dead. It's too confusing. I only know when I'm breathing with the trach; it hurts and is too noisy. If I hold my breath. I can live quietly and with less pain. Right?"

"Wrong. If you hold your breath too long, you die."

But when I breathe it makes noise and I cough. It hurts."

"Mo, we want to get that tube out and get you out of here as soon as possible. Let us do what we think is proper."

"You guys have five years to do what you want to me. This hospital has pushed me around a lot but I hope you keep getting me better."

"You're getting better every day. All it takes is time and a whole lot of effort on your part. I think you're going to be out of the intensive care unit soon."

"What about my vision? I can't see nothing. How can they let me out of intensive care before I can see?"

Twenty-Two

The next morning, Tom walked in with Dr. Kaplan and an aide. "Okay, Mo," said Tom grinning. "Out comes the trach. Off come the monitors. Time to quit faking it. Before you know it, you'll be 'outta here."

"That means we can go for a walk?"

"Uh huh. And you're getting out of the intensive care unit, but they're going to let you keep your IV for a while. I hope loss of all the machines that keep you alive won't be too much of a shock to your ego."

"I hate to change rooms or leave this part of the hospital," I wrote. "The room has been freezing but I feel safe here. It'll be scary to go to another room. Will I be all right?"

"Mo, you've moved around your whole life. You're like a water skimmer being chased by a dragonfly. Getting out of intensive care means you're on your way home." I heard Tom's words, but I did not tell him that I was not the same person who could travel around like a water skimmer. For the first time, instinctively, my body needed the security that comes from staying in one place.

*   *   *

The next evening. Carlos Bowker arrived. I wrote, "Carlos. I walked around the hospital."

Carlos looked at Tom to see if what I wrote was possible, Tom nodded. "I was with him. We went out to the hallway. It was slow and steady, but he and I and his IV, like R2/D2 attached to his arm, went down the hall. I felt like I was walking with a space man and his robot dog. He wants to go outside tomorrow, but I don't know."

"I can't believe he's out of intensive care so soon," said Carlos. "Walking has to be good for him."

"I think to recover he has to accomplish short range goals. He's been talking about walking ever since he came out of coma, I guess it's as good a short range goal as any."

"A few days ago he was in a coma. Now he's walking around the hospital. He's like a caged jaguar. It's unbelievable. I guess your doctors are real competition to our brujas."

Tom looked at Carlos inquisitively.

"Brujas are female witch doctors in my country, Tom. Here, doctors just use medicine and machines instead of natural herbs and dead swallows like the brujas. Seeing Mo improve so quickly. I'm about ready to start believing in modern medicine and abandon the old ways, but it would kill my abuelita (little grandmother) in Jalapa. It'd be like you white folk giving up religion."

"I handed Carlos a note, "Do you remember the first week?"

Before he responded, I wrote, "Maybe I should rest first." I fell asleep leaving Tom and Carlos reminiscing about that first week and their belief I'd never see today.

*   *   *

The next morning, I wrote a note to Tom. "When am I supposed to be OK? Long time?"

"Kaplan says if you keep improving like you have been, you'll be going home in a month or so."

"Why so long? Even another week sounds like forever."

"You're lucky to be alive. Let the doctors worry about how long you get to stay. This is your chance to kick back and rest for a while."

"I'm tired of being in the hospital," I wrote. "During the night, it's hard to sleep because of this thing on my head and the pain and when I finally get to sleep, the nurse comes in and wakes me

115

up. It doesn't do any good to tell her anything. I think I do pretty good but..."

Tom tried to decipher unintelligible scribbles, and I continued to write. "Today was weird. The first few days I was too screwed up to worry about my condition. Then I spent a week or so pissed about it. More than anything it's weird. During the last three weeks, which is what I remember, I've thought more about me, my family, my friends, my skills, my job, all of it. For the first time ever."

"It's about time you thought about us," Tom said, grinning.

"That's the good part, but this week was an example of the bad part. It hurt real bad when they took the tube out of my trachea. But I guess I need their help since I've got a lot of body work to do, but I'm ready to go home."

The next morning Tom told me that the doctors wanted to check for damage to my central nervous system.

"Oh shit," I wrote. "Every time they do exams on me it scares me. What if they find out I'll never walk again, even though I can do it now, or I'll never think again, which I can. I want to get out of here before they decide I'm a paraplegic."

I stayed around for the examination and didn't become paraplegic. The doctors were pleased and probably surprised that I had no central nervous system damage. A wave.

Twenty-Three

Shirley was there when I awoke. Yielding to my pleading. She and I and my IV walked down the hall, up the escalator and found the way outside.

Chilled by the bay area evening gusts when we opened the door into the setting sun, I wrote, "Why don't we stay in where it's warmer."

Back in my room, Shirley dug in her purse and pulled an inch pile of hand-addressed letters.

"Can you put them with the others under the bed," I wrote. "Someday I'm going to write back to everyone who wrote me and thank them."

Shirley reached under the bed and pulled out an eighteen- by-twenty-four-inch box crammed with envelopes. "There must be thousands here," she exclaimed. "Can we look at some of 'em." She grabbed a handful of envelopes. "It looks like all of 'em are from farm workers. We're not in a hurry, are we?" She smiled and leaned back next to me on the bed. Trying to comfort herself against the hard hospital pillow, she started to read.

"Lots of them are from people we worked with last summer in Arvin and Lamont," she said after reading one to me and leafing through the envelopes. "I can't believe there are so many."

There were only about five in the first few weeks, then hundreds," I wrote. "These letters are worth more than all the money the farm labor board or the truck driver who almost killed me could give me. It shows the amount of money we earn is meaningless. Returning to the fields to help workers improve their lives gives me something legitimate to live for." A wave.

Later, when I awoke from a nap, Shirley was still sitting beside the bed reading a novel. With her at my side, I rolled the IV through the door and down the hall. We spent an hour walking the hospital halls. While my IV and I slid slowly along, Shirley and I talked about the wreck. "Has your lawyer shown you the police report?" she asked.

"From my wreck?" I stopped and wrote. "Uh, uh!"

"I don't remember," I wrote.

"Have you seen the complaint your lawyer filed in your lawsuit?"

"No. I didn't even know I had a lawyer. I haven't seen anything. Not that I could read it if I did see it."

"Do you remember the wreck, yet?"

"Remember a little about the night of the wreck, but I'm not sure. Is this correct? I drove with you to the fundraiser for battered Latinas. When we got there we worked. When it was over, you went to San Jose and I left for Bakersfield?"

"Uh huh," responded Shirley. "We went there together. We sold tickets so people could get food and drinks. I came to San Jose and you left for Bakersfield. I should have stayed with you. This might have never happened."

While we talked, Shirley sounded angry when she said that Farm Labor Board agents were afraid to enforce the law, "It's really screwed up," she complained.

"Is anyone from the union's legal staff trashing you guys?" I wrote.

"Probably. Jerry Cohen says they're disappointed. He says the problem is the Farm Labor Board's absence of leadership."

Shirley told me she had spoken with César Chávez. He wanted to see the Board succeed. He told her to call Governor Brown.

I began writing. "Hopefully Brown will support us. He's still a friend of the farm worker. I know that when the board's general counsel was appointed by the Governor, the new general counsel told the Senate he would step down anytime Brown asked him."

"Brown should ask him to leave," Shirley said.

"We can try to convince Brown to ask him to go," I wrote.

"All any of us want is to see farm workers for the first time ever get justice," Shirley said.

"Brown will help us. The growers might have the money, but there are way more farm workers than growers. If they vote, they can have the voice in rural California they should have."

Twenty-Four

When I awoke the next morning, Kathy was at the bedside. When she asked how I felt, I immediately started writing about how the hospital would never let me sleep at night. "Come on, Mo," said Kathy. "You're making it worse than it is. They saved your life."

 Kathy apparently believed that changing the subject would distract me and stop my whining about the hospital. She told me that after my wreck the police wouldn't follow up on union leadership's belief that the collision was not an accident. "It's like a Mafia hitman," she said, "shooting an FBI agent and no one even wondering if there was a crime. Instead, Shirley was transferred out of the San Joaquin Valley for trying to enforce the Farm Labor law. It's like transferring to Alaska the person who shot FBI agent's partner because she wants the law enforced, and crime goes wild. Board lawyers and investigators are afraid to do anything the agribusiness industry frowns upon. It doesn't matter whether you're in the streets of Chicago or the fields of the San Joaquin Valley. Some people believe they are above the law."

"That sucks." I scribbled. "It's unreal to me that I won't be a lawyer for 3 or 4 months and the cops don't even care to find out what happened. I thought I was pretty tough. I guess I ain't so tough after all."

*   *   *

 Early one Saturday morning, the United Farm Workers' chief organizer, Marshall Ganz was at the hospital. "Hi, Mo." he said as he sat down next to the bed.

"Is that you, Marshall?"

"Uh huh"

"I heard you were coming." I wrote. "I'm glad I finally got to see you. I can't really see you but you know what I mean. It's nice to hear your mean voice."

Ganz told me how things had gotten harder for the workers over the past six weeks. "Do you remember what happened on the day of the wreck?" he asked.

"Time is a little mixed up. I think I remember the day before. Problem is much of it is...." The remainder of what I tried to write was not readable.

I wrote what I remembered.

"Yeah, the bartender. But I didn't talk with him much. Do you think he was somehow involved in my crash?"

"We're checking-out what happened," replied Marshall. "I don't remember what happened, Marshall. Are they going to let the man who tried to kill me go free just because he says I was so drunk I drove with no lights on? How could I drive over 100 miles in pitch black before he pulled off the dirt road blocking the highway in front of me?"

In retrospect, I realize that anguish over law enforcement officers' failure to look further into how my collision occurred was probably the result of almost always having been able to do what was necessary to get what I wanted. Since I did not grow up in a financially affluent family that could afford to spoil me, my self-confidence was more the result of being able to do what I felt I had to do. After the collision, I had to learn one of the hardest lessons of all, I was no longer physically able to personally do what I felt was necessary. I had to depend on others and the others would all too often not do what I might have done. I could have done it myself. The police failure to investigate the possibility that my collision was not an accident was part of this dependence.

Twenty-Five

One morning I awoke to see Luis Jaramillo. Luis was a friend from the Salinas office of California Rural Legal Assistance. He grew up in El Paso, attended Stanford as an undergraduate and law school at Notre Dame. He came to Salinas one summer as a law student, met and married Ann who taught bilingual education at El Sausal Junior High in East Salinas, and returned to Salinas after becoming an attorney. Together we fought the school's unwillingness to educate children of farm workers. When I left CRLA a few years earlier Luis took over the duty of monitoring the supplemental education of the farm workers' children who had been deprived of an education after being erroneously labeled mentally retarded.

"How are you doing?" Jaramillo asked as he entered the room, his youthful face beaming.

"Okay," I wrote. "I don't know if anyone has told you, but I have a very serious disease."

"I don't think you have a disease, Mo. You got hurt in a wreck, but compared to when I saw you a month ago when you were still in a coma, you look great."

"Disease, injury, it's all the same. It's taking a long while for my vision to come back."

"Is everything blurry?"

"Yeah, but the worst is it remains dark all day."

Before Luis could respond, I wrote, "You know. They took the tube out of my throat several days ago. It started out okay but it hurt when it wouldn't come out and they forced it. I feel okay now but I really thought I was going to dust."

"All the pain isn't over, Mo."

"I know, I wonder how long until it's done. I can't take too much more. I'm tired of being in a hospital."

You'll be out soon. The doctors here are very good. They know what they are doing. They want to see you out of here as much as you want to leave."

"I guess I don't have much faith in doctors anymore," I wrote. "I've been here about two weeks and they keep saying I'll be out soon, but here I am."

I think it's more like two months," Luis said.

"Whatever. The doctors took the tube out of my throat and hooked up something like Christmas tree lights on my vocal cords. That might look neat but it's stopping me from being able to talk. I am getting funnier looking and funnier sounding each day."

Tom came into the room and Luis handed him my notes. "Almost all he talks about is his physical condition," Tom told Luis that everyone who visits asks me how I feel and I tell them. Suddenly Tom had an idea.

That evening he called Shirley at her East San Jose cottage. He suggested they hold the meeting with farm labor board workers they had talked about a few weeks earlier. "We have to keep Mo distracted," Tom told her." We need to have him realize what happened in the Giumarra election and how the General Counsel's staff isn't doing anything to enforce the law. I'm sure that will distract him from being so concerned with his injuries and give him something important to recover for."

"Tom, farm workers aren't just a distraction. Their deplorable living conditions are something Mo wants to improve. That's something to live for. I'll see if we can get together with Mo this Saturday," Shirley responded.

*   *   *

The next morning, I awoke to feel Shirley next to the bed holding my hand. "Hi, Shirley," I wrote. "I wish I could talk with you."

"Soon, baby. You'll be back talking like your old lawyer self."

 Instead of asking how I was feeling, as she normally did, Shirley asked if I wanted to hear about the Giumara Vineyards election. After I wrote that I did, Shirley again told me the story of what happened in the election and all the unfair labor practices the company was charged with committing before the election. This time I was angry. Shirley was relieved to see me returning to my old self. Each note I handed her showed increased frustration. My notes revealed that I was distracted from my physical condition but for the first time in my life seemed to realize there were problems I was physically unable to do anything about. It was a very hard lesson. A wave.

 "I love seeing you pissed-off," smiled Shirley. "You're cute when you're mad. Plus, you have a good reason to recover."

Twenty-Six

Three days later, I awoke to see César Chávez's brother Richard and UFW founder and Board member Gilbert Padilla sitting silently next to the bed. I was slowly beginning to see well enough to identify visitors at my bedside, if they were close enough. "Como está, guy," asked Chávez. "How do ya feel?"

"Richard, Gilbert," I wrote. "How are you doing?"

"We're okay, but you're the one who got hurt, not us," responded Chávez. "We're up here visiting Gilbert's wife. You know Esther?"

"Como no (Sure)," I wrote. "Is she here? Where is she?"

Gilbert told me Esther was in the other wing. "We almost didn't come by," Gilbert said, "because we've heard there were so many people here visiting you. We looked in and you were alone so we stopped." said Chávez. "We can only stay a minute."

Esther would recover and one day become a member of the Fresno City Council. Gilbert had worked with César Chávez and Dolores Huerta at the Community Services Organization (CSO) during the 1950s. He was a farm worker in the Los Banos area until he joined the army in World War II, only to return and experience less pay than Braceros received. In the Kings County town of Hanford he led one of the first and perhaps most massive voter registration efforts in California's history. He joined César in Oxnard in 1960 and is one of the unrenowned heroes of the formation of the farm workers union that would become the United Farm Workers of America, AFL-CIO.

"I'm glad you came," I wrote to Gilbert and Richard that day in the fall of 1977. Gilbert Padilla and Richard Chávez leaving what I knew was a battlefield in the Sun Joaquin Valley to drive five hours to Stanford Hospital reminded me how important familia is to the farm workers' movement. Struggling almost nonstop for improved working conditions and an improved life for their children is part of the Latino value placed on familia.

No one understood this more than Gilbert and Esther Padilla and César and Helen and Richard Chávez.

"Why?" I wrote.

"We think they blocked the road with the oil truck trying to kill you and Shirley. You know some big oil companies also grow grapes.

I didn't respond for a while. Finally, I wrote. "Quien sabe (Who knows). I know there are some who don't like me, They would like to see me dead, que no? (right?) They might have tried to kill me. But if they wanted to do that, why not just shoot me?"

"They don't want to make you a martyr for the farm workers' cause. It's better for them if you have an accident and are just gone."

"Can we talk about something besides how my wreck happened?" I wrote. "You guys know a lot about agriculture. You have done more to help farm workers than anyone in history, but I'm not sure you're very good detectives."

I was largely told that César Chávez's belief that agribusiness corporations had tried to kill me and Shirley, was summarily rejected by law authorities because he had no proof. Since I was preoccupied with trying to survive and unable to go to the San Joaquin Valley and take part in an investigation myself. I had to depend on others. I would learn later that there was evidence that the collision had been an attempt to kill me, but not wanting to be paranoid, and because I felt it did not matter whether agribusiness corporations intentionally caused the collision or whether I was just in the wrong place at the wrong time, I chose to go on living a life I could have some control over rather than chase what may have been a shadow or a ghost.

During the spring of 2005, John Moore, my long time friend, fraternity brother at San Jose State and classmate at Hastings College of Law called when a series of articles on the United Farm Workers appeared in the Los Angeles Times. During our conversation, my wreck in 1977 came up. John told me that during the months after the collision he played poker with agribusiness supervisors in the San Joaquin valley. One night he was playing with a supervisor from a large melon and lettuce grower. Half-drunk, the supervisor told Moore that management from his company and management of a large grape grower met before my collision, during the summer I had successfully forced the melon Corporation to allow union organizers into its labor camp to speak with workers in the evening, the summer Shirley Treviño and I questioned the president of the grape grower about a number of unfair labor practices charges filed with the Agricultural Labor Relations Board. Moore told me that the supervisor of the melon company told him that one of the grape grower's management boasted, "Don't worry about Jourdane."

"I know the Agricultural labor Relations Act helps the union because workers can freely choose to support the union, but I don't think the growers would try to kill me just because I tried to enforce the law fairly."

"The Governor passed the Act," said Chávez, "because he feels workers should get a fair share of what they earn for the companies."

"When they do," I wrote, "their other problems like not enough food on the table and their children sharing their beds with cockroaches will be a thing of the past. Killing a lawyer won't stop the wheels of history."

"You've caused growers a lot of headaches," said Chávez.

"I've learned from you."

Chávez chuckled. "What do you want to do after all this is behind you?"

"I'd like to keep representing farm workers, but when I read the hundreds of letters sent by farm workers saying they hope I get better soon and come back to help, I realize people expect too much of me when I recover. I don't think I'll ever be able to be as good as they expect. So many expectations scare me."

Twenty-Seven

Just before seven the following Friday evening, friends from the Agricultural Labor Relations Board arrived in my room. I handed Shirley a note, "What is going to happen tomorrow? Are we meeting with the Board?"

The General Counsel still refuses to vigorously enforce the law, so some farm labor board employees are coming here to meet and talk about it. A few of us are here tonight to discuss how to convince the other farm labor board employees who will be here tomorrow that we need to do more to enforce the law."

"I appreciate being included in your efforts even though I know I can't be much help doing whatever you decide upon," I wrote. Years later I would realize that through their support my friends were helping me recover, they involved me in their effort so I would understand I had an important reason to recover. A wave.

Shirley started the meeting by reminding us, "Workers are being fired. The Union's filing charges with the Labor Board and the General Counsel is dismissing them because our agents are afraid to say anything in their investigative reports that is harmful to the growers."

"Why are they afraid?" I wrote.

"Why are you in that bed?" asked Shirley rhetorically, obviously considering my question very dumb.

"Does the union know that's happening?" I wrote.

"Yeah." Shirley shrugged. "But it's powerless to do anything. When the union tells the press that the farm labor law isn't being enforced, the General Counsel just replies that he's merely enforcing the law fairly, for the first time."

"What we have to do tonight," said Carlos, "is figure out how we can get the Board to start enforcing the law. If we handle it right, tomorrow the others will agree with our plan and push for it."

 Shirley began. "Ya know, Carlos, because you're so popular with the people who are coming tomorrow, maybe if you remind them that your life is in danger so long as you're out there alone trying to enforce the law, they'll support our goal and we could start from there rather than having a fight about whether we should do anything."

 "What'll he say if someone asks Carlos why he is in any more danger than all the rest of us?" inquired board attorney Frank Fernández.

 "Everyone knows the Imperial Valley is dangerous, and everyone knows many growers hate Carlos," responded Shirley. "Don't forget the General Counsel tried to fire Carlos until Mo represented him and the judge said the General Counsel couldn't do it. The growers are afraid Carlos is going to enable their workers to freely decide whether they want to have a union. That'll cost growers money. To them, he's the same as a coyote trying to steal their chickens. They kill coyotes. With Mo gone, Carlos is soon to follow."

 "What can we do?" asked Luis López in apparent frustration. "We can't get our fellow employees all over the state to start enforcing the law all by ourselves."

 "Many within the state want the farm labor law enforced," I wrote. "They know campesinos work too hard to be paid almost nothing and treated like dirt. Shirley says the General Counsel won't let her help them." I continued to scribble. "It sounds like we aren't protecting the farm workers, after we promised them the farm law would be behind them if they were fired for exercising rights that the labor law guarantees. Governor Brown's people have made it clear the governor wants to do what is necessary to help the Board start enforcing the labor law."

Shirley turned to Byron. "Georgiou, you're Brown's friend, Will he support us?

"When the time is right," responded Byron.

"That sounds like a candidate's press release, Byron?" quipped Shirley. She had been confronting politicians since she fought the system while a student at the University of Santa Clara, the same university Governor Brown attended. "What does when the time is right mean?"

"If pressure builds up, steps will be taken to guarantee the law is enforced."

Apparently not satisfied with what she considered a wishy-washy response, Shirley asked me. "Have you talked to the Governor?"

I wrote, "No, but yesterday, I spoke with the Governor's lawyer. I'll start at the beginning. Several days ago Gilbert Padilla and Richard Chávez told me about problems at the ALRB. I mailed a telegram to Brown. After he got it, Gray Davis called...."

*   *   *

The next morning my hospital room was packed with employees of the Agricultural Labor Relations Board gathered at Shirley's suggestion to discuss our duty to enforce the law passed to guarantee farm workers the right to unionize. That evening, Shirley returned to the hospital. I told her I was ready to go back to work. I told her that I had a plan on how to build the farm labor board agents' confidence in enforcing the labor law.

"When do you intend to put your plan into effect?" Shirley asked in a motherly tone.

"I think they are going to take a long time with my face. But in 3 or 4 weeks more. We should be ready."

"What are they going to do to your face?"

"I'm not sure, but I think it's going to change me looking weird so I can do stuff without everyone staring at me and not hearing what I want to say. I realize how seriously hurt I am and how long it's going to take, but I'm ready."

"Mo, your face is coming along good."

"Now you sound like all my friends. Everybody tells me that but it is still messed up."

"You have a lot of people on your side, Mo," responded Shirley. "We want you back to work, not lying here in the hospital feeling sorry for yourself."

Twenty-Eight

On Monday morning, Doctor Kaplan removed the wire holding my jaw closed and unscrewed the metal ring encircling my skull. I expected to finally be able to talk. A wave.

That afternoon, Doctor Kaplan stopped by to see me. When he entered, I handed him a note. "I waited months for you to take the wire off my mouth so I could talk. Everyone told me that once I could open my jaw I would regain my talking voice. Now the wire is off and I can't do it. What's wrong with me?"

"Let me hear you try, Mo," said Doctor Kaplan. "Try to say, 'how are you today, friend."

"I can't." I wrote.

"Just try."

"Okay," I wrote. "Here goes."

My fear had been loss of vision. Now, I was devastated that I could not talk. I set down the paper and pencil, sat on the edge of the bed, looked into Kaplan's eyes and said, "'ow are 'o 'oday, 'end."

I picked up the pencil and wrote, "See, Ernie. I can't do it. Rather than make sounds no one can understand, I'll keep writing notes. That way I can be understood. I guess I just have to add lost-speaking ability to my list of consequences of the wreck."

"Don't be silly," Kaplan said firmly. "It's been several months since you said a word. Because your jaw has been wired shut so long you're unable to open your mouth even though the wire has been removed. That combined with your numerous missing teeth causes you to be unable to speak clearly. Don't worry. You'll be talking soon."

"When? If only I could say a few words. Do you think my talking problem is caused by something in my mouth?"

"I doubt it. Does it feel like there is?"

"I think so. The stuff in my mouth keeps me from putting my tongue where I need to make sounds I want to make."

"Why don't you try rinsing your mouth out and we'll see if that helps. Maybe there's mucus in there."

I rinsed my mouth and tried to speak. "'ello 'end. 'ow are "ou 'o'ay."

I grabbed a pencil and started to write. "Seems like it makes it no better, no worse. No different."

"I think part of the problem is that your tongue is paralyzed."

"Anyway. Thanks for taking the bars off my head," I wrote. "When I took a nap this morning with the metal removed I was able to sleep comfortably for the first time in months. I like it. Thank you."

Several days later, an ambulance took me to nearby Children's Hospital for an examination with a speech therapist. Tom accompanied me. Not long after we arrived, I handed him a note. "All I see are kids. Is this the right place?"

"I think most people who have speech problems are kids."

"I hope they can help me. It's a bummer not being able to talk"

Just then, a nurse entered the waiting room. "Mr. Jourdane" After the doctor reviewed a report on my medical history and present status that Dr. Kaplan had provided, she asked me to try making certain sounds. Several months earlier I had been a trial lawyer who talked almost endlessly. Now, while the doctor listened, concern showed on her youthful face.

Finally, frustrated, I wrote, "I can't do it now. It's no good now. I think I'll be able to do it later. Can I come back later?"

The young doctor encouraged me to try again. After hearing me make additional unintelligible sounds, she handed me a plastic screw shaped object the size of a child's small toy top.

"Mr. Jourdane, put the narrow end between your teeth and try to turn the wide end as far as you can."

I did as the doctor requested. I was able to turn the screw very little, forcing my mouth to open a quarter inch.

"Practice doing that every few hours," suggested the doctor. "It'll help you open your mouth wider. I'm also having the hospital get you a tape player. Try talking into the recorder. Practice making sounds that are particularly hard for you."

"They're all hard, doctor," I wrote,

"Then practice making them all. I'll see you in a few days." A wave.

*　　*　　*

When I returned to my room, I excitedly wrote notes to Kathy. "It was good," I wrote. "They say it is only temporary that I can't talk. I just have to make my mouth open more, move my tongue, and practice making sounds. They tested me. There are hardly any sounds I can make now."

"Well, why don't you put down the pencil and try," encouraged Kathy.

"I think I have to learn to open my mouth first. It's no fun for you or anyone to hear me make a bunch of noises that don't make sense. Every time I try to say something, I sound like I'm trying to talk Chinese. Let me show you the neat thing the doctor gave me to help open my mouth."

I pulled out the three-inch long plastic mouth screw. "I can just get the tip in now making me open my mouth about this far." I wrote as I barely spread my index finger and my thumb. "But if I keep trying, I will be able to open it as far as ever."

I lay back on the pillow and placed the tip of the screw between two of my few unbroken teeth. I turned the screw as far as I could, feeling severe pain where my upper and lower jaw met. I held it there for a few seconds, unscrewed it, relieving the strain

134

on my jaws and took it out. "It hurts but it's going to make me a lawyer again," I wrote. Silently, I repeated to myself, "Faith, persistence and hard work," the path I had learned while scrambling perilous cliffs and swimming countless laps as a child would get me through anything.

Twenty-Nine

"You ready to go see a shrink?" Kathy, asked when she entered the room the next morning.

"What a waste of time," I wrote. "I'm okay."

"I think so, too," replied Kathy, "But let's prove it to them. It might be the only thing that's keeping you from going home."

"What's he going to ask me?"

"I'm not sure. Probably stuff like where's Mexico and where's Canada?" Stuff like that. It'll be easy."

"What's Canada?" I wrote.

"I can't read what you wrote," said Kathy after looking at the note.

"What's Canada?" I again wrote, slowly, trying to be more legible.

"What did you ask me?"

"It's another country, You know where it is."

"Do you know where Canada is?" Fear began to ooze across Kathy's youthful face.

"Oh yeah," I wrote. "We went there once." Then as if a light had been switched on, I began to scribble faster, "You and I went there a few years ago with David and Susan Steingass. We crossed Canada on the way from their cabin in Sorrento, Maine, to their home in, was it Stevens Point, Wisconsin?"

"You got it, Mo." Kathy grinned. "Show the doctor you can think like that and you're on your way home to Aptos."

Kathy helped me get into a wheelchair, and slowly passing empty patient gurneys and unplugged life-support monitors, we headed slowly down the hall toward the psychotherapy department. Kathy took two steps, moved the IV, two steps, moved the IV, two steps, moved the IV. Twenty minutes later we made it to the department. It was less than 200 feet from my room.

"Hi," Kathy said when we entered the small office. "This is Mo Jourdane. He has an appointment."

After looking over an appointment schedule, the nurse directed me to a tiny room within the larger office. "The doctor will be right with you," she said, asking Kathy if she could wait in the visitors' room. When Kathy started to leave, I said, " 'an 'e s'ay"

"I'm sorry, sir." responded the nurse. "I couldn't understand you."

I borrowed a pencil from Kathy and wrote, "Can she stay?" After studying the writing, the nurse responded, "The doctor wishes to see you alone, Mr. Jourdane. Your friend will be right outside."

Kathy hoped I wouldn't panic and fall apart, showing my mental problems. She whispered softly in a voice the nurse could not hear as the nurse walked to her desk. "It's cool, Mo. I want to get a coffee anyway. You can handle it. Just imagine yourself as a witness you have on the stand. Think before answering. Just answer the question asked and stay calm. If you're honest and stay calm, you can win the case. Si se puede."

As she walked away, Kathy smiled at me and asked, "Where's Canada?"

"What's that?" I said with a straight face, before breaking into a big grin. Kathy raised her fist with the thumb up and nodded confidently.

Thirty

I waited alone for several minutes in the office until a doctor walked in. "I've been reading about you," he said, raising his glasses to his forehead. "I understand you are a trial lawyer. Do you recall what the last trial you handled was prior to the collision?"

"Ay I 'ide answer, do'der? Id's ard do da'."

"I'm sorry, Mr. Jourdane. "I can't understand you."

I watched the doctor scribble a note, possibly writing, "Patient cannot speak intelligibly. Confirms Kaplan's speculation of brain damage,"

Having interviewed thousands of witnesses and learned how easy it is to make incorrect assumptions based on what we momentarily see, I decided I better explain. I quickly scribbled a note expressing what I had tried to say and handed it to the doctor. "Would you mind if I respond to your questions in writing?"

The doctor nodded agreement.

"In the vehicle collision, doctor," I wrote, "my mouth and throat sustained extensive injury. I am able to make some sounds, but I know you will not understand most of what I try to say. I want to talk again as soon as possible so I can return to the courtroom. I know your time is valuable, and I believe we can better spend it if I respond in writing."

"Thank you, Mr. Jourdane," said the doctor, setting down his pencil.

Meanwhile, I wrote, "The last trial I did involved discriminatory firings by Hickam Farms in Tulare County. The real parties in interest were farm workers who live in Woodlake. I represented the General Counsel of the Agricultural Labor Relations Board. I don't recall the name of the lawyer who represented the company. He was with a Fresno law firm. The trial lasted about a week."

"Thank you. Where did you go to high school?"

"Huntington Park, near LA."

"What about college?"

"Mostly San Jose State."

"When did you graduate?"

"From high school or college?

"I'm, sorry," said the doctor. "College."

"In 1965,"

The interview continued for the next 45 minutes. The doctor noted, "Good memory. Seems ready to face problems."

"How do you feel about losing your eye?" he asked, moving to more sensitive questions.

"I think it will make surfing and driving hard, I wrote, "and I have some problems with balance but I'm glad the doctors saved the other one even though it isn't too good yet."

"What about your face. Does it bother you, the way you look now?"

"No"

"Why not?"

"Looks change when you get older anyway. Mine just changed quick. I've had lots of good years. My parents always said, "Looks are only skin deep. Whether a person is a good person or not goes very deep. I can still try to be a good person although my looks have changed."

"What about the guy driving the truck you collided with? Are you angry toward him?"

"Shit, yes." I scribbled.

Thinking he almost killed me, I heard Kathy's advice. "Remain calm." I responded, "He forced me to leave important work unfinished"

The doctor picked up his pencil and notepad.

"I'm not as bothered about looking different," I wrote, "as I am about the interference with my effort to improve the deplorable working conditions of farm laborers, most of whom are poor immigrants. I am angry with the truck driver who took that struggle away from me and caused the staff of the farm labor board to be afraid to enforce the law that might lead to improvement of those conditions."

Thirty-One

Several mornings later, Tom walked into my hospital room with Dr. Kaplan. "Well buddy, today we take off the IV and tomorrow you go home." Kaplan beamed. "You passed your mental examination with flying colors. The doctor says you seem obsessed with work you were doing in Kern County and have a strong desire to return to work although you are still very physically disabled."

I felt a shock. I felt fear. "I'm going to like not being cared for. For a long time I've been just someone else's care thing." I wrote. "I'm not allowed to be a person. But it's scary to go away from here. I'm not sure I'm ready,"

"Mo," cried Tom, surprised by my mixed reaction to what he thought was super news. "Over the last few weeks we've heard almost nothing but how miserable it is being in this hospital and how much you want to get out. Now it's finally happening and you aren't sure you're ready?"

"Well, I mean," I wrote, "where will I go? Do I go back to my apartment in Bakersfield?"

"Kathy wants to take care of you in Aptos," said Dr. Kaplan. "If there's any problem, she can call me. The important thing right now is to see how you do without the IV. You can't open your mouth wide enough to eat solid food yet, so I'm prescribing the food supplement Sustacal."

"Does it matter that my cough is coming back?"

"We'll watch until tomorrow. Unless it gets bad it won't stop you from leaving the hospital. Coughing's good for you"

With that, Doctor Kaplan removed from my arm the needle that had kept me alive for the past two months.

Thirty-Two

By seven the next morning, like a child out of bed at dawn on Christmas morning, I was dressed, ready to go. Excitement lay ahead. But under the veneer of anticipation was fear. I was scared. Freedom meant change.

When the nurse walked in, I wrote, "I have some nurses I want to say goodbye to. I owe my life to you. I know that doctors do the cutting and stitching in surgeries but you are the ones who kept me alive. You fed me. You gave me the love and encouragement I refused to accept when I was crazy and complaining. Doctors receive the credit and pay they deserve but it is your kind words and gentleness that kept me going."

"Mr. Jourdane, you have fought us like the best, but we'll miss you." While we spoke, in walked four more nurses who had cared for me in the intensive care unit.

I tried to say, "Thank you," sounding like, "'an 'ou." One hugged me and began to cry, "We heard a rumor that you were leaving. We wanted to come by to say goodbye." The nurse looked me in the eye and tried to smile. "You were dead when I first saw you, Mr. Jourdane, I would have bet my paycheck you weren't going to make it. Now you're ready to go surfing."

I was about to cry. "I didn't do nothing but lie there." I wrote. "You and your friends did everything to get me better. I can't thank you enough."

"You don't have to thank us. We owe you a thanks for writing notes to us about the union problem we were having. We thought we would have to strike but your positive attitude helped us get through tough times."

As tears came to my eyes, I turned my head, trying to hide them just as Tom and Kathy walked in. "Same old Mo." Tom said, "surrounded by the ladies and trying to act all modest. What say you and I hit the road, cowboy?"

When a nurse told Tom we had to wait for Doctor Kaplan to arrive and that she was waiting for a wheelchair, I managed to say, "waid 'es. chair no." Few sounds I made could be understood. I still had to learn that to be understood I had to avoid sounds I could not make. I had to learn to talk again at age thirty-five.

Before long Dr. Kaplan arrived. "You've made a miraculous recovery, Mo," he said. "When you came in you had no nose. I thought we'd have to glue one on."

Tom and Kathy chuckled.

Turning to them, Kaplan continued. "He actually grew a new nose. I've been a doctor for more than 10 years and have never seen it happen before. The cartilage replaced itself."

Staring into my scarred and distorted face, Kaplan said, "Your nose might be a little off-center and kinda pug but you're heart's in the right place."

Smiling, I shook Kaplan's hand firmly.

"He's not saying it's all over, Mo," Kathy said.

"She's right," Kaplan said. You'll need a number of operations over the next few years. Your vision is still pretty bad. We won't know how much it'll improve for a year or so, I have the name of a doctor who's with the Center for Partially Blind here in Palo Alto. I want you to call and make an appointment to see him. He can help with glasses and exercises to improve your vision. I want you to keep practicing talking with a tape recorder and using the jaw spreader the speech therapist gave you. When you get settled in Santa Cruz, make an appointment to see a speech therapist there. With your positive attitude, your faith, hard work, and persistence, you'll be back representing farm workers in the courtroom before you know it. Do you have any questions before you go?"

I was barely hearing what Doctor Kaplan was telling me. Anticipation of the freedom I knew lay ahead, paddling out through the waves at Pleasure Point, saturated my thoughts. The thrill of dropping into an overhead swell blocked the reality of lost vision. "When can I go surfing?" I asked meekly. Kathy chuckled.

"I wouldn't if I were you," warned Kaplan. "You only have one eye left. If a loose surfboard hits that one and damages it more than it is, you'll be blind. But it's up to you."

Kaplan paused, then expressed a change of mind. "I know that what I recommend on surfing isn't going to have much bearing on what you do. For you to keep improving it's important for you to have short range goals you can reach. You keep improving and you might be back to surfing by summer."

I grinned.

"One more thing, you should walk on flat smooth surfaces. Until you get used to your vision, you're going to have lots of trouble falling, bumping into things and knocking things down. Almost all the time there will be a problem caused by your limited vision."

"My only other question is, they brought this wheelchair but I can walk. I can walk out of the hospital, can't I?"

"No. It's a hospital rule. Everyone has to leave by wheelchair. Good luck, buddy. I'll see you Tuesday."

"Bye, Do'dor." I managed to say. I started to speak, "When I'ame 'ere a ou...." I stopped and grabbed a piece of paper. Frustrated with my inability to express myself in words, I wrote, "When they brought me here a few months ago, I was as close to being dead as I could be. You and the nurses saved my life. Thank you Doctor. Thank you." As tears came to my eyes, I stopped writing and sat in the wheelchair with my head down.

Moments later, the glass door slid open. Kathy and I walked into the chilly winter sunlight. Tom pulled his VW to the curb. Kathy and I climbed in. The yellow VW moved toward Aptos with the stereo blasting the Beach Boys "Surfin' USA." Free at last, I thought. Free at last. A wave.

Thirty-Three

On the ride over the hill from Stanford to Santa Cruz, I sat wide-eyed in the VW front seat. I had traveled curvy Highway 17 thousands of times, many with my surfboard hitch-hiking from college in San Jose to the waves at Pleasure Point. Now, for the first time, watching the passing redwood trees, it struck me how beautiful California is. An hour and a half after leaving the hospital, the VW wove Trout Gulch Road along Aptos Creek bubbling and churning through the dark-green forest surrounding our mountain hideaway. Tom turned off Trout Gulch Road onto partially-paved, one-lane, Loma Prieta and maneuvered the bucking-bronco climb to the dirt road we called Westwood Lane. I felt like I had made it to heaven. The Aptos hills swept away my novel fear of change. October rains had transformed hills that were Labor Day brown when I left them in early September to a deep shade of November green. The towering redwoods, the prehistoric fern, and the brook the dirt road crossed after leaving the Loma Prieta's pothole scared asphalt ended, had not changed.

When the yellow bug turned onto the dusty drive leading home, I knew I looked different than when I was last there in early September, the weekend Star Wars was first released, but the gray squirrels, the three-toed salamanders, and the banana slugs that lived there year round had not changed. Nor had our small wooden house. I was about to notice for the first time how dimly lit it was inside, cluttered with furniture, books, and historical junk I would trip over because of my inability to see.

Leaning against the house were three surfboards, like puppy dogs awaiting my return. Lying under the ivy-colored awning was our mixed blood sheepdog Timber, who, as I slid from the car, jumped on me apparently happy to see his closest friend back home.

Twenty minutes after I entered the house, the phone started ringing. It didn't stop until Shirley's olive-brown Mazda pulled up the dirt road as the sun set over the forested hills. Kathy had gone to downtown Santa Cruz to meet friends for dinner. Twenty yards from the house, Tom and I sat near a blazing fire on an ancient railroad tie lying near the brick pit Tom built a few years earlier. Shirley wasn't alone. Lupe Pacheco was with her.

Lupe was a giant woman, only five-foot-three but weighing almost three hundred pounds. Together with Fanny Toner whose commitment to the farm workers kept her at the office late into the night notwithstanding her incredible typing speed, Mexico-born Lupe had typed my seemingly endless legal briefs at California Rural Legal Assistance. One night when we were nearly drowning in problems besieging the farm workers in the Salinas Valley, Lupe pleaded, "Can't you slow down. Boss? It seems like you're out to save the world's poor all by yourself. You file a pinchi (damned) lawsuit to help the farm workers every pinchi week." When I left Rural Legal Assistance for the Agricultural Labor Relations Board, so did Lupe. While I was in Sacramento and in the Imperial and San Joaquin Valleys, she worked with the Farm Labor Board in Salinas. Lupe and I saw each other rarely but remained good friends.

"Hi," I said, walking toward Shirley's car. "I'm 'lad you 'a'e, 'oo. Id's 'een a 'on' dine. Sorry I 'an' 'al' 'edda," I slurred, grinning. I knew Lupe could not understand my attempt to tell her I'm glad you came, too. It's been a long time. Sorry I can't talk better.

"Oh, Abogado. I don't know what you said, but I wouldn't have missed for anything coming to see you on your first day home. I saw you in el hospital, but you was sleeping. They told me you were still hurt real bad but you look super duper." Lupe wrapped her ham-size arms around me like her baby.

"Don't squish him, Ruka (Sister), kidded Shirley. Lupe's best friend and Madrina (Godmother) of her five-year old daughter.

"You're just jealous, Shirley." Lupe laughed as she slowly turned my one-hundred-and-ten pound body around by the shoulders, studying it and laughing. "I known this vato way before you."

I grabbed a pencil and began to write.

"Why aren't you talking instead of writing?" Lupe asked.

"It's too hard," I wrote. "I'm going to keep doing notes for a while. I can't talk too well yet."

"Mo," said Shirley, "we came to see how you're doing but also to talk about having another meeting to decide what we should do about the Labor Board not enforcing the law. We agreed at Stanford to picket in Sacramento but it didn't improve things. We're gonna have a meeting here, okay? We can meet Saturday. We could have a barbecue."

While we talked, the women and I heard a car bouncing up the road. Walking from the fire pit to the dirt drive, I saw headlights shining on the steep hill behind the house. I heard a loud giggle. "It's Maria Leslie," Shirley said, chuckling. "No one giggles like that lady."

The car door swung open and out jumped the slender African-American, her hair almost as short as mine and just as curly. She immediately rubbed Timber's brown neck and white belly as he rolled onto his back in ecstasy, scratching the air with his hind legs. "Hi, Timber baby. Shirley, Lupe, how did you know Mo was here?

"We called the hospital. What are you doing here?"

We flew to San Francisco and drove down the peninsula to Stanford hospital but he was gone, so we drove over the mountain. We can have a party now." María giggled. Byron slid out from behind the driver's seat.

"So how does it feel to be home, lover boy?" Maria asked as she clutched my shoulder and pulled me tight.

Sliding from her grip to grab my pencil, "Nice," I wrote.

"What is this paper and pencil shit?" María scoffed as she crumpled up the paper and broke the pencil. "You're out of the hospital. No more takin' it easy. Adios writing notes. You're going to talk. How else are you going to represent the workers in all the cases I've been getting ready for you? Me and you already have three trials set."

"I 'an' 'al' 'ood 'u' yed," I slurred.

"Did you understand him?" laughed Maria, turning to Shirley.

"I think he said he couldn't talk good enough yet," said Shirley.

"Tough shit, honky. It's a hard life. No more paper and pencil. Besides, we brought you a present and I came to cook dinner for you. Give him the present, Byron."

I opened the book that Byron handed me. I was about to say I couldn't see well enough to read. Before my eye rested very large print. A wave. "I'an 'ea' id," I said, trying to tell Byron that I could read it. "an's," I said, trying to say thanks.

"It was written for the partially blind," explained Byron while I flipped through the pages, "by a veteran who lost an eye in the war. You aren't even partially blind. If this guy could do all the things he says he was able to do, you'll have it easy."

Trying to say, it looks good; this guy was able to fly a plane, I slurred, "loo's 'ood; iz 'uy iza'le do 'ly a `lane."

 "So the loss of one pinchi eye won't slow you down from representing farm workers." maintained Maria with her wide grin. "Plus, wait until you taste what I'm fixin' fa dinna'. It'll make y'all well."

 "I'an' ea' yed," I slurred.

 Three times Maria asked me to repeat. Finally, she gave me permission to write. "I can't eat, yet."

 "This you can." she replied. You have a blender?"

"Mo, we have to go," said Shirley. "Maria's enough for you and Byron to handle in a night."

"You said, it," responded Byron, laughing as María stared venom at Shirley.

"Don't let me slow you girls down," María spit out as Shirley and Lupe rolled back on the grass in laughter. "We didn't mean to interfere with your affair with Mo."

An hour later, María handed me a bowl of pasty green something. ""wud iz id?" I asked trying to find out what it was, wishing it was a plate of fried chicken with maybe a corn fritter on the side.

"I blended some boiled asparagus and added some secret spices. It'll be yummy."

I took a spoonful. It took all my will power to hold it down. Half-hour later, María was pleading, "Come on, Mo. Try some more. We have to get some meat on those bones. You look like a skeleton."

Grinning my toothless grin, I slurred, "`an's Maria. Id was `ood bud I'm 'ull," trying to say thanks, it was good, but I'm full. That's the trouble with 60s kids, I thought, everyone has to eat healthy food.

Thirty-Four

Several days after returning home, I had my first appointment with Paul Dragavon; one of Santa Cruz's few speech therapists. Years before the wreck, Dragavon and I had worked together on Suzanne Paizis congressional campaign and Jerry Brown's gubernatorial campaign. Kathy dropped me off at his home office surrounded by hundred-year old redwood trees in the Branciforte Hills overlooking Monterey Bay. "I'll be back in a couple hours," she said.

 I nodded and slurred, "I o'e 'e 'an 'el' 'c," trying to say I hope he can help me.

 "With your spirit, you'll be back in court within weeks." encouraged Kathy, not understanding what I had said.

 Doctor Dragavon responded to my knock. Wearing wire rim glasses, Levi's and a blue work shirt, he looked like a physician from the neck up. Below his neck, he looked like a Berkeley radical. He stared at my contorted and asymmetrical face, one side swollen and sagging, the other apparently untouched. Where had once been long curly brown hair now was a cropped butch haircut.

Dragavon spent most of that first visit checking the sounds I had trouble expressing. After about an hour, he told me that he had seen a number of patients who suffered strokes; were he not familiar with my medical history he would have assumed that was what caused my condition. He summed up his analysis "You have four or five special problems, Mo. Any one of them alone would result in severe speech impediment. The wreck caused your throat to be paralyzed totally on the left and partially on the right. So you aren't able to make any throat sounds like the hard 'g' in 'get' or 'go," or the hard 'e' in 'car' or 'catch.

 "Your tongue is fully immobile on the left and partially on the right. To make most sounds we place our tongue in a particular part of our mouth. We press our tongue against the inside of our front teeth when making a 'th' sound, like in 'the.' Paralysis also causes you to be unable to rapidly move your tongue in your mouth, from where it was to where it needs to be to make the next sound. For example, I have to move my tongue all over the place to say vegetable.'"

"I haven't spoken with your doctor at Stanford, yet," Dragavon continued, "but it seems the valve between your nasal passage and your throat, which normally closes when you speak, is locked open. I suspect that's why your sounds are so nasal, like a New Yorker."

"The paralysis in your lips prevents you from making many common sounds. Like B, F, M. P, R, V, Wh and Sh. When you try to make a "P" sound without closing your lips, no sound comes out. Add to these problems your inability to spread your jaws more than half an inch and all the missing teeth, and the result is inability to speak. I understand why you want to communicate in writing."

An'ou el' 'e'a'li' Iu' do?" I slurred,

"Can you write what you just said, Mo? I may be able to tell you the cause of your problem but that doesn't make me very good at understanding you"

I wrote, "Can you help me talk like I used to?"

"There are things we can do at the start." Dr. Dragavon replied, apparently not answering my question because he did not want to tell me that no one could help me speak clearly again. "Exercise your tongue and lips. Try to move your tongue like this." He placed his tongue through his open lips then rotated it like a clock hand touching all corners.

I tried. When I stuck out my tongue, it went to the left corner of my lips like a car that lost its steering and hit the curb.

"We have to practice that one," said Dragavon.

I nodded.

"Next is getting your mouth open wider. The mouth screw they gave you at Stanford is perfect to overcome that problem. But just having it doesn't do it. You have to use it. Every hour or so, use it and try to open your mouth this wide." Dragavon opened his mouth fully. Apparently seeing the shock on my face, he added, "I don't mean you should open it that wide today, but eventually."

I tried to smile and again nodded.

"Third, is to get those lips moving. Try this exercise," he suggested, holding his lips closed on the right but open on the left. He then shifted his lips so they were closed tight on the left and open on the right.

"Next is to get back those guttural or throat sounds. The only way to do that is to talk. I want you to spend as much time as you have speaking into a tape recorder. When a sound is impossible to make, replace it with a word you can say. Instead of standing there like a fool trying to make a sound you can't make, other words will enable you to say what you want. For example, you can't say, "get" but you'll soon be able to say "obtain." You're lucky you speak Spanish. The hard G and K sounds you can't make are of Germanic not Latin origin. There are many things you will be able to say in Spanish because it's a softer less harsh language. For example, try to say, "It is cold.""

""Id' is 'old.""

"Now try hace frio." Hace frio means it is cold, in Spanish.

"Hace frio"

"Your accent's a little off but you just doubled the vocabulary you're able to use, at least when talking to your Spanish-speaking friends. You'll also learn that if you speak slowly, you're far more understandable."

"Next, quit using the pencil and paper. The only way you'll ever talk again is to practice. If you don't have permanent nasal paralysis you can build up strength in a damaged nasal valve by holding your lips closed with your finger, and blowing. You want to keep your nasal passage closed internally."

"They showed me that when I was still at Stanford," I wrote. Demonstrating, air came out my nose when I blew. I looked at Dragavon.

"That's what I thought. It is an open valve. Try blowing gently at first and if the valve can be strengthened that part of your problem may be solved."

I held my lips closed with my finger and thumb, blew gently and my cheeks puffed out. Some air again came out my nose but I smiled and tried again.

"Finally, down the line, when you get caps on those broken teeth, you'll see a big improvement. But in the meantime, do the exercises, try to get your mouth to open wider, use the recorder, and talk."

There was a knock at Dragavon's door. It was Kathy.

After I arranged to return in a week, I walked to the car in shock, opening and closing my lips from side to side. I knew I had a problem talking, but didn't expect it to be so serious, the result of so many causes, and perhaps irremediable. The fear oozed through my shoulders and chest like quicksand. It's time to see if I have enough faith and persistence, I thought.

Dragavon walked behind me talking with Kathy. She asked softly, "Look pretty bad?""

"Yep."

"Can it get better?"

"Better? Sure."

"Will he ever be able to speak in a courtroom again?"

"Probably not," responded the speech therapist.

"Any idea how long 'til he can speak so people can understand him?"

"Nope. If he gets some of the feeling back, that'll help. If he can move his lips better that'll help. If he can move his tongue that'll help. When he gets his mouth to open wider that'll help. When he gets caps on his teeth, that'll help. If he speaks slowly, that'll help. But when will he be able to speak so he can be understood? At best he'll always sound like a drunk New Yorker when talking to a stranger, especially over the phone. Help him, Kathy. Encourage him, but don't get your hopes up. Given the extensive paralysis in his mouth, he'll probably never talk well enough to be understood."

For the next couple weeks, I sat outside whenever it was warm enough. I moved my tongue and lips, blew, and spoke into the recorder. After speaking into the recorder, I listened sentence by sentence to what I had said, and repeated it, saying over and over the sounds I had trouble enunciating. Everywhere I went I carried the plastic mouth screw and slowly opened my mouth a little wider, maybe a thirty-secondth of an inch a week. I constantly walked around blowing into my closed mouth, Because my lips were paralyzed, I had to hold them closed with my fingers while doing this exercise. Each time Dragavon saw me, he was encouraging. The lip and tongue exercises seemed to help. Kathy repeatedly reminded me to slow my speech down and choose words I could pronounce. By mid- December, Dragavon could understand when I spoke very slowly.

Repeatedly, I reminded myself, "Faith, hard work and persistence." Nothing was going to stop me from being a lawyer for farm workers again.

Thirty-Five

A few days after I returned home from the hospital, John Rusev pulled into the drive. "Jourdane," he growled in his baritone John Wayne voice, "I called the hospital and they said you were out. I figured you'd be surfing at Pleasure Point."

 John chuckled at his wit. "I drove by Pleasures and didn't see you, so I came up the hill."

John Rusev was a six-foot-five-inch, two-hundred-fifty-pound college tackle at the University of California. He had been a high school teammate of Terry McDonell and both had been recruited by (then) young coach Bill Walsh and Mike White to play at Cal. Later Rusev was thought to be a high draft choice for a career in the National Football League, but injuries to both knees ended that. John's father had ridden the rails to California seeking work during the Great Depression. He ended up in San Jose. After graduation, having inherited a passion for helping the needy, John worked as a counselor with Job Corp at Pleasanton, a semi-rural area east of Oakland. One afternoon while John rode his motorcycle in Berkeley, an elderly retired Cal professor pulled his car out in front of John from a side street. John almost lost his right leg from a severe fracture. He spent one year in and out of the hospital. Rusev settled a lawsuit for the elderly driver's insurance limit, $100,000, not much given the massive hospital bills and a lifetime of limping and inability to engage in almost any sport. John immediately took part of the money and bought his father the new Volvo he dreamed of one day owning.

With a full beard and shoulder-length hair, John had been a regular at the Aptos stronghold. By the time I was home from the hospital, he was working construction days, and every night studying the Wall Street Journal, Barons, and anything else he could lay his hands on with information on the stock market. He was going to invest the remainder of his lawsuit settlement.

Reaching into the back seat of his car, John grabbed a paper bag, pulled out a six pack and offered Kathy and me a beer. "I don't know if you've had one of these since your wreck, but when I was in your place the first beer tasted like the best thing that ever entered my throat."

I grinned, twisted the cap, and took a drink through the quarter inch I could open my jaws. As beer ran down the front of my T-shirt, I immediately began choking. Hoping I wouldn't choke to death on my first week home from the hospital, I finally stopped coughing, found a pencil and wrote: "I guess I couldn't wait, But it sure tastes good. Thanks, John. I just have to drink it more carefully."

"Can you still throw horseshoes?" asked John over his shoulder as he walked to the pit and scraped the caked mud off metal horseshoes that had lay there since the previous summer.

"I 'an 'ry." I responded, trying to say I can try. I picked up a shoe and stared in the direction of the other stake. When I was ready to throw but could not see the stake 40-feet away, I handed the shiny horseshoe to John and slurred, a'e la'er," trying to say maybe later. My head hung as I walked back to the lawn chair.

"Why don't you play?" asked Kathy.

"I really want to, but I can't see, Kath," I wrote.

"Give it a try, Mo. You know how hard it is to throw it. I'll point you in the right direction."

"Naw. I'an't. (I can't.)"

"Try once." Kathy pleaded, standing and taking my hand.

"O'ay." After trying to say, okay, I walked to the nearby stake, studied the direction where I knew the other stake was planted, having thrown thousands of shoes toward it after work in our sort of 60's commune. Slowly. I swung the horseshoe back, and let it slip from my fingers. While Kathy stood watching silently, the shoe flipped over once as if in slow motion and hit the stake.

"Ringer," yelled John, as the horseshoe spun around the stake. Before he finished speaking, the shoe flew off the stake.

"Almost a ringer," he said apologetically. "What's this? I can't see the stake, shit. You faker."

"I'I 'ould zee or id 'oulda' 'een a 'in'cr," I slurred with a grin, trying to say if I could see, it would have been a ringer.

As I walked with Kathy to sit on the bench alongside the aging redwood picnic table, I looked toward her, slurring, "us lu'. I really 'couldn' see 'e "a," trying to say it was just luck. I really couldn't see the stake.

I had blended feelings. It felt good to throw a horseshoe again. I learned I could reduce the effect of my inability to see through use of feel. I couldn't see the horseshoe stake but once pointed in the proper direction, feeling the shoe slip from my fingers was all I needed. It was another step towards recovery. But, at the same time, I was reminded how injured I was and how I had to acknowledge my broken body, and harvest pleasure from memories of what I used to do, whether I was tossing ringers in horseshoes or dropping into overhead waves at Pleasure Point. Could I experience life through feel and memories instead of sight and action? Could I surf through the tumultuous white water and the glass of the smooth green shoulders of life? I knew I could. A wave. I was too optimistic to believe there was anything I could no longer do. That was about to change. I had a lot to learn.

Thirty-Six

After my weekly visit to Stanford in mid-December, I went to see Dr. McAdams at the Palo Alto clinic for the partially blind located in a residential area a mile east of the campus, The small office was surrounded by late-Nineteenth Century mansions and, just as old, towering maple and beech trees. While checking my vision, the doctor covered my left eye. "Can you read anything on the chart?" he asked.

"No," I responded.

"How 'bout now?" asked Dr. McAdams, adjusting the screen on the wall to make the letters larger.

"No," I chuckled. "My ride eye is mizzin' and I can'd see trough the glazz one."

Dr. McAdams laughed in embarrassment. "You'd think I would know that having just told you I read the report sent over by Dr. Kaplan. Your prosthetic eye is perfect and moves like a real eye, I forgot it wasn't real. Let's see what you can read with the left eye."

"I... Zero," I responded after staring for a minute at the screen on the wall and beginning to say, "I can't see" anything, then realizing I couldn't make the hard "C"" or the "th" sound, I chose a word I could say. I was doing that often with words requiring the hard C sound, T, TH, SH, SC, K, C and hard G

"Let's take a look," said the doctor as he placed drops into the eye to dilate it. "Why don't you wait out in the reception room for a few minutes and we'll see how it's doing."

Half-hour later, Dr. McAdams told me that my orbit was sound but scared; I had possible retina damage, and obvious damage to my optic nerve.

After writing a note, he commented to me, "at least there's no sign of glaucoma and the torn tissue in the orbit is healing."

"Does sa mean id won' 'e' bedda 'an id is ride now?" I asked.

"I couldn't understand you, Mr. Jourdane."

"Are you zaying I won' be able do zee 'edder than I do now?

After asking me several times to repeat what I said, Dr. McAdams answered, "Your vision probably will improve. There's still a considerable amount of mucous-like fluid on the retina. Hopefully that will dissipate. But you have a scar on the lens and a scarred optic nerve. Those are permanent injuries."

I rode back to Aptos silently.

"What's the matter?" Kathy asked as we passed through San Jose.

"No'in," I said, trying to say nothing.

"I know you're down about what the doctor at the center told you."

I shrugged my shoulders. "My vision has to 'et bedder," I moaned as I stared out the window. "I'll never drivea'ain. I'll never surfa'ain. I'll never be a lawyera'ain."

Kathy was quiet. As we headed down the hill into Santa

Cruz, she pointed toward the beach-boardwalk a mile ahead. "Can you see the blue ocean beyond the roller coaster?" she asked.

"No, and 'oing to da 'artially 'lind center isn't "oing to hel me ever zee id. Bud I feel hedder jus' knowing id's "ere."

"I hope you'll return to the Center for the Partially Blind,"

"I 'robly will. Id's hard do admid, bud thad's whad I am, 'artially 'linxi."

"Hard to admit you're partially blind? Mo, quit feeling sorry for yourself. You could be totally blind."

"I know. Than's for doing whad you had do do do ma'e sure I wasn'. I owe you a lod. Yeah, I'll 'eep 'oing do the cen'er for the 'artially 'lind. I'll 'eep 'oing undil I see a'ain."

Not sure what I said, from the tone Kathy knew it was positive. "You can do it, Mo," she responded. "The vision center is one of the keys to getting you back to work, to surfing, to living a sort of a normal life."

*   *   *

When I wasn't going over the hill from Santa Cruz to Palo Alto to see Dr. Kaplan or Dr. McAdams, I hung around our mountain cabin and read. After finishing the book Byron gave me, I was enthused. I borrowed from the Partially Blind Center, "The Boys from Brazil" and "East of Eden," in very large print.

Each day, I walked somewhere. I started just going to the barn fifty yards from the house. Unable to see more than a few yards, I tripped and fell, repeatedly. By the end of the first week I was walking half-a-mile to the mailbox at the bottom of Loma Prieta Hill to get the letters from San Joaquin Valley friends. By the end of the second week, I walked three miles down the hill to Tom and Jesse's cabin alongside Aptos Creek near where it enters the ocean. I tripped a lot, unable to see cracks in the asphalt or where the blacktop met the dirt at the road's shoulder. Falling slowed me but didn't stop me from standing and walking again. It was hard to admit I was partially blind, but through faith, hard work and persistence I would be a lawyer again, and a surfer.

Thirty-Seven

A couple days after I went to the Center for the Partially Blind with Kathy, I called Tom. "Wanna fly do Sa'ramendo wi' me?"

"Do I want to fly to Sacramento with you?" he asked, beginning to understand my strange dialect. "What for?"

"Brown's office phoned do zee how I was doin' and I tal'ed wi' 'ray Davis. He wan'z me to fly up dere for brea'fas" Sadurday. Wanna go?"

"Gray Davis? Sure, But why don't we drive? It's as fast as flying by the time we drive to the airport in San Jose, wait for a plane, fly to the Sacramento airport, rent a car and drive to the Capitol Building. Why don't you call Davis and tell him we're driving up."

Early Saturday morning, Tom and I left Aptos for Sacramento, a three-hour drive to the northeast. On the way I stared out the side window at the green hills speckled with grazing white-faced Herefords. "Can ya see the cattle?" Tom asked.

"Varely. Bud I zee da hills are real 'reen. It's li zomeone sdole three mon's a my life. Before da wre' it was all dry and hot. Now it's 'reen and 'oll. "

"Yeah," said Tom, pretending he could understand everything I said.

As we entered Sacramento, Tom asked, "Where we meeting him?"

"Know where da Senador Hodel (the Senator Hotel) is?"

"Senator Hotel? No."

"Know where da "apitol is?"

"The Capitol? No."

"Follow da zign do downdown Za'rameno."

Tom followed the downtown Sacramento sign. "Okay, we're going across a bridge, looks like a river. Know where we are?"

"Uh huh. It's the Za ramteno Riva. Go sdraid. "an you zee da 'apital sdraight ahead?"

"The Capitol's ahead of us, maybe a mile,"

"`o to da end of dis street' an' turn right." I recited from memory, not able to see where we were.

"Okay," said Tom as he turned right at the end of the street leading toward the Capitol Building. "Now what?"

"`o left at da first 'orner. I din' it's N Street."

"Got it." said Tom, "N Street." We passed along the south side of the State Capitol building.

"At da nes 'oner, durn lef'. (At the next corner, turn left.)"

"Okay, we're at the next corner but it's one way the wrong way. We'll try the next. Okay. Now we're on 16th street."

"`o two blas' and durn lef'."

Partially understanding. Tom responded, "Now we're on L Street."

"Da Senador Hodel is at da 'orner of dis street and Eleven"."

"I see it," replied Tom. "I'll find a place to park. You do pretty good navigating for not being able to see."

Five minutes later, while we walked to the coffee shop of the Senator Hotel, I said, "'rey may already be 'ere. I won' be able do zee him. He's about sis feet tall, blond hair an' real head, always wearing a dar'-'lue 'oad, whi" shird and a dar die."

As we entered the coffee shop, Tom saw a man he thought was Gray Davis sitting at the counter talking with the elderly waitress. We walked to where the man was seated.

When I was within several feet of the man, I could make out the Governor's Chief-of-Staff. "Hi `ray. How ya doin'? Dis is my brudda, Tom."

After Gray and Tom shook hands, Davis said, "We have a table. Wanna sit over there?"

"Zure," I replied.

"We've been getting daily reports on your condition from your friends at the Labor Board and others around the Capitol who've either visited or spoken with you or a member of your family over the phone. For a while we didn't know whether you were going to make it."

"He almost didn't," said Tom. "But he never had a doubt,

"'ray, my speege is real bad zo I'm 'oing to write notes, if da's all right," I said.

Gray looked at Tom for assistance after I finished slurring. "He said his speech is pretty bad and wants to write notes, if that's okay?" interpreted Tom.

"Fine," responded the man who ran the Governor's office when Brown was out of state, which was frequent since the Governor began running for president a year and a half earlier.

I pulled out a pen and pad and wrote, "Tom's right. I knew Stanford could help me because it has the best doctors in the world."

"It's unfortunate there aren't enough doctors for everyone's need," said Gray.

"Especially when there are thousands of competent people not allowed to go to medical school," I wrote. "It bothers me that Stanford, one of the best schools in the world, allows so few students a year in their medical school. We hold ourselves out as being so great but under the label of free enterprise we don't let enough people be doctors to treat all our people. All we do is make the few we let through the door of the profession charge the sick or injured eighty dollars for a ten-minute visit."

Deflecting my radical rhetoric, Davis asked, "How do you feel?"

"It's like I was real sick but got better. Since I was a kid, I've sometimes visualized doing something before I do it. Like before a baseball game, I would see myself pitching and throwing strikes or hitting and getting on base. It didn't always work but I felt more at ease when I did whatever I had visualized. In the hospital. I visualized my brothers and me paddling out in big waves at Sunset Beach."

"In Hawaii?" asked Gray, grinning.

"It was almost like doing it." I wrote, nodding. "I can't let a crash, which took only a few seconds to happen, end my whole life. I'm going to go surfing with this guy who drove me up here when he decides to listen to me rather than just my doctor."

"You think you're pretty tough, don't you, Mo?" Gray smiled. "You almost get killed in a wreck with an oil tanker, spend a few months in a hospital, and jump out of bed looking for your surfboard."

"What happened to me is like when I was a kid having a blow out and falling down on my bike on the way to the park to play ball. I scraped my knee, got up and pedaled to the park with a game to play. It's no big deal if I don't make it a big deal. I have the rest of my life to live."

"It's good to see you haven't changed," said Gray. "How do you really feel? Have you thought about the future?"

"Each day I feel better," I wrote. "But I might not be able to ever be a lawyer again. I'm thinking a lot about the future. I've thought a lot about what we do as lawyers, fighting everyone else's fight every day. Each of us has a hard enough time fighting our own battles."

"I don't know why some of us want to fight everyone else's fights, either," said Gray.

Thirty-Eight

Shirley had been visiting me in Aptos every few days. When Tom and I arrived home that night, I called to tell her about the meeting with Gray Davis. Not understanding anything I said over the phone, she agreed to come by the next day. When she arrived, we sat outside at the picnic table. "Mo," Shirley said, "you've been home from the hospital almost a month. Your speech has improved so much. We really need you at work, not here in your safe little mountain retreat."

"Merci, Shirley." I said, choosing the French word for thanks after realizing I could say neither thanks nor gracias. "I am bored, bud I can'd see or say whad I wan' well enough do wor."

Seeing hesitation on Shirley's face, I wrote, "In a few days I have to go back to the partially blind clinic and they are going to check my vision again. I think it's finally getting a little better."

"Can you see me?" asked Shirley from the other side of the picnic table,

"Barely."

"Can you tell if I'm smiling or frowning?"

"You're smiling,"

"you can't see me, how do you know I'm smiling?"

"You always smile."

"Can you read normal size print, like in the newspaper?"

"No. Plus I'an't drive do drials and do dal; wi' widnesses. Why don't we ma'c a deal. As soon as I can see well enough do drive and spe' well enough to be undersdood by a judge, I'll be ba'. (Plus I can't drive to trials and to talk with witnesses. Why don't we make a deal. As soon as I can see well enough to drive and speak well enough to be understood by a judge, I'll be back.)"

"It's a deal."

Shirley smiled through her sparkling Asian eyes. She extended her hand to shake. I gave her a hug.

The next Wednesday, I saw Dr. McAdams at the Center for the Partially Seeing. "Do'tor M' Adams,"I said, "Ine' do zee well 'nuf'o drive."

"Slow down, Mr. Jourdane. I can't understand you when you talk so fast."

"I'm sorry," I said very slowly. I have to zee well enough to drive."

"That's more like it. You will someday."

"But l'an' wai' fer zomeday."

"Slow down," said Dr. McAdams. "You can't wait? What's the rush?"

"Las' Saturday," I said slowly. "I ro' to Sa'ramento wi' my bro'er and on da way home, I felt 'ad abou' having to az'o'ers to drive me everywhere. I wanna go ba' to wor'. I have to drive to do it. How long until I'll be a'le to drive?"

"From the examination today, all I can tell you is your vision improves each time I see you. Even if your improvement slows down, we can get you glasses that will enable you to drive. I think I have a pair around here somewhere. Let me show them to you."

Dr. McAdams searched through several drawers and pulled out what appeared to be bifocals; the bottoms of the lenses were normal, the top halves were quarter inch thick magnifying glass. "Put these on and look out the window. They aren't your prescription but you can get an idea how they feel."

I slid the bifocals over my nose and looked through the window at passing traffic. "Its li' using bino'ulars. Are dey hand ho 'ct used to?"

Seeing the expression on McAdams face, I said slowly, "I'm sorry. Are dey 'ard to 'et used to?"

"Hard to get used to? Kind of," replied the doctor. "Let's wait a while and see if your vision keeps improving. Before long, you may be able to drive with regular glasses."

Listening to Dr. McAdams I visualized the blue pickup I intended to buy as soon as I could see, bouncing down the dirt road from my home with my surfboard in the back.

On the ride home that day, I pondered the difficulty McAdams had understanding me. If I'd been more careful choosing words, I bet he could have understood everything I said, I thought. I was learning that certain words were impossible for me to pronounce. From now on I have to focus on this problem. Plus, I have to remember to talk slowly, my tongue doesn't move fast enough.

Thirty-Nine

The week before Christmas, Kathy told me that she was spending the holidays in the Islands. I had forgotten she was going back to Kauai where she had a home, a job, and a boyfriend. I had accepted the reality that Kathy and I would never again be lovers, but like a child spoiled by his nanny, I had grown accustomed to always having her there to provide words of encouragement, drive me over the hill from Aptos to Stanford, or talk about life in the 1970's America, be it why she joined women picketing the Miss California contest in downtown Santa Cruz or the no-nothing American's demand we build a more fearsome barrier between San Diego and Tijuana. "Are you coming back?" I asked when Kathy told me she was leaving.

"Don't look so sad. I'll be back to check on you." She smiled. "They have phones in Hawaii, you know. You could call me sometimes."

I promised I would, and within days Kathy was gone. With Christmas approaching, I was alone with Timber in our Aptos cabin.

One morning a few days before Christmas it was raining. The phone rang. I laid down the large-print copy of "Boys from Brazil" and walked arms outstretched, feeling my way from the well-lit corner of the couch to the phone. Crossing the dark room I passed the Christmas tree Kathy and I cut on the hill behind the house.

I felt for the ringing phone resting on the eight by ten raw pine and concrete block bookshelf.

"Hi. Mo."

"Hi, John. How's Hawaii?"

"Nice, Boy are you talking good. Muffett and I are coming over. Ready to go surfing?"

"Yeah," I responded, my voice showing the first real excitement I'd felt in a month. "When?"

*   *   *

Growing up, every summer my brothers and I watched the five or ten older guys ride waves on surfboards at Doheny Beach. One afternoon, we borrowed a board from the lifeguard who was trying to make time with our full-bodied 16-year old sister. We were electrified bouncing in white water, trying to keep our wet body on the slippery board. That afternoon, John, Tom and I hiked along El Camino Real through manzanita and bright-yellow mustard up the hill from Doheny Beach to Dana Point where we talked with Hobart Alter in his tiny surf shop. Admitting we didn't have money, we told Hobie we really liked surfing. He spent an hour explaining how surfboards were made from balsa slabs glued together, sanded, shaped and covered with fiberglass and resin. He told us he hoped to soon make boards to loan like styrofoam. He explained why it's better to surf the green water where the surface is smooth to the side of a crashing wave than the white foam where the swell is breaking and the board bounces in all directions. He told us how big waves get in Hawaii and finally, how much used boards cost.

That summer, John and I saved the few dollars we earned from our paper routes. Tom searched the neighborhood alleys for soft drink bottles worth 2 cents each. By September, we had $10 between us, enough for a used board. Mom took us to Hobie's, but he didn't have any used boards. The next weekend, our sister Barbara Jean took us to Huntington Beach pier where John, Tom and I went to Gordy's Surf Shop near the beach end of the Huntington Beach pier and bought a used red nine-foot board made of balsa. As we walked from the shop, Gordy threw us a bar of paraffin. "I think you guys'll need this," he said.

"What for?" I asked. "I think the board'll go fast enough without putting wax on it."

170

"It's not a pair of skis you bought," bellowed the shop owner who looked more like Gidget's Kahuna than a businessman. "Rub it on top of the board and you won't slip off so much."

"Thanks," I said, blushing.

Sitting in the hot sun, Barbara Jean and her blond friend Patty watched us drag the 40-pound surfboard across the sand to the water. On the way, John asked if I knew the wax goes on the top of the board to keep from slipping so much.

I shrugged my shoulders. "No wonder we had so much trouble staying on that board at Doheny. Now it'll be easy."

I won a coin toss and was the first to try out our new board. Like a midwest bumpkin spending the day at the shore I dragged the board into three feet of water, jumped on, and immediately slipped off the other side. Before the day was over, my brothers and I were able to paddle far enough out in the tumultuous Huntington Beach white water to be tossed about like driftwood. It was never easy, but we were hooked.

A week later, my friend Jerry Perez, who stocked shelves in a liquor store near my home, bought his own balsa board with blue and white abstract resin. We've been surfing ever since.

Forty

Christmas morning it was still raining in Aptos. A Honda Accord pulls up the driveway. Timber splashed down the muddy road to meet the visitors. I opened the front door of our four-room redwood cabin and stood at the doorway in my tan corduroy shirt and faded Levis. Muffett jumped from the car and ran to hug me.

"Look pretty skinny, kid," the part-Hawaiian, pan-Korean part-Haole beauty remarked. She smiled as we separated, her hands on my shoulders.

"You're starting to look human again," John said. Rubbing the top of my shaved head, he smiled. "You even have a little hair growing up here." Ever since the hospital shaved my head for the first operation, I looked like a Marine recruit wounded outside Bagdad days after graduating from boot camp at Camp Pendleton. We embraced.

"Ready to 'o surfin'?" I asked, broken teeth visible through my grin.

"I talked with Tom last night. He said your doctor said you shouldn't."

Like a scolded child, I pleaded. "I'll be all ride. Do"ars don' know every ing. Dr. Kablan told me if I wan' to he sa I should spend the res' of my life sidding in a room wadging delevision. Ican live li' 'at. 'ome on. Blease."

Unsure what I was saying, John grinned. "You're free, almost white now, and 21. If you think you can handle it, I can. Let me rest for a few moments first, okay? You got a beer? Thirty-minutes later, I embraced Muffett good-bye. She whispered, "Be careful, Mo. You made it this far. Don't blow it now,"

John's rented Honda pulled out of the dirt drive with surfboards atop. I sat in the front seat already wearing my wet suit, I stared out the window at the blurred passing redwood trees. Behind the wheel, John weaved Trout Gulch Road alongside the slowly bubbling creek. "Where do you wanna go!" he asked casually. "We could go to Pleasure Point or Steamers Lane, but maybe for your first time out we should go to a sandy beach."

"I really wanna 'o to bleasures," I replied.

"Pleasure Point? It's not too scary?"

"Huh"

"You sure you see well enough to climb down the cliff from the road to the water carrying a board?

"No."

"I think we'll go to La Selva. It has a sand beach and an easy trail down the cliff."

Minutes later, John pulled off Highway One onto a country road. "You seen Kathy?" he asked. "Did she stay around after your wreck?"

"Uh huh. She's in 'auai for 'ristmas"

The Honda passed through brussels-sprout fields. Staring out the window, I saw a handful of farm workers wearing bright yellow rain gear. They were weeding the field with long-handled hoes.

I smiled.

John glanced over at me and then toward the field on which I was focused. "Make ya feel good seeing those workers standing up?"

"Ma'es id all word id. When wor'ers sdand up and say, "Basda. Enough." dey "an do anyding."

The Honda went around a curve. Ahead in a field were a handful of workers. They were bent over to the ground. I watched. "Pull over for a second," I asked my brother.

John did. Silently I watched blurred elderly farm workers, men and women stooped over picking strawberries. "Dere 'as do be a bedder way do do dat job," I thought aloud. "It boders me to see wor'ers sdill bent over wi' der faces to da mud. I sdill haven" fulfilled my commitment do end sdoop labor."

"Never give up, do ya? Now you gonna show the growers there's a better way to harvest strawberries?"

I nodded.

"Before you make a new commitment, you should consider your disabilities, especially your vision. Look what your concern for farm workers has already cost you. Those workers might be stooped today, but with the United Farm Workers help, they won't be tomorrow."

"Undil 'rowers bar'ain wi'da union in 'ood fai" the wor'ers will continue to toil with ger noses in da mud.

Not understanding me, John said, "Don't the companies have to bargain with the union in good faith?"

"Da law says 'cy do bud il da law isn envorced, id's the same as no law ad all. While Go'ernor 'rown's in Sa'ramento, at leas' he'll ensure da 'rowers obey da law and bar'ain wi" da union in 'ood fai". Bud when he's 'one, dere'll be no one envorcing da farm labor law. Farm wor'ers will he forced to return to da boy'ou and fast and pray to stop der trea'ment li'e slaves"

Understanding part of what I said, John asked, "Ya know what? Right now you have something more important to think about. You're going surfing."

Maybe for today, I thought, but if I don't recover my vision and speech, I won't be able to continue doing the most important thing in my life, trying to improve the living conditions of farm workers.

John parked atop the cliff at La Selva Beach. Two-to-three- foot high waves broke off the sandy beach below. No one was in the water. We removed the boards from the rack and walked across the cold sand to the colder water. My full wetsuit was the same color as the black patch on my eye. John had no wetsuit.

Walking across the sand from the car to the waves, my thoughts drifted back. By the time I graduated from high school, June 1960, my brothers John and Tom, my friends Jerry Perez and Jin Herdman who we called Brown Bear, and I had ridden waves up and down California's coast and seen every surf movie made: Bruce Brown's Surf Fever, John Severson's Barefoot Adventures, and Bud Browne's Cat on a Hot Foam Board; surfing movies made by surfers for surfers. High school graduations meant it was time to leave Southern California's small overpopulated waves and ride the big waves I had seen others challenge in the surfing movies. It was time to see how daring I really was. With the self-confidence my mom and dad instilled in my small body, I never doubted I could ride Oahu's North Shore.

One Friday evening in September 1960, Jerry Perez dropped me off at the Burbank airport for the midnight Standard Air flight to Honolulu. Thirteen-hours later at the Honolulu airport I met my surfing partner Brown Bear. Brown Bear had flown over on the more expensive Jet Pan Am flight. I felt the hot sun penetrate my white T-shirt while Brown Bear and I walked from the thatch roof airport carrying our new nine-foot six-inch surfboards hand made by a board maker in Encinitas, Mike Diffendorf. Surfers did not start surfing shortboards until the Australians brought them to Hawaii ten years later. "What now?" Brown Bear asked. "We're in Hawaii. Where do we go and how do we get there?"

Two days later, we were at Ala Moana, a surf spot on the Ewa or west edge of Waikiki. Three-foot swells broke from right to left as we sat on our boards facing the beach. A mild wind blew from shore to the open ocean behind us. The water and air were both 82 degrees, ideal small-wave surfing conditions. We hunkered over our boards beyond the surf line where swells hit a coral reef half-mile from Waikiki sand. I told Brown Bear I couldn't believe it, the offshore wind created perfect waves, super steep, and only three guys were out. At home there would have been 50 surfers in the water fighting for the same curl.

We rode hundreds of waves that afternoon. We would paddle out, spin around, take a couple strokes heading to our right, snap to our feet swerving 180 degrees to the left and flash across the breaking face. Split seconds later, the swell began to rupture and white water spilled over the board's nose. We kicked out or angled toward shore and popped out of the white water by submerging the board's front end. Paddling out after one of my many rides, I heard a yell. "Hey, bruda". What you folks do here?" Pushing through Ala Moana's emerald water, I saw it was Buddy Boy. Nearby, was his heavy-set sidekick, Buffalo.

I met the two Hawaiians at Doheny Beach a year before. They were spending the summer surfing California waves. "Riding waves, man. Good to see you guys are learning how to surf," I yelled jestfully.

While Buddy Boy, Buffalo, and I talked, Brown Bear paddled over. Sitting on our boards, waiting for waves outside the break, in his sing-song pidgin, Buddy Boy told us, "I talk story wid bruda' in Halieva dis mornin'. He tell me da country it breakin' da kine. We got me cuzzin's Chevy truck. Lotta room for you folks and boards. We go now. You comin"?"

An hour later, crammed into the back of a surfboard-stuffed panel truck, I thought, yow, a few days in Hawaii and we're going to the country with Buddy Boy and Buffalo, two of the best surfers in the world.

On the way to the North Shore, we stopped at a tiny wooden home near downtown Honolulu. It was where Donald Takiyama lived with an elderly woman I believe was his grandmother. She told us that Donald, the local who would become famous surfing the Pipeline, had to stay home and do school work. Having heard of Takiyama in California, I was disappointed he wasn't joining us.

An hour after leaving Takiyama's home, we crested the ridge at Waimea and starting down the several mile straightaway to Halieva, sugar cane fields framed the narrow country road. My pulse galloped hearing Buffalo talk about the waves we could now see in the distance. "Hey Bruda"," he said to Buddy Boy, giving the driver a shove on the shoulder, "It big,"

Buddy Boy just nodded, staring at what looked like white water half-way to the horizon.

From a distance of several miles, I couldn't tell how big it was. Waves usually break in water the depth of their height, veteran surfer Fil Procter had explained to me while leaning on the back of his silver panel truck at Doheny several years earlier, now I see white water a mile from shore. It's more than a few feet deep where those waves are breaking. I thought, which means those waves are more than a few-feet high. I shuddered with fear.

I was startled back to life by a loud, "Yow! Looka doz breaka's. Big, Fh?" Buffalo grew more excited by the second,

"Fifteen plus." responded Buddy Boy.

"You folks wanta go Sunset?"

"Sure," I replied, hiding my fear behind the macho veneer. From surfing movies, I was familiar with the name "Sunset". Outwardly ready for anything, inside chills ran down my arms. I knew from surfing movies that 10 to 15 foot waves at Sunset Beach broke in a sheer drop.

Sitting in the rear of the old panel truck, bouncing over potholes, we passed through Halieva's bougainvillea-engulfed shacks and small stores with their unpainted wood walls. Buddy Boy plucked a ukulele. I smelled the burning sugar cane.

Twenty minutes later, after seeing for the first time Pupukea, Ins-and-Outs, and Waimea Bay, my heart quickened when the panel truck pulled off the narrow country road at a wide deserted bay. Behind me spread the north-shore jungle stretching from the beach up to the 2,000-foot peaks five miles inland. Before me, palms that bent in the strong offshore wind broke the dazzling white sand. Staring out toward the wind-churned blue water, I felt my stomach tighten. Giant swells were breaking half-a-mile away. The swells became long steep walls inviting anyone brave or foolish enough to risk the turbid rip tides, being hit by a 40- pound surfboard after it sprung from the water like a cork and twisted 50 feet into the air returning like a dart, being thrown around underwater for several minutes as if in a washing machine, and tossed into the coral spears several feet below the surface.

Brown Bear and I looked at each other, silent what-are-we-doing-here expressions on our faces. Being with the world's best surfers and full of teenage pride, neither of us said a word. We grabbed our boards and followed the Hawaiians into the rip tide.

"Let da current carry ya out. Da rip tide'll take us all da way pas' da waves," yelled Buddy Boy.

Ten minutes later, I took off on a 15-foot swell, dropped down the sheer face and bottom turned at the base of the crashing peak. My board climbed the 10-foot wall stretching out ahead of me. I silently crossed myself, approached the wave lip or top of the breaking wave, angled slightly to the left and rocketed down the swell as it broke over the tail of my board. Finally I kicked-out, flipping my board over the wave to avoid the six-foot shore break stretched ahead and crashing onto coral spears growing from the white sand a foot beneath the deceiving surface.

Feeling satisfaction not too different from when I thrived on running from the courthouse to Salinas's Natividad Hospital 23 years later to see the birth of my daughter, I paddled back out to where Buffalo sat calmly hunched on his 10-foot balsa board waiting for his wave. He introduced me to a slender guy in his late-20s. It was Peter Cole, one of the hottest big-wave riders in the Islands. Buffalo told me Cole taught at Sunset Beach Elementary School across the street from Pupukea Beach, later known as the Pipeline. "Don't you ever get scared riding big waves?" I asked the schoolteacher.

"All the time, man. Anybody tell you he's not scared when he paddles out in 20-foot waves is talking story, crazy, or only says he rode waves but never made it to the water."

When I walked up the sand after my first day at Sunset Beach, I saw a surfer from Long Beach, Jack Webb if I recall correctly, with his back shredded like a roast beef slashed with a carving knife. "I hit coral on the inside break," I overheard him moan to a paramedic who was treating him at the side of a fire truck.

During the week before Christmas, my friend Brown Bear returned home to spend the holiday with his family. Not having the $266 it cost to fly round trip to Los Angeles, I remained in Hawaii. I was staying with some locals in a Quonset hut on Pupukea Beach. We slept so close to the Pipeline that when the surf was big, our army surplus cots shook. Sunday morning we awoke to shaking cots. We drove up the coast a couple miles to Waimea Bay. From the cliff, we watched. "That wave's gotta be 20 feet," said my local friend Kimo while we stood in the 20-knot wind. "You ready to try it?"

"I don't know," I replied, shaking my head slowly from side to side. "Part of me says, 'what, are you crazy?' but the other part says, if I don't paddle out now I never will."

"You didn't come to Hawaii to watch waves, Brudah," Kimo said smiling. I drove down the hill and pulled into a parking area where Kimo grabbed his board and slowly walked across the sand toward the waiting surf.

Feeling the fear in my midsection, I walked to the back of the wood-paneled 1950 Mercury station wagon Brown Bear and I bought for $100 and pulled out my board. Five minutes later, Kimo and I stood at the water's edge watching the seemingly nonstop ten-foot shore break crashing 20 yards off shore into three feet of water. Both to our left and to our right rose the rocky cliff that had been the bastion for our scenic view of the big waves. Finally, a momentary pause in the breaking waves and we raced from the scorching sand into the dark-green water. Before we paddled 15 yards, a 10-foot wall of water ready to explode sprung up before us. Stroking for our lives, we knew if hit by the shore break we would be thrown into the coral reef just below the surface. We pushed through the lip of the spine-snapping wall just as it broke. We paddled into a rip tide and ten-minutes later sat a half-mile off shore watching towering swells grow as they neared.

The dark shadow of oncoming waves, much larger than the shore break, sent chills through my shoulders. I paddled toward the looming shadows. I prayed I could get beyond the mammoth swells before they broke, throwing me without escape into a white-water avalanche.

"We better head toward shore and let the white water carry us," yelled Kimo. "We never make it outside those swells before de breaks."

"The white water's 10-feet high," I yelled back. "We'll end up in the rocks if we try to ride it in. We have to make it outside the swells."

As a huge Waimea Bay swell neared, it grew darker. I pulled against the water as hard as I could. When the mountain of green water was a bus length away, I looked up, staring at what seemed like a five-story wall, the top feathering like a razor with one final thrust up Waimea Bay's Mount Everest. Pulse thundered in my ears. A siren broadcast the piercing ache across my chest and shoulders. My face was a foot from the wave's lip. Suddenly, hundreds of tons of white water burst from the black swell throwing my board and my frail body backward into the relentless cauldron.

Beneath the Waimea Bay white water, my rag-doll body bounced, a sponge in a dishwasher, no idea which way to pull my arms to reach the surface. I knew ten-feet under the water stood coral spears ready to carve flesh like hot knives cutting butter.

Seconds passed. Each seemed like an hour. I can't do it, I thought. I can't do it. I can't hold my breath any longer. I thought I was tough until I confronted Mother Nature. I fought to control my screaming lungs demand that I gulp in whatever was there. I knew I couldn't breathe under water.

Ready to pass out from lack of oxygen, I pulled against one relentless white water not knowing the direction of the surface. Ready to yield to the powerful force of nature, suddenly my face cleared the surface. I gasped in air, and like an egg beater gone wild the ravishing white water sucked my limp body back down. Again I pulled. Again I could only pray I was pulling toward the surface. Again, my face cleared the water. The crushing wave had passed and my body bobbed in the smooth white foam, the residue of murdering white water.

When I returned to Honolulu that evening, I called my brother John who was in his senior year a Huntington Park High School back in California. When I told him about nearly drowning at Waimea Bay, he responded, "You can't really bitch if you get hurt. When you take chances like you do, you have to live with the consequences."

"But I think what we learned as kids is gonna help," I said.

"To survive?"

"We learned that if we want badly enough to do something, we can do it."

*   *   *

Now, with my eye covered with a pirate patch, I began to paddle through the white water. John watched me carefully. We paddled through small breakers to a spot beyond the rupturing swells.

"How's your vision doing?" John asked as we sat in the calm dark green water.

"What vision? I 'an't see any'ing. (I can't see anything.)"

"I'll help ya. Here comes a wave. Turn around and start to paddle slow."

I followed the instructions.

"Okay paddle hard."

Suddenly, the wave grabbed my board and began to thrust it forward. I instinctively snapped to my feet, twisted my ankles, throwing my shoulders from left to right. The board followed. For maybe a second I shot across the swell's face. The swell crashed. Nearly blind, I went down, choking white water but bursting with pride. I paddled out to my life-guard brother.

Sitting beyond the surf line in the smooth green water, we talked little. A light rain fell. Breaking the silence, I said softly, "'anks, John. Dis is da bes' 'hris'mas I've ever had."

Not understanding me, John smiled.

"I learned today I 'an still surf."

John grinned.

Like the feeling when you kiss your first teen love, the feeling of a bed after three days on the road, or the feeling of an orgasm with the one you love, there is something about surfing that is impossible to put in words. The feeling of your body submerged in the cold water, the ocean breeze on your face and the wave grabbing your board and thrusting it mystically forward merge into emotions words cannot express. A 13-year old at the Hook in Santa Cruz or Swamis in Encinitas knows the feeling, but few if any 50-year old doctors who have not felt the rush will ever understand. "I also learned I have to "et bedda," I told John, "Farm wor'ers are s'ill ben over. I s'ill haven' sdopped sdoob labor."

A ray of sun broke through the clouded gray sky.

Forty-One

Early the following Friday, two days before New Years, Tom, Jesse and I left rainy Aptos in the maroon Firebird Kathy left behind when she moved to Hawaii several years before. In Bakersfield, we were picking up a woman I had hung around with a lot the previous summer, Norma Arresiaga, and continuing on to Mexicali for New Year's Eve.

When we reached Paso Robles a couple hours south of Salinas, it was pouring rain. We stopped for breakfast at the Black Oak, a classy travelers' coffee shop. While Tom paid the bill, I asked for the car keys. Apparently without thinking, he handed them. Moments later when he and Jesse ran to the car, trying to keep from getting too wet, it was gone. They looked around and there it was 50 feet from where it had been. I was sitting behind the wheel.

Tom walked to the driver's side window. Before he spoke, I looked at him sheepishly. "Sorry. I 'ouldn' 'elp myself (I couldn't help myself)."

"You don't have to be sorry. It's your car. Ya wanna drive?" he asked, apparently believing I would turn him down.

"Yeah," I responded, pausing. "But I 'an't zee nuf yet. I planned on drivin' ba' do where da 'ar was but I'ouldn't zee on my right side. Dere are too many 'ars in dis lot and if one 'ame from da right, I'd be in trouble."

Not understanding, Tom smiled. "You did pretty good driving to get over here. You'll be back driving. Just be sure I'm not in your way."

Three hours later, we pulled away from Norma's South Bakersfield apartment, and just before dark arrived at Mom's North Long Beach driveway, a couple blocks from the Compton border. In the living room sat Mom's neighbor and best friend, Barbara Nelson.

"Hi. 'arbara," I said to the almost six-foot, two-hundred- pound, shorthaired Dane.

"Hi, Mo. How are you?" responded the 40-year-old former girl's-softball coach. Barbara had suffered a stroke several years earlier while teaching with Mom at Griffith Junior High in East Los Angeles. It left her paralyzed on the left side. When the stroke occurred most believed she would be totally disabled for life. Barbara missed a year of school and returned as a full- time math teacher. She became the model in whose footsteps I hoped to follow.

"Nice."

"From what I hear you took a real tumble. But my information is from Ruth, which might not be too reliable a source." Barbara chuckled.

"Jus" a s'rape," I slurred. "But it messed up my vision and tal' ing preddy much. For da first time I understan' what it mus da been li' for you."

"I didn't understand you, Mo."

He said his vision and speech got messed up." interpreted Tom, "and now he understands what it was like for you."

"For a while I talked like you're talking." Barbara Nelson responded, "I can almost understand you. Maybe because I had the same trouble. Your speech will improve."

After visiting several hours, one of the people I grew to admire and love most in the world limped through Mom's backyard and through the gate into her own yard. Norma and I went to bed. Torn and Jesse stayed up talking with mom.

"You've been around your brother more than anyone during the last few months," said Mom. "When he left the hospital six-weeks ago, Kathy told me the doctor's were worried he'd become depressed when he realized how badly he was injured. Have you seen any sign of depression?"

"Nope," replied Tom, lighting a Marlboro. "He's too cocky to be depressed."

"Why do you suppose it hasn't hit him yet?"

"Who knows," mused Tom. "From the start he's maintained he realizes how badly he was disfigured, but he's not concerned about what others think of him, so he's not depressed by it."

"He cares what others think about him," interjected Jesse. Look at how competitive he is. You can't tell me someone that is competitive doesn't care about how he looks."

"Competition is important to him," responded Tom, "but he can walk around with jam on his shirt or his hair not combed and he doesn't notice. Dressing properly or driving the right kind of car so others will approve doesn't obsess him. There's a real fine line between being cocky and having self-confidence."

"He's always been self-confident," remarked Mom. "He believes he can do anything. But I think that's because all of you children have learned you can."

"I think that's part of it, Mom. He knows he'll overcome this just like he did polio and sprained ankles. Combine his self-confidence with his absence of trepidation about what others might think, and he avoids being depressed. I guess you could say he lives happily in his own fantasyland."

"I just hope it lasts," concluded Mom, getting up. "But it scares me what will happen when he realizes he can't talk well enough to ever be a trial lawyer again."

Early the following morning, we headed south. We rented rooms at Mexicali's luxurious Hotel El Cortez and I rested while Tom, Jesse and Norma walked around the windswept streets of the dusty Mexican border town. When they returned, I was hanging on the side of the pool. Several feet away lay the tape recorder, "Been practicing talking?" asked Tom.

Thinking, hard work and persistence, I responded, "Yeah If I'm 'oin' to improve, I need to pra'tice. Dis is my firs' time swimming. I need to pra'dice it, too."

"How is it?" Tom asked, not understanding what I said.

Not understanding, Tom said, "I mean swimming. Can you still swim?"

Wanting to say yes but when I put my head under, water flows into my nose causing me to choke, I slurred, "Id's all right but water 'oes in my lun's. I'uess 'at's how people drown. But I already dis'overed if I blow out while my head's under, wader does'n 'o in. Waj. "

Tom stared blankly, apparently not understanding what I had said.

I raced the butterfly and the individual medley in high school, well enough to win the Eastern League Championship. Now, when I put my face in the water I came up coughing. Embarrassed. I grinned while Tom walked to the poolside, squatted down, and felt the water.

Jesse frowned as she and Norma joined Tom. "I'll never understand why you like this desert," she said, fanning herself with a folded magazine.

I smiled. "I li' it" I started to say I liked it because of the warm days and good people, but realized I could say almost none of it. I stood in the shallow water silently, finally saying slowly, "I love da sun an' nice gente (people) who live here."

"He's part lizard," laughed Norma. "When I first saw him in the hospital, he was a dead lizard. When I saw him at Stanford he was a bandaged up blind lizard. Now he's a Mexican swimming lizard who talks Spanish into a tape recorder. What's he going to be next?"

Several hours and three or four margaritas later, the four of us were on our way to a Mexican syndicato (union) hall for the New

Year's Eve party that brought us over 600 miles from the north. When I walked in, lettuce cutters, packers, and wrappers who work on the U.S. side of the border but live in Mexicali, both men and women, surrounded me. Over the previous couple years, I had become one of their few huero friends, "What happened?" many asked. Many more said they had sent get-well cards and prayed. Many said they were glad to see me back in the valley. Some said they had heard the growers tried to kill me. No one commented about my butch haircut, my off-center nose, and scars criss-crossing my sunburned face.

The next morning when Norma and I walked into the coffee shop, waiting at a small table, Tom whispered to Jesse, "Look at that smile?"

"Which one?" she asked.

"Both" responded Tom. "Bet ya ten pesos they didn't sleep in separate beds."

Forty-Two

When I arrived back in Aptos, exhausted from my first lengthy trip since the previous summer, the phone rang. "You missed our News Year party. It was fun."

"Sorry, Shirley. I went wi' Tom to Mejicali."

"I know. With some Chicana," kidded Shirley. "Who was she?

"You have a pretty "ood networ' of informants. It was Norma from Ba'ersfield. We wen' to a union party. "

"Well. Happy New Year. It's too bad you don't care enough about me to come to my New Years party."

Come on, Shirley. You know I love you."

"Whatever. It's time for you to come back to work. When are ya going to start?"

"Boy, are you t... hard." I began to say tough but realizing he couldn't say it. "I'm 'oing to see Ernie tomorrow. Let's wait an zee what he says."

*   *   *

The next morning, I was on my way to Stanford. After waiting for nearly an hour to see Dr. Kaplan at the reconstructive surgery clinic, I was finally escorted into a small cubicle to wait for another 15 minutes. I was learning there are far more patients than available doctor hours. I chuckled when I thought, having to wait so long every time I see Kaplan makes me realize that patients should be spelled patience. Fortunately, I had learned to bring a large print book with me when I visited a doctor.

"How do ya feel?" asked Kaplan, after I tried to tell him about the trip south.

"I want do go ba'to wor'. How soon?"

"You want to return to work?" confirmed Doctor Kaplan.

After examining me carefully, Kaplan said, "We still need to do a major operation on your face. There's a process called microvascular surgery. We transplant tissue from another part of your body and suture the veins from the transplanted tissue onto the existing veins in your face."

After feeling various parts of my body. Kaplan added, "Maybe we'll take part of a rib to use as a cheek bone and some of the tissue from your thigh to fill your jaw out. The surgery could last up to six hours. It looks like you've recovered from the last operation so we can go ahead with this one. If you recover within a couple weeks, nothing will be stopping you from going back to work around the first of the month."

"E'cept my speech and vision."

"Why don't you stop by the Center for the Partially Seeing and find out if they can get you some glasses. It sounds like you're doing all you can with your speech. If you come to the hospital a week from Thursday by 6:00 PM. and check in, we can do the operation on Friday morning."

An hour later, Dr. McAdams was examining me at the Center for the Partially Blind. "It looks like your vision is slowly improving. The first time you were here, we could correct your vision with glasses to 20:1000. When you first asked about driving, we could correct it to 20:500. Now it can be corrected to about 20:100. I think it's worth it for me to give you a prescription for glasses. Because of the apparent damage to your optic nerve, your vision will remain far from perfect, even with the glasses, but it'll be better."

"'an I drive?"

"Can you drive? You can't see that good, yet. To drive it has to be correctable to 20:30. But I think a new pair of glasses will make it easier for you to get around. Dr. Kaplan says you're in a hurry to get back to work. I think you're crazy, but that's up to you."

"Will I ever be able to drive?" I pleaded.

"I hope so," replied the doctor. "If after a few months you haven't improved, we'll try the special magnifying glasses I showed you last time I saw you. But let's wait for that."

After checking my ability to read with various lenses, Dr. McAdams said there was very little improvement in my reading. whether he corrected my vision or not. I could almost read normal size print, with or without corrective lenses. McAdams suggested that if I believed reading glasses would help, I should stop by a Woolworth's and buy a pair of cheap ones.

*   *   *

Ten days later, I checked into Stanford Hospital. After going through the blood test and signing what seemed like reams of insurance forms and liability waivers, I lay in bed draped in a green hospital gown watching McNeil-Lehrer on PBS. Dr. Kaplan came in to discuss the following day's surgery. After I commented that operations were beginning to seem routine, Kaplan commented, "Medicine might seem advanced, Mo, but a patient can die every time we administer anesthesia."

At six the next morning. I abruptly awoke when a nurse rolled me onto my stomach and inserted a needle into my buttock to help me sleep. By 6:45 an aide wheeled me down the hall to the operating room. The anesthesiologist explained what he was doing while he administered the anesthesia. I was unable to understand anything he said. The operation lasted until 3 PM. By 6 PM. I was still unconscious. The on-duty nurse in the recovery room called the anesthesiologist at home. By 6:30 PM., the doctor was back at the hospital.

Meanwhile, Tom and Jesse waited outside the recovery room. Every half-hour, they asked if I was awake yet. When I still wasn't by 8 PM., Tom called Dr. Kaplan at home. He immediately came to the hospital. The doctor had brought me back from the grave's edge. Now that everyone believed I had

190

recovered, Kaplan prayed my system hadn't been so weakened by the earlier trauma it was unable to withstand the anesthesia, particularly since he and the anesthesiologist had decided to exceed the amount planned when the operation became longer than expected.

Doctor Kaplan and the anesthesiologist spent the evening carefully monitoring my life signs. Everything seemed to be stable but I was still under the influence of anesthesia when they went home during the early morning hours. Before leaving, Dr Kaplan asked Tom to call him at home when I awoke.

I finally stirred the following day. A wave. Jesse and Tom were alongside the bed. Tom grinned after he looked at the bed and saw my eye blink. "You scared the shit out of us. During the last 24 hours, I've felt a time-machine carried me back to last September in Bakersfield. I forgot how much you like to sleep."

*   *   *

By the following Monday morning, I wanted to go home. The nurse said it was too soon. I wasn't ready. Yielding to my badgering, she called Kaplan. The doctor came sauntering in around eight. "Hi, Mo. Causin' a lot of trouble I hear."

"I wanna 'o home. I'm a prisoner."

"You shouldn't go home this soon, and I'm probably committing malpractice by letting you go. Promise me you'll stay home. Don't go walking down the street. Don't go swimming in the icy ocean, or surfing, or even take a bath while you have the stitches. Get lots of sleep and call me if you have any pain. You underwent major surgery a few days ago. I don't want to have to start over because you go home and play too hard. Your face, leg and ribs are all very tender."

"'anks, Ernie."

"One more thing. You can't leave until someone comes to get you."

"I already 'alled Tom. He's registering for s'ool but 'athy said she'd be here. While I'm waitin', maybe you could look at my wrist. It's been real sore since I remember."

"Your wrist? Which one?" asked the doctor with a puzzled expression on his face.

Kaplan tenderly examined my right wrist, repeating, "Does this hurt?" as he moved his thumb and index finger up and down my lower arm and hand.

Each time he asked, I winced.

"We better X-ray it," said Kaplan. I frowned, expecting another delay in leaving but shrugged my shoulders.

Forty-five minutes later Kathy arrived. Dr. Kaplan walked in with a hand specialist. "We looked at the X-rays," said Kaplan. "You need surgery on that wrist."

"Is it 'bro'en?" I asked.

"Is it broken?" confirmed the hand specialist. "I don't know if you can see this X-ray, but let me explain what it tells us. See this light area?" The hand specialist pointed out a white mass in the wrist area shown on the X-ray. I squinted. "That should be a solid line, like up here," the specialist said, pointing to a part of the X-ray displaying my upper forearm.

"What's wrong wi' it?""

"The bone has been crushed," interjected Kaplan, "We were so concerned with saving your life and reconstructing your face, we never thought to look at your wrist. I guess your head injuries were causing so much pain, you didn't mention your wrist hurting until today."

"Anyway," said the specialist, "it's amazing your hand hasn't gone limp. Your wrist is destroyed. We can operate on it a week from today. Dr. Kaplan explained to me the problem you had with anesthesia a few days ago. This time we'll have to operate with you awake."

"You what?" I cried.

"Take it easy, Mr. Jourdane. We can prevent the nerve under your arm from transferring pain from your hand to your brain. It'll be like going to a dentist and having Novocain. It won't hurt."

Forty-Three

An hour later, I was on my way to Aptos with Kathy. "It's unreal about my wrist," I complained as we sat in San Jose traffic. " 'an you believe da hospital never knew id way' broken?"

"Can I believe the hospital never knew it was broken?" confirmed Kathy.

"Uh huh."

"Mo. The reason they didn't know your wrist is broken is that you never told anyone it hurt. So if you're going to blame someone, you better start with yourself. Anyway," she continued, "they did a super job on your face again. You're a little swollen but you look like a different person than you did last week. Your left check looks like your right one instead of being sunken way in like a cave and your nose is in the middle of your face instead of pointing off to the left side. Dr. Kaplan's a sculptor.

*   *   *

The next Thursday evening, I was back in the hospital. At seven Friday morning, an orderly wheeled me into surgery, with no general anesthesia. After what felt like an hour of probing under my right shoulder, the doctor found the nerve that relayed pain from my wrist to my brain. As I lay on the stretcher watching the doctor calmly prepare to cut my arm open, I thought, I'm too much here. I know I can't have anesthesia but this is going to hurt like hell.

A few minutes later, I lay rigid fearing the worst. I heard a power saw cutting through my ann. I screamed. "I feel it. It hurts."

"It's your imagination, Mr. Jourdane," replied the hand specialist as he turned the loud saw off. "You just hear the saw. During operation number four, the specialist told me repeatedly that I couldn't feel the bone in my arm cut and my open flesh probed. For the rest of my life. I will swear it was the worst pain I ever felt, worse than having a dentist drill with no Novocaine into a raw nerve to fill a cavity when I was eleven. But who will believe a patient when what he says conflicts with a doctor. After the operation, the specialist told me he had replaced the bone with plastic an inch of my right radius immediately above the wrist.

Forty-Four

The next week, I told Shirley I was going back to work. She sounded shocked. "Does anyone know? Are you okay? I mean didn't they operate on your face and arm a few days ago? I didn't mean to push you into going back so fast. Shouldn't you talk to your doctor first?"

"I did," I responded. "I saw him yesterday. Ile removed the stitches from my wrist. He says I 'an return to wor whenever I wan". Da only 'ing he doesn' know is 'at I'm 'oing do Delano.

Ten days later, Tom drove me to the Greyhound bus station in Gilroy. While he slowly slalomed his VW along the Pajaro River on the pine-tree-lined winding road from Watsonville to Gilroy, he was saying, "so I start back to school next Monday. After taking the semester off last Fall to be with you at Stanford, it's gonna be hard to go back." Tom grinned. "I must really like you. I mean to voluntarily give up a semester at San Jose State."

"You should. You're my brudda. You know I'd do da same for you." Returning Tom's grin, I continued. "I'm "lad you're returning to s'ool. You not only had your exlu'ation interrupted by Vietnam but now by my pinchi wre"."

Tom understood a small part of what I said. "Anyone would do the little I did," he said, becoming serious. "As hard as Vietnam was, having my older brother almost die in Bakersfield while playing gladiator for the farm workers was a whole lot harder."

Minutes later, we arrived at the Gilroy Greyhound station, a one-story, one-room wooden building on old El Camino Real in the heart of the small village. After hugging Tom good-bye and promising to call that night, I caught a bus to Fresno, where I changed buses. I was in Delano by four that afternoon. A wave.

I walked alone down the dusty main street carrying my blue Nike bag and checked into the Star Motel on the North edge of town. The following morning at eight sharp, I walked into the

Delano office of the Agricultural Labor Relations Board on the main street of town. It had been four and one-half months since I had walked out on a hot September afternoon to ride to Santa Maria with Shirley.

The only person in the office when I arrived was the chunky receptionist. "Señor Jourdane," she exclaimed when she looked up and saw me standing before her. "I didn't know you were coming back so soon."

"I'm ready to wor¹. Dis is where I should be." I smiled my partially toothless smile. "Been busy?"

"Not too," she replied, apparently still in shock, not looking me in the face. "This time of year, you know how it is, not many workers around. I didn't know you were coming back."

"Almost no one does," I responded. "I didn't know I was until a few days a'o. Who's in charge now?"

"Bob Dresser still, but he hardly ever comes down from Fresno. Shirley pretty much ran the office until the General Counsel transferred her to Salinas. Now, the only people who are here most of the time are John Moore and Frank Pulido. They are here regularly, but everyone else does their own thing. Most of the time, no one except Mr. Moore and Mr. Pulido are around."

I was surprised. When I left Delano the previous summer the office was packed with scurrying attorneys and investigators. "Probably no one except Mr. Moore and Mr. Pulido will be here until this afternoon," the receptionist mused. "Want some coffee?"

" 'han's. I'll 'et it." I replied.

"It's okay. I'm not doing nothing."

Walking to the coffeepot with the receptionist, I recalled the numerous labor trials going on in Delano a year earlier; now it was like an empty church two hours before mass. "Dere aren't any trials 'oing on?"

"There aren't any trials?" The receptionist asked, glancing in my direction.

I nodded.

"I don't think so. Mr. Moore and Mr. Pulido try but they can't do them all. I think they had to go to Fresno today to try to get Mr. Dresser to issue a complaint in a case Mr. Moore and Mr. Pulido have been working on."

"What happens if a wor'er 'omes in and says he was fired for subording da union?"

"I'm sorry, Mo. I didn't understand you."

Off a nearby desk I grabbed a pen and paper and wrote, "What happens if a farm worker comes in and says he was fired for supporting the union?"

"Mr. Pulido investigates it. If there is merit Mr. Moore drafts a complaint, but he has to send it to Fresno, and usually Sacramento tells Mr. Dresser to reject it. It's a joke."

Was it the writer Thomas Wolfe who said you can't go home again? Things you remember change. They are different than we recall. Or, maybe we change. We are different. Maybe our memory of how it was is all a fantasy.

"Why has it changed so much?"

"After your wreck, Shirley was transferred to Salinas and it seems like everyone but Mr. Moore and Mr. Pulido got scared to do anything. Instead of coming down to build up the people's spirit, like you always did, Sacramento people came and took away the cases and transferred the people out. It seemed like the law ended the day you had your wreck."

I shook my head sadly. Maybe that's why César Chávez thought the growers wanted to kill me, I thought.

I spent the morning reading farm labor board opinions issued during my absence. When no one arrived by eleven, I called Dresser.

"Agricultural Labor Relations Board," answered the Fresno receptionist crisply.

"Hi. Is Bob Dresser in?"

"Who's calling?"

"Mo Jourdane."

"Oh, hi Mo. I'll get Mr. Dresser. Where you calling from?"

"Delano."

"Why are you there? I hear you're still real hurt."

Before I responded, an FM-disc-jockey voice came on the line, "Robert Dresser here."

Hi, Bob. Dis is Mo. How ya doin"?"

"Fine, Mo. How about you? Where are you calling from?"

"Delano. The ALRB office. No one but me and the receptionist is here."

"What are you doing in Delano?"

"I returned to my job. Dis is where I wor'. Dat's why I'm phoning you. What do you want ine to do?"

"Let me talk with John Moore. He's here. He's been down there a lot more than I have. We'll call you back in a few minutes."

Twenty minutes later, the receptionist told me there was a call on line one. I picked up the receiver. It was Bob Dresser. "Jourdane," he said, sounding defeated. "I just got of the line with the General Counsel. He's transferring you to Salinas."

"You don' need help here?" I asked.

"Yeah, but Sacramento says it's been a lot quieter in the San Joaquin Valley since you and Shirley are gone. He wants to keep it that way."

"Why won' he tell me himself?"

"He told me to tell you, so I'm telling you, that you, you are transferred to Salinas. He told me to tell you it's too bad you got so hurt, but a lot of the discontent disappeared in the valley when you and Shirley were gone."

"You mean he hears fewer 'rowers 'omplaining dat da law is being enforced?"

"We'd love to have you stay in Delano, Mo. We need you to handle cases, but Sacramento ordered me to tell you that you are transferred to Salinas. So I guess I'm telling you."

Holding back my anger and frustration, I set the receiver down, hugged the receptionist good-bye, walked to the motel, picked up my things, walked to the Delano Greyhound station, and was on the next bus to Fresno where I caught another bus to Gilroy. I called Tom as the sun was setting. "Guess what?"

Arriving home in Aptos. I called Shirley. She laughed when I told her what had happened. "You weren't surprised, were you? They're afraid to have us in Delano, Mo. I got the same kinda shit after your wreck. Anyway, it'll be good having you in Salinas. I'll call Lupe Martinez and tell him you're coming in tomorrow."

Lupe Martinez was the mid-30's director of the Salinas Region for the ALRB. He was a stocky Latino from Ios Angeles who had been a public and federal defender before joining the Agricultural Labor Relations Board in Salinas. Overseeing the Salinas office, he enforced the Agricultural Labor Relations Act in an area stretching along the coast from Oxnard in the south to the Napa Valley in the north. I was hopeful that the reception I received from Martinez would differ from that in Delano.

Forty-Five

As the sun glimmered through the Aptos redwoods the next morning, Tom pulled up at the stronghold. He was taking me to Salinas where I planned to stay in a motel until I found an apartment. During the 28-mile ride from Aptos, my thoughts traveled back to the thousands of trips I had driven over the same two lane country road over the seven years I worked with California Rural Legal Assistance.

As we approached Salinas, I could see the Agricultural Labor Relations Board office, an out-of-place stucco building planted in the middle of a lettuce field like a cactus growing in a rose garden. New black asphalt surrounding the creme building overflowed with beige state Plymouth sedans and Dodge vans. Gesturing toward the building, I told Tom that was my new worksite, if I needed a ride back to Aptos I would call him.

Just after eight, I walked into the office. Unlike Delano, the Salinas office was full of investigators and lawyers working on their cases. All were preparing for trial or on their way to talk with witnesses. The first person I saw was Lupe Pacheco.

"Mo, mi amor. (my love)" cried Lupe. "La Shirley me dijo que iba a llegar (Shirley told me you were coming.)"

"Hi, lover," purred Shirley as she walked out to the reception area, having overheard her comadre. "Welcome to Salinas. Ever been to this cowboy town before?"

I chuckled. "It's li' I never left. Is Martinez here yet?"

"No way, vato," Lupe grinned. "You forget he's da bossman. He'll pull up in his Mercedes around nine or ten to make sure all us peons are working. Want some cafe (coffee) while you're waitin' for him. Come on. We can wait in his office. It's plush."

I sat in Martinez's soft-leather chair talking with Shirley and board agent Luis López about what was happening in the Salinas Valley. "We have all kinds of unfair labor practice trials coming up," said López who was in charge of the investigators in the office. "You can start working on one right now."

"Let me see Martinez firs'. I don' want him to believe I'm movin' in and trying to run da office. Plus, I'm not able to tal' much yet. I think it'll be a while before I'm ready to do a trial"

"Mo, you talk fine," said Shirley. "I have several cases set for trial you can help me on. I'd much rather have a disabled lawyer who knows the law and believes the clients than some physically fit lawyer who's right out of law school, learning how to do a trial at the expense of the farm worker he doesn't believe."

While Shirley was speaking, Lupe Martinez walked in. "Nice to see the Farm Labor Board's Bonnie and Clyde at home in my office." He grinned, giving me a hug. "I'm glad you're here, man. I talked with Dresser. He told me what happened in Delano. I was surprised you didn't tell 'em to fuck-off and walk. I'm glad you didn't."

"Than's Lupe. I'm ready to wor' wherever da Labor Board lets me. I'm not sure if I 'an see or tal' well enough to handle a trial, but if you have a file. I'll find out right now."

Martinez opened a metal file cabinet drawer and looked through neatly lined up manila folders. "Here's a good one. Not too difficult. Two workers fired by a large south county lettuce grower claim the company hired former teamster goons to run the personnel office and weed out all the United Farm Worker supporters."

I spent the day reviewing and searching for witness statements in the skinny file and researching the applicable law. López made arrangements for us to meet with the farm workers that evening. Around five, he took me to an old motel several miles from the office. I registered and we rode to Gonzalez, a pueblo 20 miles south of Salinas. That night, we spoke with farm worker witnesses. While we were leaving the witnesses around ten, I told them, "La audencia empieza el Viernes a las nueve. Les junto en la Laurel Inn 'offee shop en la 'alle Main eer' a de la 101 a las ocho." When the workers looked at Luis and me with questioning expressions, Luis explained what I had said.

While we rode back to Salinas, Luis commented, "Ya know, Mo. You speak pretty clearly when you talk slowly."

"I haven't done a trial since I lost my ability to spea' and see. How am I 'oing do as' 'uestions? How am I 'oing to ar'ue 'onvincingly to the judge? How am I 'oing do observe da witnesses' demeanor or rea'tion to my 'uestions. All 'at is 'rucial to being an effe'tive trial lawyer?"

Not understanding me, Luis replied, "You can do it, Man."

I smiled nervously, I have to do it, I thought. Four months ago they said I was going to die. I have to be able to be a lawyer or it's not worth living. Have faith, Jourdane.

Forty-Six

The next morning, we appeared at the hearing at 9:50 AM. By 11:15, the company had gone on the record agreeing to rehire the two workers and reimburse them for lost pay. At noon, López and I were having lunch with Shirley.

"Well, what do you expect, Luis?" asked Shirley. "Nothing changes. They see Mo and run for the hills. He settles almost every trial he does."

I didn't say what I thought, if it hadn't settled, I never could have won. I can't do it yet. Will I ever be able to?

When I walked into the office after lunch, Lupe Pacheco told me Martínez wanted to talk with me. I went to Martinez's office where he sat comfortably behind the large mahogany desk. Expecting to hear the General Counsel had decided I was still too disabled to work, I asked uneasily, "What's up?""

"I need someone to supervise the lawyers. I've been trying to do that job and run the entire office, but it's too much. Will you take the Regional Counsel position?"

"No."

"Why not," responded Martínez, apparently surprised by my abrupt rejection of his offer. "It's easy."

Thinking, he knows I can't speak or see clearly enough to handle trials, so he wants to keep me in the office. I told Martinez, "I was Chief-of-Operations for this entire agency when I worked in Sa'ramento. I left be'ause I wanted to be a trial lawyer. I still wanna be a trial lawyer, not a bureaucrat."

"You can handle trials and still oversee the other lawyers. You know that all the supervising job involves counseling and giving a little help while the lawyers are preparing for trial."

I smiled. "And advising the investi'ators on how to proceed with investi'ations and meeting with you and the investi'ator handling the case when we decide whether to issue a complaint or dismiss the unfair labor pra'tice charge."

"Come on." insisted Martinez, apparently understanding part of what I said. "It'll be a big help."

"Until you find someone else, I'll do it." I told Martinez. "I'll do the job temporarily, not be'ause I want the title but be'ause Hi' wor'ing with the o'er lawyers and investi'ators while they investigated unfair labor practice charges and prepare for trial."

By February 5, four days after returning to work and less than five months after the doctors told my family I'd be dead by the week-end. I was preparing my own cases for trial and supervising the lawyers for the Central Coast region of the Agricultural Labor Relations Board.

Forty-Seven

That evening, I returned to Aptos. I knew I could call Tom to come get me, but decided I had to be more independent. After work, Shirley drove me to the Salinas Greyhound station where I caught the bus to Watsonville. As the sun set into the Pacific Ocean across the lettuce field to the west, I walked the mile from the Greyhound depot to Freedom Boulevard and caught the Santa Cruz local bus to Aptos. When I arrived at Trout Gulch Road I climbed down from the bus into the night. Since my eye did not dilate to allow more light in as it darkens, night meant it was pitch black. I decided to call Tom and get a ride three miles up the hill to my home. There was no answer. I began walking. Step by step, I held my arms out in front of my body like a blind man without a cane. After 20 minutes, I made it to the post office, a couple hundred yards from the bus stop. I'll never make it, I thought. I can't even see the broken line in the middle of the road. While sitting on the post office steps trying to think of some way to get home, I was surprised when an apparent stranger walked up. "Mo Jourdane?"

I looked up but couldn't make out the face. "Hi," I responded.

"How you doing, man? I heard about your wreck. It's good to see you back in Aptos."

"Than's, but I have a real problem right now. You may he my hero of the day if you 'an help solve it." I was still unaware who I was talking with and too shy or proud to admit I couldn't sec a friend who stood in the dark a few feet away.

"Whata ya need, man? I'll help if l can."

"Well, in the wre' my vision 'ot pretty messed up. Especially at night. I just rode the bus here and I have to "et up the hill, but I 'an't see well enough to ma'e it wal' ing. 'an you 'ive me a ride?"

"Can I give you a ride? Sure. I have to drive right past your house to get home. Jump in." The stranger began walking toward his Datsun pick-up.

"ary? It's you. Shit. I 'an't see well enough to know who I'm tal'ing to." Gary was an old surfing buddy who lived in the only house up the hill from the Aptos stronghold, on the same dirt road. He laughed.

"You fooled me, man. L assumed you were seeing me when we talked. I guess your vision got hurt pretty bad."

"It'll et better," I replied confidently, while I got in the pick-up. "I have faith."

Forty-Eight

Over the following days, I spent much of my time counseling and training the less-experienced investigators and lawyers in the Salinas office to negotiate settlements of unfair labor practice charges and prepare for trials. Every evening, overwhelmed with my need to recover my ability to speak. I spent hours carefully pronouncing words into a tape recorder and exercising my lips and tongue. I kept hearing Dr. Kaplan, "Faith, hard work, and persistence." One evening while I walked through the lettuce fields between the Farm Labor Board office and my motel room in town. I recalled him saying if a dentist capped my broken teeth, I would talk better. I was convinced that when the General Counsel found out I couldn't talk well enough to handle a trial, he would fire me. The next morning I called Dr. Kaplan and arranged to begin seeing a dentist near Stanford.

Pondering on my inability to speak clearly, I was sitting behind my desk when Ladislao Pineda walked up and asked, "Wanta do an easy trial?"

Ladislao and I met ten-years earlier, the day I arrived at the California Rural Legal Assistance office in Salinas. Fresh out of law school, I shyly waited outside the office for the attorney who hired me. Ladislao was the first community worker the founders of CRLA hired when the Ivy League idealists prepared to open offices across rural California in 1965. When I arrived in Salinas on my first day as a lawyer in 1967, Ladislao walked to my car window in the Salinas office parking lot. Over the years, he taught me about the farm workers' struggle.

"You always say de' are easy." I smiled. "But I'm the one who has to try 'em and it's not always so easy. Whada we have 'is time?"

"A mushroom company. I'd say let me tell you about it and you decide but Martinez assigned it to you so you get to do it."

"Tell me about it anyway. I'll get us some 'offee."

"A year ago several of the hundreds of workers at the mushroom company began to organize for César's union. Many of them are undocumented."

"Union members or mushroom 'ompany employees?"

"Come on, huero. The mushroom workers. The job there is ideal since they work in the almost pitch black growing sheds. If the migra (immigration agent) comes, they just hide. Anyway the workers who organized for the union were fired. During the following months, other union supporters carried on the organizing effort."

"In the mushroom houses?""

"Si, mon (Yeah, man), Wearing their miners' hats with the beam glaring from the light affixed to the front, they secretly went from worker to worker during lunch and obtained signatures of workers who wanted an election. By January, they had signed up most of the workers and submitted the signatures to the Board. The union says that after we contacted the company to tell them a petition for an election had been filed, the company fired more Union supporters and began making repeated threats to those still there."

"Li" what?" I asked, with growing interest.

"Workers say a supervisor told 'em, 'Vote for that fucking union and we'll have the Border Patrol here tomorrow,"

"Pretty bad."

"There's more. Witnesses say that when the payroll clerk passed out checks, he told the workers, "Vote for the Union and you'll be out of company housing before dark.""

"It's 'etting better." I grabbed a pen and began scribbling notes. My strong desire to help farm workers reap justice thrust into the shadow my overwhelming fear of inability to speak well enough to be understood.

"Workers say that the general foreman told a group of them, "Vote for the union and we're going out of business,"

"How did the wor'er respond do the threats?"

"They were scared. Like moles, they huddled in the dark growing sheds and talked. Many decided not to take the risk."

"Didn't they know that the ele'tion would be secret so the "ompany won't know how anyone voted?"

"Many weren't sure how secret anything the State does is."

"What happened in the ele' tion?"

"I'll get to that. Let me tell you one more thing first. On the morning of the election, the workers had to pass by two uniformed guards sitting outside the polling place with shotguns across their laps. Many of these workers do not have papers authorizing them to be in the United States. Many of the workers were afraid to vote. The Union lost a close election."

"I assume the union's challengin' the cle'tion," I surmised.

"Sure, but the day after the election, the Border Patrol raided the mushroom growing houses, taking away handcuffed pickers.

Desperately, I tried for weeks to settle the mushroom company case. Finally it was time to put my money on table or fold. I didn't sleep the night before the trial was scheduled to begin. "I have to do it," I told myself, over and over as midnight turned to one, two and three. At dawn I dialed Ladislao's home number. I felt sick. I would tell him we had to continue the trial. That way I would still have a chance to enter a settlement. I'm too disabled to be a trial lawyer, I thought.

Forty-Nine

After Ladislao's phone rang once, I hung up. "I have to do the trial," I told myself. "I have to do it."

At 9 AM, I sat red-eyed at the counsel the table beside Ladislao. My stomach churned nervously. Silently I prayed for an earthquake or tornado. When the earth didn't shake and the wind didn't blow, I reluctantly told the court that the general counsel was ready to proceed. My voice quivering, I called our first witness. As the middle-age farm worker slowly walked to the witness stand, I whispered to Ladislao. "I 'an't do it, Lyle. No one is 'oing to understand me."

"Just talk slow, Mo," encouraged my friend.

Haltingly, I asked, "Would you... state your full name, please."

The interpreter turned to the witness, saying, "Diganos su nombre, por favor."

The witness replied, "Alfonso Ramírez Zapeda."

I felt like screaming. They understood. They understood me. I can be a lawyer again. In a trial that seemed to last forever, I fought for the jobs of the workers who had been fired, and challenged the threats on behalf of the workers who had not been deported or fired but had been treated like rebel slaves by the victorious company since the election. Daily, I had to make it through hard times, but surprisingly, if I spoke slowly, the interpreter, the court reporter and the judge understood my questions and objections. Ladislao's encouragement made the difference. A wave.

One evening I was having dinner with Maria Correlejo who during her teens had been one of the prettiest Latinas in the Southern Salinas Valley. She had put on some weight but still had an Elizabeth Taylor face framed with flowing black hair. She asked what good it did to fight about the threats after the workers were already deported. "Well, the union's challenging the ele'tion be'ause of 'em. The Board can 'et fired wor'ers their jobs ba' with ba' pay and ma'e the 'ompany apologize for the threats."

"I didn't really understand you, Mo. Make the company apologize?" María scowled.

"Uh huh. There are thousands of undo'umended wor'ers this Valley. If we don't do anything, when other 'ompanies hear what happened at the mushroom company, what's to stop them from doing the same. It 'ills 'ompany management to have to apologize to Meji'anos. They spend thousands of dollars for lawyers' lees to avoid having to 'ive an apology."

"Maybe, but won't the other companies see threats worked at the mushroom company; it kept the union out."

"They already know tha". We have to show other 'rowers that if they threaten their employees we'll sue 'em."

"You're hard to understand when you get excited, Mo," said the 26-year old mother of five who had become my friend over the years. "Tell me if I'm right. You're challenging the threats so other companies will see you prosecute when threats are made?"

"Right"

"And if you win, the company has to apologize to the workers."

"Right"

"All this just so other companies will see that to beat the union all they have to do is make threats and, at most, later say I'm sorry."

"Yeah. prob'ly." I responded dejectedly.

"Even worse, you can't do anything for the workers who were deported."

"You're right, but no law is perfe't. Since there have been employers and employees, wor'ers have been treated unfairly. The aim of the farm labor law is to allow wor'ers to be part of

Company decisions. The 'ompanies earn lots of money from the wor'ers' labor. In Russia, They had a revolution trying to solve the problem. The Agricultural Labor Relations Act is a small step and it's far from perfe't but it's a step. Would it be better to have no law and have wor'ers in the field with 'uns?"

"Get me a gun. I'll join them. Your fucking farm labor law. Just like every law passed by the White legislators, the poor people of color are the ones hurt. You tell the workers, sure, choose a union. Have an election. We'll protect you with a secret vote. Then, when half the workers get deported, all you can say is, 'sorry. There's nothing we can do to help you.' What shit."

The mushroom trial was held Monday through Thursday. This gave me Fridays to go to Menlo Park and have caps put on my broken teeth. Each week, I took buses and the train to the Bay area. The dentist began by performing root canals on the destroyed teeth. This completed, he inserted posts into the teeth roots and added the caps. In the end, I had teeth across the front of my mouth that looked like I had been born with them and was able, for the first time in over six months, to make the th sound.

Eventually, the mushroom trial ended. The company appealed, first to the Board and then the court of appeals and the Supreme Court. In the end, we would win the suit, but the paper victory did nothing for the deported workers and their children in Mexico who depended on them to put food on the table.

*   *   *

With Kathy spending most of her time in Hawaii and Tom back in school, my weekly trip to Stanford had become a real adventure. Nearly blind, I got up early and walked through the black world unable to see the ruts and bumps in the dirt on Westwood Lane and the cliffside edge of Trout Gulch Road as it weaved three miles down to the center of Aptos, a stop sign, a hotel and bar, a market and a laundromat. There I caught the local bus to downtown Santa Cruz. Fortunately, there was only one bus on the line headed toward Santa Cruz so my inability to read the bus destination did not make the trip impossible. When the local bus reached the corner of Soquel and Water Streets, I walked a block to the Greyhound depot and bought a ticket for the ride over the hill to San Jose. Unable to see the curb at each corner, through shuffling and feel I walked a mile down Santa Clara Boulevard from the Greyhound station to the Southern Pacific depot and caught a train to Palo Alto. Although daylight helped, I was still unable to see the dips and rises as I walked through the Stanford campus on a forested trail the mile from the train station to the hospital. There, I saw Doctor Kaplan. One-way, the trip that took just over an hour in a car took me from six in the morning until one in the afternoon.

One Tuesday in early May, Kathy was in Aptos. She drove me to Stanford. "Aside from my slurred speech that ma'es me sound li'e a drun'," I told Kaplan, "tears run down my chee'. It's pretty embarrassing."

Doctor Kaplan chuckled, apparently surprised that anything embarrassed me. After examining me, he said there wasn't much he could do about my speech and urged me to keep practicing on the tape recorder. Regarding tears dribbling down my cheek, he explained, "Our eyes tear constantly so they don't dry up. Normally, the tears just run from your eye through the tear duct to the nasal passage. In the wreck, your tear duets were destroyed."

"Without a tear duct, tears run down my cheeks?"

Right. We can insert a glass tube called a Jones Tube from your left socket to your nasal passage. That should relieve the problem on that side. Because of the prosthetic eye in your right socket, a glass tube won't work there. But we can raise that lower lid a little and it should reduce the problem on that side."

"Whenever you want to do it, I'm ready."

"How 'bout next Monday?"

"Should I 'ome to the hospital Sunday evening?"

"No. I have another surgery Monday at the Surgicenter in downtown Palo Alto. We can do this one there, too. You can stay in a motel and save the cost of spending several days in the hospital. Kathy or someone will have to come and stay with you at the motel."

On the ride back, Kathy said she was bothered by the lump in her breast that she first noticed several years earlier. "I know I had a mammogram and it came back negative, but maybe I should have a biopsy done while you are having surgery on your tear duct. I'll take my car and you can ride with Tom if he doesn't have school. You guys need to stay overnight in a motel, so I'll have a way to get home."

Fifty

At six the next Monday morning, I stepped from Tom's VW and walked into the Surgicenter. A few hours later Kathy walked into her appointment with the cancer department at Stanford Hospital.

After a blood test, a blood pressure check and the rest of the pre-operation ritual, I removed my clothing, donned a gown and lay on a stretcher. At seven the operation began. By eight, it was over. A wave. Meanwhile, Kathy was walking into the cancer center at Stanford I Hospital. While I was in the recovery room, Kathy was having a biopsy done on her right breast. Forty minutes later the biopsy was complete. As he placed a bandage on her breast, the doctor said, "If you call me about four this afternoon I can tell you the results. It'll probably be negative, but be sure and call around four this afternoon."

During the late morning, a nurse escorted me to Tom's waiting VW parked outside the front entrance. I was wobbly. The nurse gave Dr. Kaplan's home phone number to Tom, telling him, "be sure to call Doctor Kaplan if there is any problem."

At four o'clock sharp Kathy was on the phone with Kaplan. "Hi, Ernie, how did it come out?"

"Well, it's positive, Kathy." responded Dr. Kaplan after a moment's delay. "But the lab has only done a preliminary test. I want to see the specimen. II'I find the test results positive, we'll do a confirmation. In the meantime don't worry about it, okay?"

"Ernie, it scares me. How can the test be positive? The mammogram a few years ago was negative."

"Let's talk about that after I see the specimen. No use wasting our time and getting upset now. It might be all for nothing. I'll call you tomorrow after I've had a chance to examine the tissue."

*   *   *

"What's up, Tom?" Doctor Kaplan asked when Tom called his home at 4 A.M.

"About ten minutes ago I heard Mo groan so I turned on the light. When I looked at him, I saw blood all over his face and pillow. I don't know what to do. I learned in Vietnam how to stop bleeding by cutting off the circulation, but if Mo doesn't get blood to his head he'll be brain dead."

"Keep applying direct pressure," instructed Kaplan. "I'll be right there." Dr. Kaplan lived in Portola Valley, about five miles on a curvy road from the Palo Alto motel. He arrived less than ten minutes after Tom set down the receiver.

Doctor Kaplan took over. Minutes later, with me still asleep, he explained to Tom that to diminish swelling, he left a tube protruding from the incision. He attached the tube to this rubber globe taped to my neck. Excess blood would seep from the incision into the globe rather than causing swelling. During the night, I must have rolled over and the tube was dislodged from the incision. The blood-filled globe ran onto my pillow and face. "I'm glad you were here and didn't panic," Kaplan told Tom. "Bring him by Stanford in the morning and I'll take a look at him."

As Ernie drove off, Tom stared blankly out the window and thought, if you only knew how much I panicked. I almost cut off the blood to his head when I should have just applied pressure to the cut, I could have killed him. When I saw all that blood, it was too much like being back in that Vietnam jungle.

*   *   *

Meanwhile, Kathy's night was sleepless. With daylight, she picked up the ringing phone. Dr. Kaplan told her he had studied the tissue taken from her breast and personally analyzed the tissue himself. There was no doubt the cells were malignant. He asked Kathy to return to the hospital so they could determine how widespread the malignancy had spread through her body.

After Kathy's sobs drowned out the doctor's voice, Kaplan told her this wasn't 1920. It was likely they could remove the malignancy through surgery, the medically preferred solution, or they could treat Kathy with radiation and chemotherapy making the chances about fifty-filly she could live for five years. Doctor Kaplan asked if Kathy could come to the hospital tomorrow.

"Why not today?" Kathy sighed in a defeated tone.

"I have a surgery this morning. We could take more tissue from you this afternoon and you can stay over in the hospital tonight while we analyze it. Can you do that?"

"I'll be there, Ernie. Thanks."

Kathy sat silently drinking coffee and smoking Winston after Winston until I arrived at our Aptos home around noon. "Hi, baby." she said, trying as hard as she could to sound cheerful. "They say they can take care of it by removing my breast. Nice, huh? Aw fuck, Mo. Why me? I'm only 35-years old." Kathy managed to say before the torrent of tears and thunder of sobs began.

I put my arms around her slender shoulders, holding her tight. "What shit, baby. You're loo 'ood and too young and too healthy for this to happen. But know what?"

"What?" she sobbed into my shoulder.

"To'ether, we can beat anything. You'll beat 'ancer. We can win if we try hard enough. All you have to do is set a long range 'oal and short range 'oals and ta' da first step toward reaching them. It's li' running any race. You have to ta' the first step to win." Faith, persistence, and hard work, I thought.

That afternoon Kathy went back to Stanford. The next morning she learned the cancer had spread. Not only would they have to remove her right breast but also the tissue anal muscle from her shoulder.

I took the buses and train to Stanford to join her. "I know it sounds like a lot," recited the monotone-Stanford specialist Dr. Kaplan had brought in to study the test results. "If you want the best chance to get rid of it," he continued, "you'll have surgery. Dr. Kaplan tells me he already explained to you the odds if you limit yourself to radiation and chemotherapy. Now that we know the cancer has spread, the odds escalate against you the longer you postpone surgery."

"I don't know what to do," thought Kathy aloud, her voice shaking, tears clouding her once-sparkling azure eyes.

"You should decide soon."

On the ride back to Aptos, Kathy cried. Over and over, like a rhythmic chant she mumbled, "They aren't removing my breast. They can't."

While she continued to drive, Kathy's chant strayed into a stream of conscience, "Even if I let them remove my breast," she wept, "that's not enough. They have to take more. I'll be a cripple. I can't live that way."

By the time we reached the Aptos Stronghold, Kathy had decided she could beat cancer without surgery.

"I'm strong," she said. "I have to be strong. My first goal is to research everything that's ever been written about cancer."

Kathy called Doctor Kaplan. "It scares the shit out of me just talking about it, Doctor, but we can beat it. Si se puede."

That evening, Kathy went to the University of California at Santa Cruz library and began working on her short-range goal. She began reading every book and every article she could find that discussed the interrelationship of cancer and diet. "I'm going to beat it," she said, her now strong voice hinting not the slightest doubt. "And I'll have both my breasts when I've done it." Richard and Annette Block's Cancer Survivors Park in Sacramento did not yet exist, but Kathy had innately decided to live by the principles the Block's would one day post. "Visual imagery has been demonstrated to improve the chances of success. Prayers by individuals unknown to the patient have been clinically demonstrated to improve the chances of success. So prayer by the patient could certainly help and cannot hurt. Make certain your subconscious attitude is receptive to successful treatment and keep a positive outlook. You must, on your own, make the commitment that you will do everything in your power to fight the disease. Nothing halfway. Nothing for the sake of ease or convenience. The biggest and hardest thing that you will be required to do in the entire battle is to make up your mind to really fight it. When you have done this, you have accomplished the most difficult thing you will ever have to accomplish throughout your entire treatment."

The day before Kathy's treatment began. I asked if she would be able to drive home.

"They say there won't be any noticeable effect this early. Later it'll make me weak and maybe I'll have to stay near Stanford, but for now I can go back and forth. I know it will work." Kathy maintained. "Radiation and chemotherapy treatment, and my dict. I've learned so much about the effect of what we cat on our bodies. I know I'll beat it. Besides, they'll probably find a cure to cancer before my radiation is over anyway."

"How lon' will you do radiation?"

"For nine weeks. I'll be taking chemotherapy at the same time. Then I'm done. I plan on staying in Aptos for now. When radiation kills the cancer, I'm outta here and back to Hawaii. Hopefully, I'll never have to see a radiation machine again."

I was more scared for Kathy than she appeared to be for herself. I agreed with her that her plan would work, and they probably would discover a cure to cancer before her treatment was over. I thought but did not say that I knew so little about cancer, I did not feel nearly as confident for Kathy as I felt about recovering myself. I also knew that Kathy and I could not freeze our lives like a movie scene. We had to go on living and face whatever devil jumped up before us. We had to have a pay check and medical insurance for Kathy's medical bills. I returned to Salinas to represent farm workers and Kathy stayed in Aptos. I visited her on weekends. Naively, I never expected my friend who drew cartoons for the farm workers in their effort to organize into a union would be visiting her during the week.

Fifty-One

One Saturday in July, Tom came by with David Konno. "What're ya doin' Sunday?" Tom asked.

"I don' know. Wanna 'o surfin'?""

"Want to come with us to the City?"

"That's right;" I smiled. "Tomorrow you loonies are running the San Francisco Marathon. No way. I'd...." Not being able to pronounce a hard G when I started to say, "I would get tired watching," I said, "I'd be too tired just watching people run that far. You 'an tell me all about it tomorrow night, if you're still alive."

"When're you gonna start runnin', lolo (slang term for insane person in Hawaiian)?" kidded Konno, knowing that I thought running was the dumbest way to pass time yet discovered.

"I don't think that's 'onna happen real soon. It's no fun suffering. Besides I don't have the time to waste out on some road with drivers missing me by inches while they ta' in the sights of beautiful Santa Cruz. I'd rather surf, even if I don' see the waves."

*   *   *

On Sunday evening Tom was back. "Still wal'ing." I kidded, grinning with pride in my brother while I watched him limp from his VW to the front door.

"It was super. We finished in a little over four hours."

During the following week while in Salinas I thought a lot about why my brothers liked running so much. John had run the Honolulu Marathon the year before and now Torn in San Francisco. Back in Aptos the following Saturday, I searched the barn and found a pair of antique low top Keds. I put the black basketball shoes on for the first time in more than ten years, walked down the steep Loma Prieta hill to Trout Gulch Road and started jogging very slowly toward town. Puffing deeply, I made it to the first curve. I walked for a hundred yards and began jogging again. Not only did my lungs scream for relief. but the sensation of slicing knives penetrated my cramping calves. A car approached and I limped over onto the left shoulder and began to jog after the car passed. On my third step, I tripped over a crack in the asphalt and fell. I lay in the gravel and dust out of breath. How stupid this is, I thought. Hobbling up Loma Prieta hill, knees bleeding and my right ankle beginning to swell, I thought. You gave it your best. You tried to run and it's as dumb as you always thought. I think you best improve your vision and stick to surfing.

*   *   *

A couple weeks later, Tom and Jesse came by on a Saturday afternoon. "Wanna run?" I grinned when they walked through the door.

"Yeah. Right." Tom smiled.

"I'm serious. I been runnin' a little in Salinas after wor'. I fall about one day out of three but if we run in the middle of Trout Gulch I'll be alright."

It took five minutes to convince Tom I was serious. "Why don't we drive to the eucalyptus grove a mile down Trout Gulch toward town," he finally suggested. "We can leave the VW there, run to our house and I can run back and get the car later. While I'm gettin' the car, you could walk from our house down to the beach break at Rio del Mar with my board and ride some waves. I'll pick ya up there and give ya a ride home."

"Wait a minute," I gasped with a look of terror on my face. "I'm not li' you "uys. I only run a little. I've been joggin' maybe a mile at most every other day. How far is it from the eu'alyptus trees to your house?"

223

Well, it's two miles from the trees to the Bayview Hotel and maybe another half-mile to our house. You can do two and a half miles. Especially since it's all down hill."

"I'll try. I 'uess, there ain't no law that says I 'an't stop and wal' if'l 'et tired. But you 'uys should know before we start. I don't really thin' I'll ma'e it."

While I was in the bedroom getting a sweatshirt, I overheard Jesse ask Torn. "What'd he say?"

"I didn't understand what he said either," whispered Tom, "but from the tone of his voice I assume he agreed to run. I never thought I'd see this day. It's about as awesome as his crashing into that eighty ton oil rig and walkin' away from it in one piece."

"Tom, He didn't exactly walk away from that wreck in one piece."

"Well, you know, what I mean, he is still walking. He might have a few parts missing but he's still pretty much in one piece."

Ten minutes later the three of us were jogging through the redwoods lining the creek as it hugged Trout Gulch Road. By the time we reached the Bay View Hotel, I was ready to walk. Jesse and Tom urged me on. "This is what I was afraid of," I panted, trying to get a breath as I plodded behind the two real runners. "You 'uys are 'ruel, forcing me to 'eep 'oing. (You guys are cruel, forcing me to keep going.)"

"You can stop if you want," panted Jesse. "We'll meet you at our house."

" If I 'an see well enough to find it." I puffed, barely able to see the other side of the road.

Once we reached Tom and Jesse's cabin, Tom grinned. "You surprise me sometimes, Mo. I never thought I'd see you do what you just did."

"'ome on," I responded defensively. "Faith, persistence, and hard work. Plus you 'uys have never stopped pushing me since my wre"

"Since your wreck? Maybe, but you better get different shoes. Those are the shoes you wore to play basketball in the ninth grade. They aren't exactly running shoes. With no cushion and your toes stickin' out the front, you're sure to have an injury that takes far longer to heal than the scraped knees you get when you fall on Trout Gulch."

That afternoon, Tom and I went to Big Five. Ten minutes after we arrived, I bounced out wearing a brand new pair of Brooks Chariots. Walking to Tom's VW, I told him, "These shoes feel lighter than air. They're neat. It's too hard to surf since I'an't see the waves, and I 'ant play ball now since l 'an't see the ball 'omin', so maybe with these hot shoes I'm ready to run."

Tom laughed.

Fifty-Two

The next week I was in the Salinas office talking with Shirley. "Ya know, you can almost talk normal now," she said smiling. "It's about time."

"Than's. It ma' es me feel 'ood to hear ya say that. Plus, no one's bothered me about what I'm doin' for a long time."

Shirley frowned. "No one's been harassing me either. I remember you telling me about Reagan trying to shut down California Rural Legal Assistance because you guys were doing too much for farm workers. You said it made you feel proud because if no one's after you, it means you aren't doing much. I guess after we got kicked out of Delano, we haven't been a threat to those who don't want the farm labor law enforced."

"Maybe the 'rowers have finally accepted the farm labor law. Maybe we've played our part and it's time for us to step aside."

"Let's wait and see what happens this winter. A lot of contracts the union and growers entered after the union won elections a few years ago expire in January. We'll see if the companies renew the contracts or start the fight all over again." I was too speechless to ask for more information when Shirley said, "I hear Kathy's seeing Albert." Albert Escalante was the brother of one of Shirley's closest friends in San Jose.

*   *   *

When November came, I was on my way to Calexico. Riding the Greyhound across the state, I stared through the dirty window at the golden California hills peppered with giant black oaks. It was a beige blur with labs of black. Although my vision had improved enough to enable me to very slowly read law books, I no longer saw colors and I missed the beauty of a California autumn. As the depressing feeling of lost vision began, I looked at the paperback in my hand, Lie "Down with Lions", that told about the Russian invasion of Afghanistan that ended ten years later after the brave self-reliant tribes held off the super power's modern armament and before the United States invaded the independent nation to kill Ben Laden the terrorist. I thanked God I was not injured in Afghanistan and that I could still read. My life had changed from an out-there surfer-trial lawyer to a reclusive reader who jogged a couple miles a day.

 Unknown to me, Kathy's life too had changed. She had fallen in love with Albert Escalante, a United Farm Workers' volunteer who I met a couple years earlier in the Imperial Valley. Escalante was my friend. Together we played pool near the De Anza Hotel in Calexico and drank beer and tequila in Mexicali.

After my wreck Escalante had come to visit me in Aptos. He met Kathy.

*   *   *

 Carlos Bowker met me at the Greyhound depot in El Centro and drove to the nearby All American motel. The next morning, Carlos and I met Luis Lopez at Imperial Valley's one-runway airport. Throughout November, Luis and I tried cases based on unfair labor practice charges. Each evening, we ran from the hotel into the lettuce and asparagus fields. In my eyes, Luis was a real runner; he ran ten-kilometer races. While I trudged slowly through the red dusty sunsets, he ran ahead, ran back, ran sideways and backwards urging me to move a little faster.

 "Ya know," I panted, slowly climbing the motel stairs one evening, raising a leg one step, raising the other to that step and painfully repeating the process for all 22 steps. "Before this winter is over, I'm 'onna run from El Centro to the border."

 López laughed.

227

Fifty-Three

One evening, Luis and I were having dinner in a Mexicali cafe we visited most every day. We saw the chief UFW organizer Marshall Ganz, and union board member Jessica Govea. Walking toward the front door, we stopped by Jessica and Marshall's table. In response to my nonchalant inquiry. "What's happening?" Marshall replied, "Tomorrow's our first negotiating session with 28 growers who joined together to bargain as a group."

"Who're in the 28?" I asked.

"Almost every large lettuce grower in California. César's coming to town for the meeting."

"You already have 'ontracts with most the lettuce 'ompanies, don't you?"

"Yeah. All 28. But the contracts expire this winter. The workers are asking for a little more money because the companies are making millions forcing the workers to toil long hours in the sun. I hope the companies are willing to share a small portion of their incredible profits with those who bend over all day bringing in the crops."

*　　*　　*

During November, workers across the Imperial Valley set up picket lines on the country roads adjoining the fields. The day before Thanksgiving, union lawyer Tom Dalzell called "You have to do something to protect the workers," he demanded.

"What's the problem?"

"This morning. The growers went to court to get an injunction to stop union members from picketing on the roadside near their fields. The judge said the workers could peacefully picket, but when the farm workers on the picket line entered their cars to go home this afternoon, sheriff deputies followed and stopped them, scouring their cars for any possible mechanical violation. They checked the tire tread, the brakes, the headlights, tail lights, everything."

"Just li'e the 'rowers, the 'ops are smarter than they used to be," I responded. "Remember when the 'rowers 'ot a temporary restraining order that ordered the wor'ers to stop pi' 'eting a "antaloupe field. When the Sheriff deputies went to arrest wor'ers for violating the order Jerry 'ohen showed up and had the deputy in charge read the order prohibiting the union and its members from pi' 'eting a parti'ular 'antaloupe field. He then pointed to the field beside the road. It was filled with ready-to-pi watermelons. The farm wor'ers 'ontinued to pi' 'et, the 'onvoy of deputy sheriff 'ars pulled away, some deputies laughing, some an'ry, many asking why lawyers 'an never 'et it right."

"I didn't understand much of what you said, Mo," Dalzell responded, and asked, "can the farm workers file an unfair labor practice charge against the sheriff for interfering with their right to organize and strike?"

"You can file an unfair labor practice charge, Tom, but I don't think the General Counsel will file a complaint against the sheriff. I'll talk with the General "ounsel. If you showed 'rowers are 'onspiring with the sheriff to deprive the wor'ers of rights, you'd have a 'ase, But it'd be pretty hard to prove."

The Union filed the unfair labor practice charge. Over the weekend the General Counsel was out of town. On Monday afternoon when the General Counsel still had not returned, at the urging of a fearless field agent David Arizmendi I approved filing the complaint charging the Imperial County Sheriff's Department with committing an unfair labor practice. When the General Counsel returned on Wednesday, he angrily ordered the novel complaint dismissed.

*   *   *

Several days before Christmas, Luis and I had just returned to our room from dinner when I gasped, "Oh, shit."

"Que paso?" asked Luis, inquiring what was wrong.

"My eye jus' "ame out."

"What?"

Remembering to speak very slowly, I repeated, "My eye just fell out."

"Your real one or the glass one?"

"The pretend eye. I thought it was there permanently. I don't thin' it's supposed to 'ome out. I better phone my do'tor."

I called Stanford Hospital, leaving a message for Dr. Kaplan to call. Twenty minutes later, the phone rang. Kaplan told me that we shouldn't let the prosthetic eye stay out too long. The socket would close up. He suggested we try to put it back in temporarily while he was on the line.

I tried. Luis tried. We couldn't fit the small plastic orbit into the seemingly smaller socket. I picked up the receiver. "Ernie. We 'an' l'et it to 'o in. What should I do?"

"Okay," replied the doctor patiently, apparently thinking as he spoke. "There's no one I know in the Imperial Valley who can help. You could go to the emergency room down there, but it's Saturday night so there's probably no one there who can help you." Kaplan then told me to catch the first plane to San Jose or San Francisco. Saying he would pick me up at the airport, he asked, "Do you think you can see well enough to travel and catch a plane at night?"

"Luis says he'll drive me," I said. "We'll get there faster. There aren't a whole lot of planes out of the Imperial Valley airport. He said if he drives me. I'll arrive in the Bay Area rather than ending up in Mexico City because I went to the wrong gate." I could see myself stumbling around a foreign country with one eye I could hardly see out of and the other in my hand.

Twelve hours later, Luis and I arrived at Stanford Hospital's room. Waiting to see Doctor Kaplan, I glanced at a young African-American patient sitting in the bed next to mine. He stared at me wide-eyed, his mouth agape. I smiled and said Hi.

"Hey, man," responded the youth. "That doctor just take yer eye. How come you just sittin there? How come you ain't a hollerin' and a shoutin?"

"It's a phony eye." I grinned. "It 'omes out."

"Oh, man," sighed the guy. "Scared the shit outta me." The apparently relieved patient lay back down giggling, holding his shoulder.

"What are you here for?" I asked.

"I was shootin' craps wi' ma homies when some fucka' shoot me. Bang. For nothin'. The motha'fucka up and shoot me. But my shoulder, it get betta' You eye ain't neva gonna get no betta."

Kaplan came in, he told me that when they initially inserted the eye. He connected it to the muscles in the rear of the socket. The artificial eye moved like the eyes I was born with. What happened in the Imperial Valley was that the muscle rejected the implant. Doctor Kaplan couldn't just replace the prosthetic eye. Tossing the unusable device into the trash basket, he said. "We have to make a new one. It won't move like your old one did, but I think it'll look better than an empty socket."

Kaplan inserted a white plastic ball a little smaller than one that I would play jacks with into my socket and said, "This'll keep the socket from shrinking closed tonight." Holding out a piece of white gauze and a black eye patch, he said, "Take your choice."

The next morning, Dr. Kaplan sent me across the hall to see Tom who made prosthetic or artificial eyes. After examining my vacant eye socket. Shult had me hold my head back and filled the socket with warm wax. I watched in fascination as he whittled an eye of wax after it had hardened. When satisfied with his artwork, Shultz carried the eye out of the room. When he returned moments later, I asked what was happening.

"I used the wax to make a mold, filled the mold with plastic and right now your new eye is cooking or hardening in a kiln."

"Is that all there is to it?" I asked. "I've only been here half an hour?"

"After the plastic is hard, all we have to do is paint it, put it in again, and we're through for today. You'll walk out of here without that patch over your right eye."

Shultz went out to get the molded plastic. When he returned he sat in front of me, studied my left eye, grabbed a paint brush, painted the lens hazel to match my remaining eye, studied my left eye again, painted blood veins onto the white of the plastic eye, again studied my left eye, added some green to the plastic lens, held it up against my left eye and smiled. He placed the plastic eye in the oven momentarily and returned, asking me to tilt my head back. He installed the prosthetic eye and handed me a mirror. I looked at the new eye. Through my misty vision I was impressed. It looked like I had never lost an eye.

Fifty-Four

By early January, the Union negotiators had met with companies repeatedly. There was no movement on either side toward reaching a new contract. César Chávez recognized the hardship that would result from a strike in the fields but felt the workers had to act precariously if they were going to get a reasonable response from the corporations in their negotiations for a contract. On January 19, 1979, farm workers walked from the fields across the valley. Over the following days, turmoil in the fields escalated. The striking farm workers' children grew hungry. The striking workers grew bitter against neighbors who were taking their jobs.

In mid-February, a group of striking workers entered a field to try to speak with the scabs. The workers saw a foreman run to his pick-up, grab a rifle and fire toward them. Seconds later, Contreras lay dead. The sheriff conducted a cursory investigation. The foreman was not charged with a crime. A few days later, El Dia de Enamorados or Valentines Day, 9,000 farm workers joined the pall-bearers carrying Rufino's body in a wooden box down the narrow-country road from the Calexico to a cemetery several miles north of town. In the words César Chávez uttered at the cemetery over Rufino's lifeless body, "February 10 was a day of infamy for farm workers. It was a day without hope. It was a day without joy. The sun didn't shine. The birds didn't sing. The rain didn't fall. On this day greed and injustice struck down our brother, Rulino Contreras." César paused, his head bowed solemnly. His dark face rose. "What is the worth of a man? What is the worth of a farm worker? Rufino and his father and his brother together gave the company 20 years of their labor. They were faithful workers and helped build up the wealth of their boss, helped build up the wealth of his ranch. What was their reward for their service and their sacrifice? When they asked for a just share of what they themselves produce, when they spoke out against the injustice they endured, the company answered them with bullets. The company sent hired guns to quiet Rufino Contreras."

"Labor together produces the fruit of the land. The human beings who torture their bodies, sacrifice their youth, and numb their spirits to produce this great agricultural wealth. A wealth so vast it feels all of America and much of the world. And yet, men, women, and children who are the flesh and blood of this production often do not have enough to feed themselves."

Again César paused. "But we are here today to say that true wealth is not measured in money or status or power. It is measured in the legacy that we leave behind for those we love and those we inspire. In that sense, Rufino is not dead. Wherever farm workers organize, stand up for their rights, and struggle for justice, Rufino Contreras is with them. If Rufino were alive today, he would tell us, "Don't be afraid. Don't be discouraged. Don't cry for me. Organize.""

In many ways, the farm workers' spirit lay dead in the mud with Rufino Contreras.

Fifty-Five

With the harvest coming to a close in late-February, it was time for Luis and me to return to the Salinas Valley. Before I left the Imperial Valley I had one thing I had to do, run from El Centro to the border.

Early on my last morning in the Valley, wearing my red nylon trunks and no shirt, I started in downtown El Centro, jogged to Fourth Street, and headed south. After I had run two miles, I passed under Interstate 8, the motorist's link between the Pacific and the Atlantic Ocean. Lettuce fields replaced the residential neighborhood. I saw a sign, Calexico, eight miles. I continued my slow and steady pace as the desert sun bore down on my frail body. I planned to drink water at Carlos Bowker's home in between El Centro and Calexico.

Forty minutes later, I shuffled left onto the deserted Heber street through older housing, passing a gas station, a Circle K, and a bar. When I used to surf, I thought I'd sit out there and talk story with other surfers while we waited for a wave. I never realized how it really was a social sport, like golf. Running is a very lonely sport, since I can barely talk. I'm learning to live without a social life. Now I barely see, and I'm trying to forget surfing. Thank God, I can run.

I stopped at Carlos's house and gulped down luke-warm water. Leaving pesticide residue in the glass, I was on the road again. Four more miles and I will enter Calexico, I thought. Another mile to the border. I ran on through a fog of smoke from an asparagus field being burned to prepare it for next year's planting and through the blank stare of thousands of black and white Guernsey's slowly chewing as they watched the crazy human run past the their dairy home.

As I passed the cemetery where days earlier the farm workers buried their murdered brother, I wondered if their suffering in what sometimes seemed like a futile effort was worth it. After reaching the outskirts of town, I continued down the deserted street, passing A's Hotel and McDonalds. Several hundred yards ahead lay Mexico. I could see ahead the green and white Border Patrol vans lined up outside the immigration office at the border crossing, waiting like poised black widows, to seize the helpless but hungry immigrant. When I reached the 12-foot chain-link fence separating Mexico from their brothers and sisters in the United States, I sat on the curb alongside the road and cried. I had done what I had thought all winter about doing, but I was overcome with apprehension over the danger ahead if we did not find a way to heal the deep and division between the starving workers who felt forced to go on strike to feed their children the bare necessities, tortillas and frijoles, and their poor neighbors who felt forced to take the jobs the striking workers left behind. It was February 28, the day they declared they had reached impasse with the Union and refused to bargain further. The Agricultural Labor Relations Board would later find this declaration of impasse that the growers to disregard the union and treat workers as if the union did not exist, was an unlawful effort to destroy the union and was therefore an unfair labor practice.

*   *   *

Throughout the spring, I tried unfair labor practice cases in the Salinas Valley. One Sunday morning in early March, I lined up at the back of the pack of several thousand lightly clad runners near the courthouse at First and Hedding Streets, north of downtown San Jose. The gun went off and I moved with the mob, first walking. then trotting, then jogging, and finally running. At mile three, I passed my old college, San Jose State. I'm in trouble, I thought as I panted by San Carlos Street, a couple hundred yards from my old fraternity house. I went out too fast. By mile five I was struggling through downtown San Jose, fighting not to walk. I very slowly crossed the finish line near the federal courthouse where I had spent exciting days fighting for farm workers, sixty-three minutes after the starting gun was fired. A wave.

Riding over the hill to Aptos, I bragged to Tom and David Konno, both of you had run the six-point-two miles in around forty minutes. "I might be slow but it don't matter. I ran a ten-'ilometer race. But I'll tell ya, there ain't no way I'm 'onna (gonna) try to run a 26-mile marathon. I don't how "uys and John do it."

"Forget about running for a while." Tom grinned. "Come with us to Hawaii."

"When ya 'oing?"

"The twentieth of next month."

"Who's going?"

"Jesse and I and David, and you. Since Kathy's living with Escalante I figured she won't be going."

By then, I knew Kathy was sharing a rented home with Escalante. Kathy and I had separated as husband and wife a few years earlier but remembering I had lost her still hurt. Repeatedly I had to convince myself that Kathy was my friend not my wife. You're permanently disabled, I thought. She still drives you over the hill to Stanford Hospital, but you can't see well enough to join her drinking wine at the Cooper House when you return because it is night and too dark. Mom always said you have to accept some things the way they are. Every dark cloud has a bright side.

"Yeah, I'll go," I said to Tom.

Fifty-Six

On April 20, I was on the United Airlines flight to Honolulu. My brother John met us at the airport and took us to his apartment a block from Kapiolani Park, just towards Diamond Head from Waikiki. We stayed the week with him.

On Friday morning, John took us sailing on Lava Le, the 47-foot New Zealand sloop with its owner, a dentist, and raced. After passing Diamond Head on the sleek-close-to-the-water ultralight boat with the spinnaker blown full, John asked if I wanted to have some good fun. "Sure," I replied, knowing little about sailing but willing to try anything, once.

"Put this harness around your chest and climb out on the spinnaker boom," said John. Attached to the harness was a half-inch line coiled on the deck.

"I don't have real super balance anymore," I divulged. reluctant to scramble across a wobbly aluminum pole directed 90 degrees from starboard, ten feet above the rapidly passing green water.

"You can do it," encouraged Tom. His smile became a grin as he added, "You have nothin' to worry about. All of us are experienced lifeguards if you have any trouble."

I started to slide out the boom as the sloop bounced over the swells. I moved slowly, almost falling several times, able to catch myself and hold on, only to slide a few more inches and almost fall again. Once I was out near the end of the boom with the harness around my chest, John tossed me the other end of the rope attached to the harness. "Tie this onto the boom," he said.

I did.

With attentive Jesse fearing the worst, thinking John must not realize how injured I still was, John yelled, "Okay. Is the rope tied on good?"

"I thin' so."

"Okay. When I say go, jump."

When I hit the wind-chopped surface below with my mouth open, my lungs filled with salt water. I began to cough as I ricocheted across the green. I'm gonna drown, I thought. I'm gonna drown and John doesn't even know I'm in trouble

But John knew I needed help. He was not the reckless buccaneer I feared. Through an experienced sailor's eye, he saw me hit the water and come up coughing. He immediately dropped the sails and the sloop coasted to a halt. "Tom, throw him the ring buoy," he yelled. "It's right behind you."

I saw the ring tossed from the deck and hit the rough sea several yards away. Choking on the water that flooded my lungs, I tried to swim toward it. Panic. My splashing left hand touched the ring, but it slipped from my grasp. Ready to give up, my lungs begging for air, I frantically made a final lunge. My right hand touched the buoy. Again, it slipped away. A wind- blown white cap covered my face. My head sunk beneath the surface. Suddenly, the tip of my finger felt the quarter-inch nylon cord tightly encircling the wildly bobbing buoy. Desperately, I tried to dig my finger under it. My head momentarily cleared the water. I gasped for air. Coughing. I felt the buoy moving away. I clung to it tightly and was slowly pulled toward the sloop. When the buoy reached the stern, I tried to climb the side of the hull. I fell back into the sea.

"Use your feet to climb the side of the hull like Spiderman," John yelled.

Five minutes later I lay on deck shivering.

"Shit, I'm sorry," said John. "I almost killed you. After seeing you thrown under wave after wave surfing yesterday, 1 didn't imagine you'd take in water. We do it all the time. We just jump and slip along like a rock skimming the water after you toss it."

"It ain't your fault, man. I swallowed the water like a baby all by myself. I thin' I better sti' to surfing." I coughed. "At least I 'an hang onto my board if I'm in trouble."

Surfing in Waikiki that afternoon, I realized that a partially blind surfer amidst many surfboards in the water is not a whole lot safer than a disabled spinnaker-boom jumper. "I'm sure someone will lose their board and I won't see it 'oming," I confided in Tom as we paddled out together.

*   *   *

Over the following days I found running safer than water sports. Every day we ran. One day running from Waikiki to Hanama Bay, a little over ten miles east of Diamond Head, we reached the top of Coco Head. I caught up with David who stood waiting for me. "Now I know your secret," I panted. "Japanese runners have stronger legs than Haoles. Running up hill is easier for you than us white folk."

Konno grinned.

"You know I panted, "My goal ever since I left the hospital has been to surf like I used to. Maybe I should change my goal.

"There's no law saying you can't." What's your new goal going to be??

"To run a marathon."

On Sunday, we all ran the annual King Kamehameha Run, an eight-mile loop around Kapiolani Park, over Diamond Head to the Arco station in Kahala and back to the Honolulu Marathon finish line. I finished not too far behind my brothers and Konno.

Monday, we went across the island to Haleiwa to visit the country, have shave ice at Matsumoto's store, and ride waves. After a bad wipe out, I paddled over to Tom's board and told him I was going to shore.

While Tom continued surfing, David and I ran through the steaming sugar-cane fields to Waimea Bay, a nine mile round trip. Most of the way, I complained about the heat and the humidity and the hills and the pain. David encouraged me to keep Back at the beach at Haleiwa, although fatigued, I wanted to try to surf one more time. Five minutes later, after riding a small wave that closed out when it hit the inside coral reef called the Toilet Bowl, I paddled to where Tom sat on his board. "Where's your eye?" he asked in a startled tone.

I felt my right eye socket. The prosthetic eye was missing, "Oh shit, it must've popped out in the toilet Bowl. I better phone Emie."

Tom and I paddled to shore. From the pay phone outside the shave-ice store. I called Dr. Kaplan. After I explained the situation and where I was, he told me to go to Niilani Hospital in downtown Honolulu and ask to see a doctor who had been a student of Kaplan at Stanford. "I'll call him and arrange for him to place something in your eye socket so it doesn't tighten and close before I see you," he said. "Then go to the airport and get back here as soon as you can. We have to replace your eye within 24 hours. Call me when you arrive. You have my home number."

The Honolulu doctor handled my urgent problem and I went to the airport. Walking through sliding green-tint door, I eyed disgruntled passengers packed like cattle in a feedlot. The United Airline mechanics were on strike. All United flights from the islands to the mainland had been canceled. While I stood in a line that stretched past the airport, Tom talked with some sailors camped out in the terminal. They told him they had been there for two days trying to get home. They only had two weeks leave and had already spent much of it waiting in line.

Finally, the United Airlines agent told me, "I'm sorry, sir. I understand you need to see your doctor, but we have no planes flying and all the other carriers to the Mainland are booked beyond capacity. All I can recommend is you get in one of the lines and wait as a stand-by passenger."

Walking from the counter. I feared that before I saw Dr. Kaplan my eye socket would close too much to replace the lost eye. I would spend my life with a black patch over the shriveled eye socket. I explained to Tom what the agent said. He told me of his conversation with the sailors. I had given up when John offered to call Larry Loganbill.

Loganbill was the world's tallest surfer, six-six former All-American water polo player. He surfed and life guarded in high school with John, joined John and I as a Theta Chi at San Jose State, and joined John in Hawaii to teach at Kamehameha, the school for Hawaiian children created by Princess Kuhio, the last of the Hawaiian Royalty. "I hope he has as much power as he has height." I said in response to John's offer.

I doubt it." John smiled. "but he has a friend who's high up in Pan Am. Maybe he can help you."

I shrugged my shoulders. "Whatever," I said, walking to a pay phone with John.

"We have to stay near the pay phone." John said when he replaced the receiver after talking with Larry Loganbill.

Fifteen minutes later the phone rang. After a few words John set down the receiver and walked from it grinning. "God or somebody's on your side. Larry's friend told him Pan Arm always keeps a couple seats open for emergencies or in case someone real important needs to get somewhere. United already told you that you aren't an emergency so you must be real important."

Less than twelve hours after losing my eye in the Haleiwa surf, I walked into the emergency room at Stanford. Dr. Kaplan awaited my arrival.

After Dr. Kaplan was sure that my eye socket had not constricted so much that I would need surgery before I could obtain a replacement prosthetic eye, he sent me across the hall to see Tom Shultz who looks and talks more like Jack Nickelson than an anaplastologist. Shultz whittled a new eye from wax just as he had several months before, cast the wax mold into plastic, painted the hazel iris and blood veins, and again placed the eye into the oven. Once he had made the eye and assured himself that it fit comfortably in my eye socket, Shultz told me that since I was so reckless, going surfing with a prosthetic eye, I had to have a socket in which the false eye fit like a hand in a glove. "The socket will mold around the prosthesis with time, but we have to keep it in until the molding is complete."

Shultz connected a half inch stern protruding from the newly-made prosthesis. To the end of the stem he attached a plastic disk a quarter-inch across. He called his creation a champagne glass. He placed the champagne glass into my eye socket, crossed the base with tape attached to my forehead and cheek, and covered the champagne glass with gauze and tape. A wave.

For next two months, I tried cases with gauze covering my right eye socket.

Fifty-Seven

At 6 AM., 11 days after I returned home, I shaded my eye the glaring sun as I rode to Greenfield with Luis López to run the Salinas Valley Marathon. Greenfield lies deep in the broad valley, 40-miles south of Salinas. The race began on a narrow two-lane road running through grapevines a few miles southeast of town. The 300 runners ran west through the green fields followed the foothills nine miles north to the Soledad Mission, went east a few miles then south through the city of Greenfield with its 2,000 farm worker population. I started out near the rear of the pack with a gauze bandage covering my right eye socket, and stayed there. By mile ten, I realized I was not in shape to run a marathon. By mile 17, I was walking through the 100-degree heat. At mile 20, Tom Dalzell, a UFW lawyer I started the run with, pulled up sitting in a car driven by his girlfriend Maria Maldonado. "Want a ride?" he yelled.

I shook my head and waved. The car moved ahead a couple-hundred yards and pulled over. When I reached it, I jumped. "No law says I have to finish a marathon," I panted. "It was a dumb idea. Never again."

Never didn't last long. A week later, I sat among the redwoods when my brother Tom drove up the Aptos dirt drive, "How ya doin"?" he asked, sitting down on the ground. "I feel like shit for having not finished in 'reenfield," I lamented.

Before Tom replied, I added, "I decided I'm going to train and finish a marathon."

"There's one in San Francisco in August," said Tom. "I'll run it with you if you want"

I called John in Hawaii. "John, you attended the Honolulu Marathon 'linic before you ran the marathon there, didn't you?"

"The Uh huh. Why?"

It astonished John to hear I tried to run a marathon. He was not surprised when I confessed that I had not finished. "What should I do to really run one?" I asked.

"Well, they had us train for almost a whole year. Are you running more than 20 miles a week?"

"Yeah," I boasted.

"How long have you been doing it?"

"Three or four weeks."

"When do you want to run your marathon?"

"In Au'ust."

John laughed. "I know you think you can do anything, Mo, but two-months training isn't enough to run a marathon. Maybe if you run 500 miles a week until August, you might finish."

"I'll try anything, once. When it's hard, all I have to do is remember how bad I feel not finishing in 'reenfield."

*　　　*　　　*

A little over two months later, on August 19, I was in San Francisco to run the Mayors Cup Marathon. Since talking with John in June, I ran through Salinas streets, over Aptos hills and on the wet sandy beach of Rio Del Mar. During the training I fell, scraping my knees over 15 times and turned my ankle so bad on one occasion I didn't run for a week. On the night before the race, Tom and I splurged, staying at the Hilton in downtown San Francisco. We loaded with carbohydrates, eating dinner in an Italian restaurant in North Beach.

At 6 AM. the next morning. Tom and I were on Treasure Island Road along the west edge of a coast guard base about two miles east of San Francisco below the Bay Bridge. As the sun peeked over the Oakland Hills, we heard Mayor Diane Feinstein fire the starting gun. We joined the thousand runners climbing the hill to the Bay Bridge. Packed like Cannery Row sardines, we headed

245

slowly toward the skyscrapers several miles ahead. We descended to the Embarcadero and grabbed small Dixie cups of water as we passed Fisherman's Wharf. We jogged through the army barracks in the Presidio, climbed the hill to the Golden Gate bridge, crossed the mouth of the bay with its unforgettable view, returned to the Presidio, ran along the rocky Pacific Coast and entered Golden Gate Park.

I felt pretty good for the first 20 miles. In a eucalyptus grove overlooking the coast just south of the Golden Gate Bridge, I hit the wall I had heard so many experienced runners warn of. The last six miles became more painful with each step. I managed to jog into the Polo Field at Golden Gate Park and finished in three hours and forty-six minutes. A wave.

On the ride back to Aptos. I accepted the cramping in my calves as the cost for my detonating pride. "Okay," I said to Tom. "I did it. Now I've run a marathon. Never again. I'm in retirement."

Fifty-Eight

During the winter 1979-1980 the farm workers' strike continued in the Imperial Valley. Meanwhile, Kathy had completed her radiation and chemotherapy treatment at Stanford and returned to Hawaii.

When I returned to the Imperial Valley in the fall of 1979, Carlos Bowker met me at the bus station, I told him that I had to find an apartment. "My sister lives in some apartments on Imperial Highway just north of town," he responded. "It's near the office and real cheap. We better go over there now," he added. "Bud Antle workers from Salinas and scabs from Arizona and Mexico are arriving. The apartments will probably be full by tomorrow."

I jumped into Carlos' sedan and we headed north. Just before entering the lettuce fields, Carlos pointed to a scattered single level apartment complex in the middle of a dusty dirt field. It looked more like a farm labor camp than an apartment complex, no grass, no trees. "That's it. It doesn't look like much but it's only a hundred-a-month for a studio and you can walk from here to work. They don't have a swimming pool like the Holiday Inn, but it's cheap."

* * *

A little over a month later, I called Kauai to wish Kathy Merry Christmas. Her roommate Carol told me Kathy was back in Fresno. Her cancer reappeared so she went to her mom's home.

Minutes later the phone rang in Fresno. Kathy's brother Bill answered. Bill was 12-years younger country kid than Kathy, a blonde-haired country kid of ten when Kathy and I started going together. Over the years, I had taken him surfing in Santa Cruz, skiing Yosemite's Badger Pass, and taught him how to toss horseshoes in Aptos. Now he was a bearded graduate of the University of California at Santa Barbara.

"Hi, Bill, is Kathy there?"

"Oh. Hi, Mo. Yeah. She's in the bedroom. I'll get her."

Moments later, Bill was back on the line. "She's sleeping. Mo. Want me to wake her?"

"No, let her sleep. Tell her I phoned. I'll try later. How's she doing?"

"Pretty bad."

That night I was on a Greyhound bus to Fresno with transfers in San Diego and Los Angeles. Just after seven Christmas morning, I arrived in Fresno. Carrying my blue Nike bag with an extra shirt, a pair of socks, running shorts, some boxer shorts, and my tooth brush, I slipped into the restroom, donned my running shorts and jogged to Kathy's family home on the other side of town. I arrived just after eight. Kathy's mother, Lottie, responded in her bathrobe to my knock. "Mo, I didn't know you were coming," said the half-awake blonde, wiping her eyes. "Where's your car?"

"I too' the bus."

"Why didn't you call us. We would have picked you up at depot."

"It was early, Lottie. Plus, I like to run. Is 'athy still asleep?

"Come in. I was just going to make some coffee. You can wake her up. She'll be surprised you're here."

As Lottie went into the kitchen, I went to Kathy's room. She was lying on her side in the middle of the same double bed she had slept in while a high school student. She looks thin but she's still beautiful, I thought, leaning over and kissing her cheek. "Mmmm," she murmured as she rolled her head to the side, still asleep.

"Hi, 'ath." I whispered.

Slowly she opened her emerald eyes, smiling. "Mo, what're you doing here? I thought you were in Mexico or somewhere,"

"Close, but I heard a rumor you were home and I wanted to see you."

"I'm glad you came." Kathy took my hand caressing it gently with her finger. "I've been here for a week, but I didn't want to bother you at work. I hoped you'd call Hawaii today and Carol would tell you I was here,"

"How ya doin'?

"Okay, considering they keep saying I'm gonna die soon. But they'll find a cure just in time and the cavalry will come riding across the valley with it just like in the movies."

Kathy will make it, I thought silently. She will recover.

"You'll surprise 'em. You 'an do anything.

"I wish," Kathy said softly, apparently thinking out loud as she spoke. "I'm only 35-years old. I tried to do all the right stuff. It doesn't make sense. I'm not an alcoholic or a druggie. I eat lots of fruit and vegetables and not much red meat.

"It's not fair, Kathy."

"Even if I die now, I've had a better life than most people live to be 80. We're lucky we had such good moms. They didn't spend all their time sayin', 'No. No. No. Don't do that."

"They spent their time making sure we were happy instead of worrying that we weren't perfect," I said.

"You've probably recovered so well from your wreck because your mom taught you things don't have to be perfect."

"Yeah. She always believed life was good as long as things work out okay," or asi, asi." It was okay' if my room wasn't perfectly clean or my hair wasn't combed or I got a 'B' instead of an "A" in English. It was okay if I lost a race or missed a tackle so long as I tried my hardest. She believes life is good if you do 'okay."

"And it's okay if speech isn't perfect or you have a few scars on your face, because you're still alive when you should have died. You weren't ready to die but I think I am."

I did not know what to say. Kathy's gentle tone while saying she was ready to die hit my chest like a bludgeon.

Obviously unaware of the numbing impact of her words, Kathy continued. "I'm glad my mom told me about the danger of getting pregnant when I wasn't ready to have a child and I know your mom told you about getting someone pregnant when you weren't ready to be a father. I always wanted to be a mother but I'm glad we decided to wait until our careers were established before having children."

Kathy continued with energy I feared had abandoned her lithe body. "Remember when my mom let me hitchhike to Mexico with you and we got a ride with Anastacio Alvarez who looked so fat when he picked us up in Mexicali? He kept losing weight as we went through the checkpoints and he pulled out pairs of nylons or cartons of cigarettes to pay off the federales who wanted to examine his car. For sure they could've found all the stuff he was sneaking into the country. We could've all ended up in a Mexican jail if he'd have run out of stockings."

I tried to chuckle, but her acceptance of impending death closed the valve of humor. Kathy continued, "And when we got to Mazatlan and stayed in that little trailer and made love and woke up in the middle of the night when we heard the scary noise and you peeped out the window and it was only a mule eating cactus on the side of the trailer? And we eventually got married and lived in Carmel. I think the best part about Carmel was Point Lobos. I remember going there with your brother John. He was like a science teacher explaining all about the lichen and moss and how each is a step in the development of the earth. He knew so much. And I remember going there with Terry after we lived in Aptos and he was into photography and took all those pictures of us at the coast on a cool day. I think a bunch of them are still in the barn in Aptos. Remember Terry, you and I were going to look at the house and they thought we were three hippies and no one wanted to go with us to let us look at the house and we went by ourselves and bought it?

And what about that guy who owned the junk store down on Soquel where we went looking for a refrigerator and he yelled at you, "Can't you read?" pointing at the sign that said, "No dogs or hippies. And you said, "I'm a lawyer," and he said, "I don't give a shit. The sign says no hippies and that means you. Get the fuck out a here." And David and Susan came to live with us. It was so neat. And we played horseshoes all the time. And we went to the Fourth of July parade with them and sat on the bridge and cheered when nine-year-old Clarice rode by on her horse. And remember when we went to Mexico with Rusev and Terry and Marsha and you and Terry were having a bucking bronco contest riding the wild surf near Manzanillo and you claimed the crabs stole the car keys while you guys were surfing? You can tell me the truth now. You guys just lost them, huh?"

"Kath, I promise, the crabs took 'em."

Kathy smiled. "You were always so honest with those big green eyes and that boyish grin. The crabs probably did take the keys. I always admired your honesty. Ya know, I really liked sharing our lives. When I get my head together we'll have lots more fun. If only you had shown the persistence with me that you had in your cases and surfing. If you'd tried as hard to keep me as you did to win the short hoe case or to get beyond the breakers to ride the waves, there's no way I could've walked away from you. But you weren't. You let me go, and I had to follow my own path. I'll always love you, Mo Jourdane. I'll always love you."

Kathy reached for the table next to her bed, delicately picked up the cup, and sipped the lukewarm tea. "Remember the time when you and John and I sat like baboons in the rain on the rock in the hills above Honolulu. The wind was blowing so hard through the valley below that the rain was rising instead of falling. And then we went to the supermarket to buy stuff to make enchiladas and it didn't even have anything we needed but all the bright yellow and red advertisements kept jumping out at us and we couldn't stop laughing. Plus remember when we went surfing at Sunset after we left the supermarket and rode fifteen waves? I've experienced too many high points to ever complain that I'm dying too young."

I sat half listening, hearing some things I knew were true, and some things, in the words of Terry McDonell that he attributes to Ken Kesey, were "true even if they didn't happen," because they had made Kathy face death without bitterness or fear,

I sat silently, beginning to understand what it's all about. Death is unavoidable. "If I try to do anything," Kathy said weakly, "I have to rest. I feel best when I'm in bed, reading or just sleeping. All the time I have pain. They give me codeine but it still hurts and if I have too much. I get spaced and don't remember stuff. But I'd rather be spaced than go through the pain."

"Is the pain what brought you ba' from Hawaii?" I asked.

"Not really. I came home because the doctor told me the cancer's metastatic. It's spread to my spine and I could fall going to the bathroom or kitchen and become a paraplegic. It scares me. If that happens, I want it to happen here."

I stared at Kathy, not knowing what to say. I thought, Ever since my wreck everyone's been telling me they feel sorry for me and all that because I lost an eye and scarred my face, but watching you suffer, unable to do anything to help, hurts more than anything that happened to me. "It's not fair," I finally said weakly.

"Hey, man. No one ever said life is fair. I could have let them cut off my breast and maybe I would have beaten cancer, but would spend my life as a one-breasted woman. Would that be more fair? I have no regret for doing it the way I did. I've had a good life. I'm ready to die," Kathy murmured as she fell asleep.

Has she given up? I wondered. You can't recover if you give up, Kath. But I think she has decided there is a time to give up and she is ready to die without regret.

I went to the family room and watched Supermarket Sweepstakes with Lottie. Neither of us felt much like talking.

Fifty-Nine

I returned to the Imperial Valley. While my thoughts were flooded with anxiety over Kathy confronting death, the crisis in the Imperial Valley left me with little time to brood. The strike was in its second year. The union placed a full-page ad in the Valley newspaper, *La Voz*, setting forth its economic proposal. The growers responded with ads in the valley papers saying they were bound by President Carter's anti-inflation limit. Growers claimed that the farm workers' union was demanding they violate the law by paying too much. Farm workers were the lowest paid workers in the United States. They were asking for five dollars an hour. When the striking workers were forced to return to work to put food on their table, their employers refused to rehire them. Over and over, when I tried to help workers recover their jobs, I heard, "the strikers have been permanently replaced," or, "a labor contractor hires all our employees now. Talk to him."

The giant carrot grower Maggio, Inc. sued the United Farm Workers for disrupting its business. "Can a company sue a union because union members exercise their right to strike?" Carlos asked one evening after hearing the story on the radio news. "It sounds crazy to us laymen who were taught in school that the law is blind; it doesn't favor one group over another."

"I guess you can sue for anything. It might be thrown out of court, but who knows."

"It's wrong," maintained Carlos. "We told the workers they had the right to strike, and they exercised that right and now they have no jobs and their union is being sued because it waged an effective strike that cost the company money. Everyone loses in a strike."

*   *   *

Throughout its life, the United Farm Workers has faced severe adversity. For decades, César Chávez, Dolores Huerta, Gilbert Padilla, Marshall Ganz, Jessica Govea, Richard Chávez, Carlos and Linda Legrette, Eliseo Medina, Jerry Cohen, and tens of thousands of members and volunteers with the United Farm Workers fought the toughest foe around, the agribusiness industry. They survived the killing of union organizers and the growers and Teamsters' joint effort to run them out of the fields. They survived years of strikes and jailing, heckling and arrest when they engaged in a nonviolent boycott, and they survived the California Legislature's closure of the Agricultural Labor Relations Board. But would the United Farm Workers have to survive the most vicious enemy of all, loss of confidence?

Sixty

In January 1980, I flew from the Imperial Valley to San Jose and again took the train to the hospital. This time I was not there to see Dr. Kaplan. Kathy had been flown to Stanford Hospital from Fresno. She was near death. Escalante and I sat beside her bed until almost midnight. She drifted into a coma. On February 11, holding her hand at 11:20 AM., I felt her pulse stop. Escalante tried. No pulse. I felt Kathy's breast. There was no heartbeat. I called the nurse. The doctor came in and confirmed Kathy had peacefully ended her fight with breast cancer.

Lottie, Kathy's mother, was staying in the Riviera Motel a mile away. I had to tell her. I ran. When I walked into the room panting deeply, she stared at me. She knew. I held her as she cried. Finally, she said she had to return home. No, she didn't want to go to the hospital. No, she didn't want to see Kathy's body. I walked to the hospital. I cried. I cried from the moment I walked out of the motel parking lot until I entered the hospital, a mile away. It was the second time I cried during the past couple years. This time it was not tears of joy.

I took the train to San Jose and the bus over the hill to Santa Cruz. I called John Rusev from the bus station and told him it was over. John came down and we got drunk in the bar adjoining the Greyhound depot. Sadly, I told Rusev that Kathy's cancer had been discovered too late. As the empty beer bottles filled the table, I rambled that you can't beat the devil if you don't know he is haunting. Until Kathy discovered the lump in her breast was malignant, she had no idea that the devil was approaching. All the confidence and all the best doctors and all the will to live could not beat the invisible devil.

Kathy wanted her ashes thrown from the Sleeping Giant near Kapaa, Kauai, a mile from where she and Carol had lived. One cold winter morning. I walked down the hill from the Aptos stronghold, caught the local bus to Santa Cruz, the Greyhound to San Jose, and ran to the crematorium. Carrying the ashes that were Kathy Flynn I took the train north to Burlingame, walked from the depot to the San Francisco airport and arrived in Hawaii the next morning. I flew Aloha Airlines to Kauai where I met Kathy's business partner and close friend Carol and Escalante. Together, we rode to Kapaa and hiked up the desolate Sleeping Giant. We tossed what was left of Flynn into the wind from the highest peak of the spiritual Hawaiian monument deep in the overgrown jungle. After several days on hold, Kathy would continue the cycle of life.

Maybe I had finally accepted the most basic prognosis for life. We are all going to die. But if Kathy had something incredibly strong to live for, like I had the farm workers' struggle, she probably could have delayed the inevitable, not because she was afraid to die or thought it was not fair, but because she would have had to finish the task she was here to accomplish. For me, that task was improving the life of farm workers.

After Kathy died, I had returned to the Salinas Valley questioning life. Why are we here? Why can it be so unfair? When my mind was unable to come up with answers, I pondered the law I had believed in so strongly and what I had witnessed the previous winter in the Imperial Valley. California's new Farm Labor Law was not working. Violence was returning to the fields. So too were the vermin of the sixties, farm labor contractors.

The State of California expressed the purpose of the Agricultural Labor Relations Act; to encourage farm workers to join and support unions. Yet, through ever-mounting paperwork and seemingly endless delays, the growing bureaucracy that administered the Agricultural Labor Relations Act was defeating the farm workers. I feared the courts, having learned in law school that during the 1920s courts had destroyed unions under the guise of preserving private property.

One March morning, I stood near the front desk of the Salinas Farm Labor Board office when farm workers began jamming their way through the door. "Senior Jourdane," yelled one. I recognized the voice and walked to the counter. "Como 'sta, Mi'uel? Hace mucho tiempo. (How are you, Miguel? It's been a long time)."

"Pues, estamos aqui, pero tenemos problema serio. Podemos hablarte? (Well, we're here, but we have a big problem. Can we talk with you?)"

I joined 40 farm workers in the vacant hearing room behind the office. I heard my old friend Miguel Delgado tell me in Spanish, so everyone crowded in the tiny room could understand, "You know I have worked for Murphy Tomato since you worked at CRLA. Waving his arm around the room filled with farm workers, Miguel continued, "some of these men have worked there far longer than me. Now the company is firing all of us."

"Why?"

"Two years ago we had an election and voted for the United Farm Workers Union. The company appealed and your Board finally held the election valid and ordered the company to bargain with César. Instead of bargaining, the company began using tomato harvesting machines I hear it got from the University of California at Davis."

"Can they pick tomatoes by machine?"

"Barely. The company picks them when they're still green so they won't get squashed as they bounce through the machine. The tomatoes taste like cardboard. With the machine, the company no longer needs tomato pickers. What can we do?"

I helped the workers fill out an unfair labor practice charge claiming that machines were brought in to retaliate for the union activity and that the company had not met its legal duty to bargain with the union certified to represent its workers before bringing in the machines. Two weeks later, the Farm Labor

Board office in Sacramento dismissed the charge. When I heard this, I stormed into the director's office, throwing the dismissal letter down on his desk. "What's this?"

Lupe Martínez glanced up from a brief he was reading and shook his head. "I think the workers got screwed, too," he said, "but Sacramento decided there's nothing the Farm Labor Board can do about mechanization. That's a company decision."

I looked at the director sadly. "I can't do it. I can't be part of it anymore. I'll send ya my resi'nation." I walked out and took the bus to Aptos. As the Greyhound passed through the celery and lettuce fields, I stared out as the landscape that had changed like my life. Maybe everything buds, blossoms, becomes ripe and dies, I thought, reflecting on my exciting years as a surfer and farm worker's lawyer. Over the past few years I was nearly killed in a collision with a phantom oil rig, lost an eye and vision in the eye I still had, lost my ability to speak clearly, lost the ability to surf, lost the ability to drive, and now, lost faith in the law enacted to provide minimal justice to farm workers. By the time I reached Aptos, I felt confused. I had to get away and think. Should I get out of the fields for a while, maybe forever?

*   *   *

After nearly a decade of success, the proverbial light at the end of the United Farm Workers tunnel seems to have begun to flicker about the same time as my wreck. While I was in a coma, the nearly 3,000 grape harvesters at Giumara Vineyards in Kern County had an Agricultural Labor Relations Board election. Did they want to be represented by César Chávez and the United Farm Workers or did they want to work with no union? The union lost the election by 227 votes with 172 uncounted votes that were challenged because a party to the election did not feel the voter eligible to vote. The union filed 46 unfair labor practice charges. After a hearing, the Agricultural Labor Relations Board set aside the election finding the company "discriminatorily discharged one employee, discriminatorily failed or refused to hire or rehire twenty-one employee-applicants, delayed or interfered with the work of two employees, interfered with statutorily-protected employee rights by engaging in threats and surveillance, and, by all of the foregoing acts and conduct, created an atmosphere in which its employees could not exercise free choice in the election."

But the union's momentum had been broken. After the loss at Giumara. United Farm Worker victories in the fields were rare. When a number of union contracts terminated on December 31, 1978, the companies as a group began negotiating the terms of renewed contracts with the union. While most of the lettuce companies negotiated as a group, Bruce Church Inc. decided to negotiate alone with the union. For two years the United Farm Workers and Bruce Church negotiated. The union was asking the lettuce companies to pay the hourly workers $5.12 an hour, an amount the growers felt was outrageous. In February 1979, the Bruce Church workers struck in an effort to nonviolently put pressure on the company.

During the summer of 1979, protesting the growers' refusal to enter contracts with the UFW, ten thousand farm workers and other supporters marched to Salinas's Hartnell College from San Francisco 100 miles to the north, San Ardo 70 miles to the south, San Juan Bautista, and Watsonville. Joining Chávez were Governor Jerry Brown and actress Jane Fonda. At the rally, Chávez announced the signing of a contract with Salinas Valley's Meyer Tomato Company. Union attorney Jerry Cohen, one of the best labor lawyers in the country, noted that the contract "makes a lie of the industry claiming they could not afford our demands." On December 27, 1983, the Agricultural Labor Relations Board held that Bruce Church, Inc. had not been negotiating in good faith.

Meanwhile the strike was having minimal effect on the agribusiness entities. Because of the extreme poverty in Mexico and Central America, caused in large part by the United States world economic dominance, hundreds of thousands of men and women cross the border seeking jobs. Agribusiness corporations in the United States are able to pit these impoverished immigrants against the low-paid workers who are members of the United Farm Workers. When UFW members go on strike seeking tolerable working conditions, their chance of success is reduced because they are easily replaced with the hungry Mexican and Central American immigrants. Facing this dilemma and committed to nonviolence. César Chávez sought to urge Bruce Church, Inc. to enter a contract with its workers through a boycott of Red Coach Lettuce.

Twenty years earlier, the grape boycott had broken the will of Delano growers and led to a number of contracts. To ask shoppers not to buy Red Coach Lettuce is a primary boycott. A boycott is more effective when the union asks the shopper not to buy at a store that sells the boycotted product. This is called a secondary boycott. It is effective because grocery chains lose income when they are boycotted because they sell a particular brand of lettuce. This causes the chains to put incredible pressure on the grower to do what is necessary to resolve the labor dispute. Because they believe the secondary boycott is too effective and upsets the balance between labor and management, some states have outlawed secondary boycotts. To end the dispute with Bruce Church, Inc., through non-violence Chávez asked shoppers to stay away from markets that sold Red Coach Lettuce.

The secondary boycott is illegal in Arizona. The union was careful to limit use of the boycott in states where it did not violate the law, but apparently someone overlooked eager volunteer activity in Arizona. Bruce Church, Inc., filed suit against the union in Arizona claiming it had engaged in an unlawful secondary boycott. After a thirty-one-day trial, a jury held against the union and ordered it to pay Bruce Church, Inc., a little over $5,400,000. The union appealed and the Arizona Supreme court reversed the award finding the trial court erred in allowing the jury to find the union must pay damages for acts engaged in outside Arizona. Arizona did not have jurisdiction beyond its borders. The court sent the case back to the trial court to see if the union had caused any damage through acts performed in Arizona.

While the case was being retried, César Chávez underwent two days of grueling cross-examination by Bruce Church attorneys. During the night of April 22, 1993, after the second day of examination, the nonviolent struggle to improve the treatment of farm workers died. An attorney representing the union who later became San Diego City Attorney, Michael Aguirre, said "César Chávez was facing an unfair set of pressures on him... that's what killed him."

Six days after César's death, 50,000 farm workers and supporters accompanied his body as it was carried from a central Delano park to Forty Acres, the union headquarters several miles west of town. Bishop Roger Mahoney, performing mass said final rites over César's casket. With a short- handled hoe resting atop the wooden box Richard Chávez. had made to bury his brother, César was lowered into the ground.

In 1995, the newly elected replacement as President of the United Farm Workers, Arturo Rodriguez, in the style of his predecessor, led a march of farmworkers from Delano to Sacramento. In May 1996, under new leadership, Bruce Church, Inc, ended a 17 year struggle and entered into a contract with the United Farm Workers. Arturo Rodriguez, the new union president, hoped to build a "partnership of cooperation."

However, few other companies where the United Farm Workers is certified to represent the workers have entered a contract. In the summer of 2002, believing the companies were refusing to bargain in good faith. Dolores Huerta at the side of Arturo Rodriguez again marched with farm workers across the San Joaquin Valley to Sacramento to urge Governor Davis to sign a law that could end the stalemate.

In an editorial, the Salinas Californian urged Governor Davis to sign the bill, saying, "It's the right thing to do." The Salinas daily went on to explain that growers who bargain in good faith have nothing to fear. If Governor Davis signs the new law they will "continue to resolve problems in the way they've done it for nearly 30 years under the auspices of the State's landmark Agricultural Labor Relations law." Governor Davis did sign the law. Now, if a company refuses to bargain in good faith with the union chosen by its workers in a free and fair election, a neutral party or arbitrator appointed by the state will step in and settle the conflict.

The growers have vowed to challenge the law in the courts. The farm workers and their union, the United Farm Workers. continues to struggle. Through persistent, hard work, and hope, the workers and the union will overcome.

Sixty-One

During the spring of 1980, confused over the destiny of my effort to improve the lives of farm workers, I fled to Hawaii. Running along the coast over Diamond Head on my first morning in Waikiki, I flashed back on my high school dream to be an Olympic swimmer. I had memorized Spanish while I swam to escape the pain that comes with swimming hundreds of laps a day. Lap after lap I chanted trabajo, trabajas, trabaja, and quiero, quieres, quiere, and vivo, vives, vive. I didn't make the Olympics but I improved my Spanish.

In college, I surfed whenever possible to take my mind off the academic pressure. I didn't become valedictorian, but I improved my surfing.

Now, for the first time, I thought, I don't know what to do with my life. It's so messed up. I can't see. I can't talk. The farm labor law isn't working. Kathy's dead. I ran, focusing on how far away stood the next telephone pole rather than on my problems of my life. I thanked God I could run. Running will get me through it, I thought. In a couple weeks, I'm gonna run the Maui marathon in three hours and twenty minutes, for Kathy.

On most mornings. I ran from the two-story, run-down hotel on Lewers Street to Kapiolani Park. I ran around the park. I was a mile from the hotel to the park and two miles around the park. I ran around it four more times and returned to the hotel. During the afternoons, I often carried to Kuhio Beach the surfboard loaned to me by my California surfing buddy Larry Loganbill. For several hours I sat in the water and paddled for waves I could barely see.

The next week, my sister Barbara came to make sure I was okay. Within days, my brothers Tom and John joined us. Tom had graduated from San Jose State and was managing the B. Dalton bookstore in Salinas. John had returned from the Mediterranean where he had been racing on Ondine, a 79-foot Fast Coast sloop. My brothers had come to run the Maui Marathon with me.

At 5AM. on March 19, before the sun crept over the ocean to our east, John's wife, Muffett, dropped us off at the Wailuku High School gymnasium for the six o'clock start of the Maui Marathon. Six hundred runners lined up in the dark. Except for the handful of elite runners who were there to win, the pack moved slowly when the gun went off. It remained dark for the first half-hour of the run. Up the hill through Wailuku. I ran between my brothers. As we reached the crest, the wooden missionary school became visible on the horizon. A couple hours later, in the hilly sugarcane field above the Lahaina mill at mile twenty-two, I slowed. Running became hard, each step painful. The cane road finally flattened out as I approached Kaanapali. With the fish line just 70-yards ahead, a man in his sixties tried to pass me. We raced. I lost.

A chunky Polynesian nurse grabbed me when I staggered across the finish line. Over my protest, she firmly escorted me to the emergency tent. My normal 104 over 68 blood pressure was 120 over 89. My normal 55 pulse was over 120 beats a minute. My temperature was surprisingly low. The volunteer doctor ordered me to lie down.

Half-hour later, Muffett found me in the tent, wrapped her arms around my still sweaty shoulders and hugged me.

"Know how fast you ran?"

"No."

"What was your aim?""

"I wanted to run three hours and twenty minutes, for Kathy."

"You ran 3:19:34. Congratulations."

Sixty-Two

The next Tuesday I flew to Stanford Hospital for surgery number six, another bone graft. Dr. Kaplan was in the reconstructive surgery office when I limped in. "Well, you're walking." He smiled. "I guess you survived the marathon."

"Yeah. Barely,"

"How was it? As hard as they say?"

"Yeah, but it was fun in a weird kinda' way."

"Are ya glad you did it?'"

"Yeah. But I'm mostly 'lad it's over. I'm ready to lie around a hospital for a while and recover while you 'uys take care of me."

"I think you planned the timing of this surgery for exactly that reason." Kaplan smiled. "Let your insurance company pay while you recover from a marathon. Is that what you learn in law school?"

"I think you planned this surgery, not me." I smiled defensively, needing sleep badly. "What are you 'onna do to me anyway?"

"Take part of another of your ribs and build up the side of your face around your temple. When we replaced your cheekbone with a rib in the last bone transplant we weren't sure how much your face would reject the foreign element."

"So tell me about the marathon. Was it the Honolulu Marathon that med student from here at Stanford, Duncan McDonald, wins every year?"

Doctor Kaplan operated the next morning. I stayed at the hospital until the following Sunday. Tom drove me to Aptos where I spent a few days alone thinking about my years representing farm workers and life in the Aptos stronghold with Kathy, Terry, Tom, Susan and David; I felt good in Aptos. This old house has seen a lot, I thought one morning. I can still feel the cheerful spirit in every room.

On Tuesday I flew to Los Angeles to visit my mother. By Thursday, eight days after my bone transplant, I was running on the asphalt bike path through the smog alongside the concrete Los Angeles River as it crossed Long Beach.

That evening, my high school friend Jerry Pérez and I were playing pool. I told Jerry about the problems with the Farm Labor Board. "I 'uess it's time to do something with my life." I mused, waiting for a response.

"Haven't you been doing something, being an attorney, I mean?"

"Yeah. Kinda". But I don't really want to go back and live in Aptos or Salinas. I have too many years representing farm workers and being with Kathy in both those places."

"Where do ya want to go?"

"I'm not sure. I thought about moving to Hawaii, taking their bar exam and working for Hawaiians on land problems. A friend offered me a job helping native Hawaiians with a suit involving their access to the coast being blocked by developments. Plus, some pi' farmers are being evicted near Hawaii Kai so developers can build more condominiums for Haoles from the mainland. They want me to represent "em. The pi' farmers, I mean."

"Pig farmers?"

"Uh huh."

"I guess you can abandon California's farm workers and move to Hawaii, but you know as well as I about Island Fever, about how small Oahu gets when you're there for a long time."

"I think I need a real change. Maybe I'll 'o to Sacramento and try to find a job."

Sixty-Three

A week later, I walked across the bridge spanning the Sacramento River to a West Sacramento motel, checked in, and ran along the river. Heat reverberated from the 90-degree asphalt. I like it here, I thought. Maybe I'll stay a while.

"So I'm ready to move out of the fields and take a real job in the city," I told Marty Glick the next morning sitting in his office a couple blocks down Capitol Mall from the capitol building.

Marty was a longtime ally working with California Rural Legal Assistance. Together we had done the Diana case and banned the short-handled hoe. About the time I left CRIA, Marty joined the faculty at Stanford Law School and within a few years Governor Brown appointed him as Director of the States Employment Department with its thousands of employees seeking to help unemployed Californians find jobs and receive unemployment benefits.

"I never know if you're serious, Mo," responded Marty. "If you're ready to walk away from the farm workers, I need you right now."

I felt satisfaction that Marty Glick apparently had enough respect for the legal talent I had shown over the years to not let my severe injuries bar me from continuing as an attorney, Though he never directly expressed it, the faith in me he demonstrated helped me look beyond my disfigured face and inability to speak or see as clearly as I once did. The faith shown by friends outweighs all the words a psychiatrist or psychologist could have expended. My friends at the Agricultural Labor Relations Board pushed me to return to work and my friends like Marty Glick gave me the chance to prove I could still be a lawyer. A wave.

*   *   *

During the following weeks, when I wasn't sitting at a typewriter drafting proposed regulations for the Department of

Employment I ran in preparation for the Magical Musical Marathon. Less than a month after arriving in Sacramento. with a patch over my eye I ran with Luis López the 26.2-mile race on the bike path along the American River. Two miles from the finish line, the bike path crosses a small road. In the middle of the path on each side of the road, there are cement posts to prevent vehicles from entering the bike path. Looking ahead toward the finish line instead of looking down for obstacles in my path, I hit the cement post. I flew through the air for about ten feet and landed on my knees and hands. I slowly got to my feet realizing I'd injured my right ankle. I began to walk and then slowly jogged the remaining two miles.

Sixty-Four

Throughout the summer, I continued to run 70 miles a week. I ran the ten-mile Buffalo Stampede in just under 63 minutes. I planned on using the ten miler as a training run for the upcoming Sacramento marathon. During the Buffalo Stampede, my prosthetic eye popped out. I didn't realize I had lost my eye until I was having a Coke after the race with Byron and Maria Leslie. As it grew dark that evening, Byron and I were slowly walking the race route with our eyes to the ground. We found three pennies, a used condom, and 42 paper running visors but never found my artificial eye.

The following day, I was on the Greyhound to San Francisco and the train to Palo Alto. After examining my face, Dr. Kaplan told me my socket still wasn't holding in a prosthetic eye. "We'll have to reshape your eyelid," he said. "Hopefully, that'll correct the problem."

The next day, an orderly wheeled me into the operating room for surgery number seven. Again I wore a gauze patch over my right eye socket for the next month, missing the Sacramento marathon. In October, I took the bus to San Francisco and the train to Stanford for Dr. Kaplan to check on the surgery. Outside the Palo Alto Amtrak station, under a bush I hid a Nike bag with my running shoes and walked to the hospital. I was on my way to run the Fresno Marathon. When I returned a couple hours later, the bag was gone. I walked to downtown Palo Alto to buy new running shoes. The next day I had not run more than five miles of the 26.2 before the new-shoe blisters erupted. I finished in 3:11 but couldn't wear shoes on the Greyhound bus ride back to Sacramento. I was recovering from the wreck but had not yet learned that none of us can pass blindly through life without paying the price.

On Christmas Eve, 1980, while I was jogging with Byron Georgiou on the Sacramento River, he told me that the Governor wanted me to handle a lawsuit for him. "He's going to call you at home tonight," Byron said.

The summer before my wreck, I had gone to Sacramento to talk with Governor Brown and his administrative assistant Gray Davis about going to work in the Governor's office. I told them the Delano fields were in the middle of the grape season and I couldn't leave then, but perhaps we would talk when the season ended. I collided with an oil rig, and during the time I was in a coma in the hospital recovering, the Governor hired Byron. When the Governor's Secretary of Legal Affairs left the Governor's office in 1979, the Governor appointed Byron as his replacement. The Governor wanted me to join his office as Byron's deputy. A wave.

"It'll be fun to be a trial lawyer again." I responded to Byron while we ran along the Sacramento River. "If you talk with him, tell Brown I'm leaving tonight to spend Christmas with my family. If he wants to talk with me before I leave, he should before eleven."

At 11 PM., I left Sacramento on the PSA flight to Los Angeles, my Nike bag filled with presents. The governor had not called. At 12:50 AM., my mother pulled into her Long Beach driveway after picking me up at the 1.A terminal. When we walked through the door, the phone rang. "It's for you, Mo." she said, handing me the receiver. "It's a woman. How do your friends always know the minute you get in town?" Mom handed me the receiver but stood close by pretending to look at junk mail lying on the table, curiously listening to one side of my conversation.

"Hello, Governor."

"Yeah, I spoke with Georgiou this afternoon."

"Yeah, I have thought about it."

"Thank you. I'd be an honor. I'll see you Monday morning."

"That was a female voice, not the Governor," said mom when I set the receiver down.

"It was the governor's secretary. She just made the call. I agreed to represent Jerry in a legal hassle he's in."

The pride emanating from my mother's light-blue eyes showed me that she finally realized I was recovering from the devastating effects of my wreck that doctors expected to be insurmountable.

Two days later the Governor handed me the complaint filed in a lawsuit against him. A group of Southern California taxpayers claimed the Governor's purchase of computers and monitors to use in the Governor's Office was a misuse of State funds. "Draft whatever we need to file," he requested. "Show me what you have when you're done. I'd also like to hear any suggestions you might have on filling the vacancy on the Agricultural Labor Relations Board." Before I responded, the governor turned to more pressing business.

Sixty-Five

One hot Friday afternoon late the next summer, I sat outside eating a sandwich downstairs in my apartment complex. I turned when I heard a familiar voice behind me. It was Virginia Gonzalez.

Virginia had been a secretary in our office in Sacramento when the Agricultural Labor Relations Board opened five-years earlier. Outside the sandwich shop that afternoon, she introduced Olivia Flores, a law student living for the summer with Virginia and her young daughter.

"Mo, why don't you tell Olivia about what you're doing," Virginia said as she turned and walked to a nearby table where friends had just sat down. "I'll be right back."

I chuckled. "Same old Virginia."

"Is that how she always is?" Olivia asked.

"I take it you're not from here? Sacramento, I mean," I said, infatuated by the dark Latina's smile.

"No. Los Angeles, but I go to law school at Hastings in San Francisco."

"Yeah, that's how Virginia's always been. You like law school?"

"It's okay."

"What year you in?

"My last. This is it. I'm working as an extern for Justice Reynoso in the Court of Appeals this fall. When I return to school I'll graduate."

"Reynoso's good. You're lucky to work with him."

"I know. I've known Justice Reynoso for pretty long. He's my mentor. I almost dropped out my first year of law school, but he encouraged me to hang in there and now, well next year, I'm going to graduate, thanks to him."

Sixty-Six

That fall, wearing my old pair of Brook's Chariots I prepared for the Pepsi Twenty. Several days before the Pepsi race I saw Olivia near the capitol building while I returned from a lunch run along the American River. Before we parted she asked if I was going to Virginia Gonzalez's wedding the following Saturday. The wedding was scheduled in Elk Grove, 20 miles south of Sacramento. When I told Olivia that I planned to, she asked if I wanted a ride. "I was gonna take the bus," I responded shyly. "I'm going to run a race not too far from Elk Grove Saturday morning."

"I'll pick you up for both. That way I'll have someone to hang with at the reception."

The following Saturday morning, Olivia was at my apartment at 6 AM. in her dark green Volkswagen bug. As we rode through orchards south of Sacramento, I apologized, "I didn't realize it was this far. I really appreciate you taking me."

"It's okay. Did you stop driving after your wreck?"

"Pretty much. I can drive, but my license is expired and I'm afraid to take the driving test to 'et it renewed."

"You don't have to take a driving test to renew a driver's license."

"If you lose an eye. you do. It would be really hard to drive now anyway with the sun so low like that."

"It's hard for everyone to drive when the sun's low like that," said Olivia, squinting. "Just be sure to take the driving test on a cloudy day."

After winding through the cornfields and pear groves south of Sacramento, the race finished in an elementary school parking lot. Fifty yards from the finish line, running into the still low sun, I hit a speed bump I didn't see, stumbled to my feet, and with blood running from both my knees, limped across the finish line.

At 3:30 in the afternoon, I stood wearing long pants covering my bandaged knees in front of my apartment complex. I was talking with the security guard when Olivia pulled up. "Hi," she said as she pushed open the passenger door. "Climb in. I didn't think about it this morning when you were wearing your running shorts, but I'm sorry my car's not cleaner now that you're all dressed."

"It's okay. I'm not into keeping cars real sanitary either. As long as a car runs and you can move the junk out of the way. it's fine."

While driving to Elk Grove, I asked Olivia what part of Los Angeles she was from.

"Echo Park," she answered. "Close to downtown."

"That's a pretty tough area, isn't it?"

"We were poor. My mom is from Panama, My dad from El Salvador. They came to the United States just before I was born, but my dad died when I was two. My mom got a job in a sweatshop sewing all night long."

"But you went to college, right?"

"To USC."

"Isn't SC expensive?"

"I was on scholarship."

"But I know there are costs a s'olarship doesn't pay."

"By the time I was in college my mom had started selling clothing at the swap meet with money she saved from her sweatshop job and my dad's social security."

"The swap meet in Echo Park?"

"You don't know much about Echo Park, do you? All we have are liquor stores and churches. There's no swap meet in Echo Park. My mom sells in Calexico, Chula Vista, Paramount, Bakersfield, all over."

"Do you have brothers and sisters?"

"Two younger brothers, Julio and Mark."

"Sounds like it worked pretty well for your family. I mean your mom was a woman alone raising children. Pretty hard, especially if you live in Central LA and are an immi'rant"

"I guess."

"For sure. She was able to raise you and your brothers and get you through college,"

"My mom's a workaholic."

"She works more than she has to?"

"Tu sabes. We don't even see her on Christmas or Thanksgiving because there's money to be made. She thinks money's more important than being home with us."

"You might believe that, but I'm sure you're real important to her. She could've stayed home waiting for her welfare check and not worked and you'd probably be a mother in East LA."

"I am proud of her. To our family in Panama she is the goose that laid the golden egg."

"If all moms were like yours, our schools would be fuller, our prisons wouldn't be overcrowded with ne'lected kids who've become adults, and America wouldn't be screaming about the welfare cheats."

"My mom would like to meet you."

"I'd like to meet her. I have a lot of respect for women like her."

Olivia frowned. "If I'm ever a mom, I'm staying home with my kids. Kids need their mom home."

"You better marry a rich dude."

Olivia looked at me and winked.

Seven hours later we were both tipsy. While walking off the dance floor after dancing the Mexican polka to a Norteno ballad, Olivia kidded, shaking her long black hair to cool herself, "How'd a gabacho like you ever learn to dance to that music?"

"I guess I've spent some time around Mexicanos; growing up in LA and then hanging with farm workers for about ten years. A little of your culture rubbed off on me, no matter my color."

"You're lucky."

*   *   *

That winter I planned on running the American River 50- mile uphill race from Sacramento into a Sierra foothill village Auburn in April. Training for the 50 miler, I ran as many marathons as possible. At four AM., on the first Saturday in January, I walked half-blind in the dark several blocks between my apartment and the downtown Sacramento Greyhound depot. I caught the 5:00 AM. bus to nearby Davis and found the start of the race. In the 40-degree chill, I ran an even-paced fun run along the creek through the University of California Davis campus and the surrounding alfalfa and rice fields.

After the race, I took the Greyhound bus to the Bay Area to visit Olivia. She picked me up at the Oakland Greyhound depot, took me to her Berkeley cottage and made eggplant parmesan with a Greek dinner better than I had eaten in Athens, Mykonos, or Rhodes.

Over the Presidents' Holiday, Olivia and I went skiing at Lake Tahoe with my long-time friend Frank Pulido. It was my first attempt to ski since the wreck. I couldn't tell by sight whether the slope went up, down or neither. Most of the time I saw only white glare. Fortunately, the shadows helped when I most needed the help, in moguls. I spent the day taking the chair up the hill with Olivia, and slowly turning and stopping as we made our way down the mountain. She had rarely skied. I had once worked at Mammoth Mountain and raced down the slope. Now, because of my vision, Olivia and I skied about the same. Riding up the icy Sky Express lift that rises into gusty wind at 10,040 feet for the second time that day, I thought, well, I had to find out. Skiing will never be a fast-daring sport for you again. I guess it's like surfing. It'll be fun but scary in a different way.

On the ride back to Sacramento. I told Olivia and Frank about how I no longer did things I loved, surfing, and skiing, driving, playing ball, "Last week," I continued, "my brother called and asked me to crew a yacht back from Mexico with him next fall. As much as I wanted to do it, I had to turn him down."

"Why?" asked Olivia in a scolding tone. "You talk about how you've always taken chances, but now you're afraid. You only live once, Mo. I think you should call your brother and go for it. If you're going to recover, you have to try things even when they are hard because of your injuries."

Sixty-Seven

The following November, John raced to La Paz on Crazy Horse and was delivering the ultra light racing sloop back to California when Frank Pulido and I flew to La Paz near the southerly tip of Baja California to meet him. We were his crew.

Leaving La Paz, we rounded the southern tip of Baja California the following afternoon and headed north 600 miles to Long Beach. On the fourth day out, Crazy Horse was sailing into a 30-knot gale.

That evening at dusk, I was at the wheel, thrilled by the wind but concerned by the growing swells crashing off the rocky point ahead. By dark the point was less than a mile away. The boat was rising and falling over 15-foot swells. I can't see anything when it's dark, I thought. "Why am I doing this?" I asked myself. "What if I'm steering the boat too close to those rocks? If one of those waves hits us, adios million-dollar boat and we're dead"

John came on deck. With binoculars he looked toward the threatening cliff looming ahead. "What are we at?" he barked.

I glanced down at the illuminated compass. "280 degrees."

Pointing ahead of the bow of our boat vaulting like an empty styrofoam cup in a flood-swollen gully, John told me the point was named Abre Ojos or Open Your Eyes. "It's like Waimea Bay in Hawaii," he said.

"Swells travel all the way from Alaska and hit it?" I asked.

"Yeah, I've seen 25-foot waves here. It's famous as a burial ground for old fishing boats. Go to 270,"

Quickly, I moved the wheel to the left, thinking, aw, fuck. 'Open Your Eyes, right. A 25-foot wave over our port side will be the ball game, and I'm still too proud to admit to my younger brother that I can barely see. I silently prayed we would make it beyond the point.

Starting to descend the stairs, John apparently saw the fear on my face. "I'll stay up for a while," he said calmly, not saying it was for the crew's survival.

Feeling my way to the built-in bench in the cockpit astern of the steering wheel, I strained to hold back a sigh of relief.

The next afternoon, Thanksgiving Day. Crazy Horse entered Bahia de Tortuga. We needed fuel and food. We dropped the sail and started the diesel engine.

An hour later, we were back on board. Pulido opened the newspaper-wrapped groceries we had been able to find in the only store in the tiny one-dirt-road fishing pueblo. He frowned at the two cans of tomato sauce, spaghetti noodles, and a loaf of bread, "I guess we were dreaming to think we could get turkey," he said.

"It's not exactly the Thanksgiving dinner my grandma used to make on her Vista farm with turkey, dressing, sweet potatoes, cranberries anal fresh buttermilk biscuits," I said as I lit the small stove's single burner to boil water for the noodles.

At ten that evening we departed north toward Cedros Island and San Quentin. By the time I took the wheel at 4 AM. off Scammon's Lagoon, the wind had died. There were no noticeable swells. While John and Frank slept, I listened to the dolphin dive and splash and play, chattering in a language I did not understand.

A couple hours after my shift at the wheel began, I was at the helm watching the gauges. Depth 68 feet. Wind six knots from the north. Speed eight knots. All was smooth as Crazy Horse sailed across the emerald surface. I looked starboard, squinted, and could make out waves crashing on the misty shoreline. Their thunder had warned me they were there. Suddenly, I saw white water ahead. Hearing a wave crash to my left, I turned and saw white water rushing toward the boat. I panicked, "Fuck. What'd

I do?" I muttered. "There are waves breaking all around us. I gotta wake John. But I can't leave the wheel and go below."

I hit the window beneath my knees, hoping to awaken someone.

There was no response.

I pounded on the window. I screamed. "John, John. Wake up?"

After seconds that seemed like hours, the glass window slid open. "What's happening?"

"I need help. There's white water everywhere."

John sprang from the bunk and bound up the stairs three at a time. He jumped behind the wheel, pointing to a line behind me, and yelled, "Grab that sheet. Drop the main sail and hold on."

The sail hit the dock and slid into the churning white water. The boat swung sharply starboard. John started the diesel engine, thrust it into reverse, and went to full throttle. He swung back to port and for several minutes revved and cut the throttle, spinning the steering wheel from side to side like a Porsche racer at Le Mans. When the 70-foot sloop was free of the surging rapids, John calmly offered to take over the wheel. "It's about time for you to get off," he said, glancing at his watch. "Let Pulido sleep. Why don't you go below and make us some coffee."

Fifteen minutes later, I returned and handed John a steaming cup of black coffee. "Wish we had some brandy to put in this right now." I kidded. "You got us out of that just like you were on a seven-foot surfboard in a Doheny Beach curl not a 70- foot boat worth a million dollars in white water somewhere south of border,"

John smiled.

"I was being real careful," I said apologetically. "I really tried to stay away from the shore."

"It wasn't your fault." Pointing to the white water now safely off the stern, John continued. "A new sand bar has formed over there. It's not shown on the charts. It seems to be shaped like a crescent moon stretching down what was our port side and curving ahead ultimately joining the beach."

"Like Cabrillo Point in San Diego but underwater?"*

"Sorta, but Cabrillo Point has a lighthouse to warn you. The white water you saw was breaking on the sand bar. If we would have kept going straight we would have hit sand and been beached. I'm glad you woke me. You can't see shit," John grinned, "but you were a lifeguard long enough to know you have to ask for help when you're in trouble. Don't ever forget that, man."

I thought about my fear at Abre Ojos but remained silent.

All too slowly, I was learning that to recover I had to ask for help when I needed it, something I had rarely done before. A wave.

Sixty-Eight

Throughout the winter, I anticipated that the governor would appoint Court of Appeals Justice Reynoso to a vacancy on California's Supreme Court. In early spring, the Governor appointed Hastings College of the Law Professor Joe Grodin. Grodin was a former Teamster lawyer who worked with Byron and me at the Farm Labor Board. After announcing the appointment, Byron told me that because of our labor law background and my attendance at Hastings some think the governor appointed Joe Grodin at our request. "Grodin's our friend," Byron said, "but I know you also supported Cruz Reynoso for the Supreme Court position. I hope you'll tell your Hispanic friends to have patience. The governor agrees that Reynoso's a natural for the position, but he can't appoint anyone who's soft on crime."

"Byron, Justice Reynoso isn't soft on crime. Do people think that he's soft on crime just because he's Latino and was the director of California Rural Legal Assistance representing the poor? Are all civil rights lawyers and lawyers who represent the poor soft on crime?"

"If he had law enforcement support, he'd be the governor's next appointment to the high court."

That evening I called Olivia and told her what Justice Reynoso needed. Together, over the next several months, we let the word out. By summer, the Governor had received letters endorsing Justice Reynoso from the state's most powerful law enforcement groups.

*   *   *

One Saturday morning in January, I ran from the downtown condo I rented a couple blocks from the Capitol to the tiny house near Sacramento State College that Maria and Byron were renting from our ALRB friend Dan Stone. I think it was Byron finishing the Sacramento Marathon the previous September that led María to decide she was going to be a runner. We jogged from her house to Sacramento State. While crossing the nearly treeless campus, I told María I was taking the bus to Berkeley the next day to visit Olivia. "You guys are getting tight," kidded Maria.

"Too tight," I confessed.

"Come on, Mo. You need a woman to care about you."

"It scares me."

"You're scared of Olivia?"

"Naw. She's cool. It's just that getting too close to anyone scares me."

"Because of Kathy?"

"I guess. I got hurt real bad, twice. First she left me and went to Hawaii, and then, when we were getting close again, she dies."

We ran without talking. Finally, Maria stopped. I turned toward her and walked back. "Mo, I know a lot of bad stuff has happened to you. You've been incredible in overcoming most of it, but just like you wouldn't let your wreck stop you from trying to surf, you can't let losing Kathy stop you from being with a woman. Olivia is good for you. Take a chance. Just like you always tell us, what do you have to lose?"

Throughout the winter, when we weren't spending weekends gathering support for Justice Reynoso, Olivia and I were in Aptos. The city girl loved the fern covered creeks, the towering redwoods, and the freely roaming deer, rabbits, bluebirds, endangered three-toed salamanders, and even the slimy foot-long banana slugs. Most of all, she loved Adele Ellis. The single mom who lived across the dirt road where she had reared two near-perfect children Clarice and Mark.

One Saturday morning in June, I took the Greyhound from Sacramento to Oakland. Instead of meeting Olivia and continuing on Highway 17 to Aptos, we met and rode across the Bay Bridge, past the San Francisco airport, and rented a hotel room in Burlingame. We picked up my running number for the next morning's Sri Chinmoy Marathon, drove the portion of the route run on public streets, and loaded on pasta at an Italian restaurant in San Bruno.

Sitting in the darkness on a cement wall running along the San Francisco Bay outside the hotel, with the northerly blowing hard, Olivia cuddled against me to keep warm. Our rambling conversation turned to Olivia's family. "You know," I said, "as well as I know you, I know almost nothing about your family and how your mom ended up in LA."

Olivia smiled. "My grandfather, Rufino, came from Seville in Spain, they think. They say he was part of a royal family, but I think he might have been a gypsy. I'm not sure about my grandma. I think she was Spanish, too, or Arab, or maybe Spanish of Moorish blood. Maybe she was a gypsy. I'm sure I have gypsy blood in me from someone."

I smiled. "Do you still have family in Panama?""

"My grandparents still live in a pueblo northwest of Panama City. It's called Atalaya. All my mom's brothers and sisters are still there, too.

"What about your dad's side?"

"He was from El Salvador. My mom met him in Costa Rica. After they met, he came to the United States to work and within a few months went back to Panama and got my mom."

"And you grew up in Echo Park until you attended University of Southern California?"

"Si, mon."

"With that kind of homegirl talk you weren't one of the sorority girls, I'll bet?"

Olivia laughed. "During my senior year in high school I came closer to the California Youth Authority, the prison for kids, than to a sorority house. I had always been a goody- two-shoes, attending Catholic school and getting all A's. Then my senior year I almost blew it all." She paused.

"What happened?"

"I was hanging around with some pretty tough girls. Most of the kids in our neighborhood were Mexican, so even though my parents are from Central America I grew up as a Chicana. I wore lots of eyeliner and too much lipstick. My hair was puffed way out like a Chuca. I wore Levi's and a leather jacket and too much jewelry." Olivia stopped again, appeared to be thinking, and continued.

"I was going with a homeboy. He drove a 63 Chevy, all nosed, decked, real low. Really cool, but my grades fell from A's to incompletes. I don't know why college let me in after I fell apart academically in my senior year of high school. I guess the A average I had before caused then to realize I could do it"

"You must have done well on the College Entrance Exam, too,"

Olivia chuckled. "I think they called it that in the old days. By the time I took it, it was called the SAT. Yeah. I did okay on it. But I'd probably have gotten pregnant and been a housewife in East LA with four kids but for my friend Gloria."

"Tell me about her."

"You might know her mom and dad, Dolores and Joe Sánchez. They're really successful in business. They live in Los Feliz, a wealthy neighborhood not far from Echo Park."

"Joe Sánchez is the guy who helped the Union during the Imperial Valley strike, isn't he? The grocer who made sure the striking families had food?"

"Yeah. He's real close with César, and Dolores Sánchez publishes the largest Hispanic paper in the country in East LA.

Anyway, I went to school with Gloria since seventh grade. We were best friends. She was pissed when she saw me turn into a homegirl and she told me so. At first, I wouldn't listen, but she didn't give up. She got me to apply to college on the last day I could."

That night, for the first time, I told Olivia I really liked her. That was as far as I was able to go. I was too shy and had been too badly hurt when Kathy died to tell the woman I loved how I felt. I was falling for this Los Angeles homegirl. If only I could put my feelings into words, I thought. We learn a lot in our lives from our parents, from friends, from people we work with, but some of us never really learn to express how we feel.

*   *   *

Early the next morning, I stood five yards from the starting line when the sun slipped over the Oakland hills. Recollection of the fragrance of Olivia's silky black hair hypnotized me. The loneliness I had endured since Kathy left over five years before melted. I was blinded by the sun, but thinking about Olivia I didn't consciously realize I couldn't see. God, it was good being with the woman I love last night, I thought. Before my wreck I jumped into bed with too many sensuous women, believing what the books and movies said about the pleasure of body to body contact, no matter who you're with. But I learned last night that when I love the woman I'm kissing and touching, it's a different experience.

As my thoughts rambled, I heard the starting gun. Surprised, I sprinted the first mile through affluent Foster City in less than six minutes. Feeling relaxed, I slowed and comfortably finished five miles in thirty-two minutes. If I run seven-minute miles from here on, I thought. I'll break three hours. Last Sunday I ran 20 miles along the American River at that pace. I know I can do it.

As the sun moved higher in the sky, I unconsciously slowed down my pace, my mind drifting to a friend in Hawaii telling me

287

that real runners finish marathons under three hours. The rest of us are just joggers. I didn't run a marathon until I was almost 40, I thought. I've been trying to break three hours ever since. It's been my goal. I have to do it, but maybe I'm too old and I am just a jogger.

At mile 24 I was running on a bike path along the bay. Every muscle in my frail body throbbed. About to give up my goal of breaking three hours, in the distance I heard music corning from an African-American teenager fishing on the edge of the harbor. Beside him lay a portable radio playing the theme song from "Chariots of Fire."

I crossed the finish line in 2:57:12. A wave. I walked through the spectators to where I could be alone and cried. It was the third time I had cried in the past several years. Tears of joy had returned. Thanks to a kid fishing with his portable radio, I broke the three-hour mark; and I realized I was in love with Olivia the same morning.

After I ran, Olivia and I stopped at the hotel to shower and pick up our bags. While I checked out, the Front Desk handed me a message. "Please call the Governor immediately. Urgent."

I crossed the lobby to a pay phone. It was just afternoon Sunday.

"Where are you?" stormed the Governor.

"St. Francis."

"How soon can you get back?"

"A few hours, if I have a ride."

At 3 PM., Olivia dropped me off at the side of the capitol building. I kissed her good-bye and said I'd call and tell her what was going on. "After watching you, I'm not sure I want to be a lawyer," she said softly. "If the Governor isn't calling you at three in the morning to ask about a case, he's hunting you down and ordering you to get back to work on your rare day off."

I grinned. "I'll call you."

Sixty-nine

In December, Byron dropped me off at the Sacramento airport. I was flying to Honolulu for the marathon. On the way he told me he had talked with the Governor at his home the evening before.

I smiled, thinking about the tiny one-bedroom apartment across K Street from the capitol building that the Governor called home. The State's highest executive refused to live in the Nancy Reagan planned mansion on the American River miles east of the Capitol, Governor Brown felt it would be like the president of the United States working in the Whitehouse and living across the Potomac River on a Virginia plantation. It was too far from the Capitol for a working governor.

"... and since the State Bar found you qualified," continued Byron, "that vacant municipal court seat in Monterey County is yours, unless you're willing to recognize I've learned a little about the political survival of judicial appointments and let me recommend that the Governor appoint you to the bench in Los Angeles or the Bay Area where you won't have agri-business out to get rid of you from the day you start?"

"I'll think about it while I'm in Hawaii,"

My brother John met Olivia and I when we arrived in Honolulu. He took us to his condo near the yacht club in Waikiki. Sunday morning at 2:30, the alarm on my Casio awoke me. I yawned entering the kitchen where John and Olivia talked while John made coffee. I could hear the rain streaming onto the lanai. "What're we doing?" I complained to wide-awake John and Olivia. "I think we just went to bed."

"We gotta be at the park by 4:00 for the bus or it's a long walk to the starting line at Aloha Tower." John smiled. "I don't know about you, but I don't want to walk five miles in that downpour."

I chuckled. "So you're gonna take a bus five miles to avoid the rain so you can line up in the rain with thousands of other shivering bodies and run in the rain for twenty-six miles."

*   *   *

On Tuesday evening, Olivia and I were at the Honolulu air terminal. Our flight to San Francisco had been delayed several hours. "So now that you've finished law school and are a successful marathon runner, what are ya gonna do with your life?" I asked while Olivia and I carried cold beers to the cafeteria table.

"I don't know. I guess while I'm studying for the bar exam I'll keep working for legal aid in Solano County. There are a lot of poor people who need lawyers much more than the wealthy ones who can afford them."

"You sound like me ten years ago." I smiled. "It's hard to work full-time and study for the bar. Maybe you should come live with me while you're studying."

"Let me think about it."

*   *   *

Before December ended, I took the bus to Oakland to talk with Olivia. Sitting on the dock at Spencer's Fish Food on San Francisco Bay, I told her I was moving to Salinas. "Have you thought about living with me while you study for the bar?" I asked.

"Yeah. I want to, but you're going to be a judge. How can you be a judge in Monterey County and live with a Latina you aren't married to? Everyone in town will be talking about it."

"Who cares?

"I care. If they want to get rid of you because you fought to improve the living conditions of farm workers, let them. But I don't want them to throw you out because you brought a Chicana to town to live with."

290

"So what if we get married?"

"Are you proposing?"

"I guess. We can see a judge friend of mine right now and he'd marry us. We could move to Salinas and live together happily ever after."

That afternoon, Superior Court Judge Leach married Olivia and me. That evening, while sitting at Luis and Susanna López's kitchen table, I casually mentioned Olivia and I had married that afternoon.

"You fucker." grinned Luis. "Nothing in life's a big enough deal to celebrate for Mo Jourdane. Come on, huero (whitey). I have a bottle of tequila. We have to toast, even if we can't get drunk any more now that you're going to be a pinche judge, "Your Honor."

When Olivia and I arrived at our Aptos home during the early hours the following morning, Olivia looked at me and smiled teasingly, "Aren't you even going to carry me across the threshold to our wedding-night bed?"

I took the small Chicana, running my fingers through her long black hair, pulled her face to mine and kissed her deeply. "I love you, Olivia. Welcome to Aptos and the Jourdane family."

Seventy

In February, I was in Salinas to be sworn in to the Monterey County Municipal Court. A wave. I walked across the lawn surrounding the courthouse with Olivia, Shirley Treviño, Carlos Bowker, and Luis López, overwhelmed by the hundreds of farm workers chanting, "Que viva El Mo (Hurrah for Mo)," "Que viva el Juez (Judge)."We crossed the courtyard through which the Soledad Brothers had angrily shuffled in ankle chains and handcuffs 10 years before when charged with tossing a guard off the third floor walkway at Soledad prison, the courtyard through which César Chávez proudly walked in handcuffs when he chose nonviolence in his effort to obtain for farm workers the opportunity to freely choose their union.

We passed through the expansive tinted glass courthouse entrance and entered the hallway packed with hundreds of common folk I had assisted with their common problems. We made our way to Department One. When we reached the courtroom door, Olivia and I hugged our friends and slipped through the mob. Like Mexican, Filipino, Black, and White sardines packed in a nearby cannery row, my friends and former clients filled the courtroom. Stopping to speak with well wishers, I made my way to the counsel table. I was surprised and felt an inner warmth when I saw my old high school surfing buddies Jerry Perez and Jim Corlett sitting among the crowd. Off to my right I could see my mom, dad, brother and sister in the jury box with the special guests, California Supreme Court Justice Reynoso, and the Monterey County Judges I had appeared before as a fledgling attorney and was now to join.

*   *   *

At 8:00 AM. the following Monday, I took my place on the Monterey County bench, Department One of its Municipal Court. Twenty-seven arraignments were scheduled my first morning on the bench.

Within a year, the Governor elevated me to the superior court. One afternoon, I was presiding over a jury trial for a Vietnamese immigrant charged with unlawfully fishing with a gill net when the phone rang in the courtroom. My bailiff whispered to me that Olivia was at the hospital. I recessed the jury trial, ran several miles from the courthouse to Natividad Hospital, and coached Olivia through the birth of our four pound, seven ounce daughter, Jacquelyn Flores Jourdane. Jonathan Julio Jourdane followed her three years later. Waves of recovery.

Now, Jacquelyn is a twenty-three-year old graduate of UCLA. She is a graduate student seeking a master's degree and teaching or counseling credential. In high school she played tennis and softball. She is a Southern California beach girl, beautiful like her mother. Jonathan Julio is a twenty- year old junior majoring in economics at Stanford University. A couple years ago at the Kennedy Center in Washington D.C., he received top honors for Academic Excellence from the National Hispanic Heritage. Over the past two years. he has twice been the M.C./motivator at Stanford's all night dance marathon raising funds for seriously ill children, walked around the Stanford track for 24 hours to raise money for cancer research, and is currently a residential assistant who counsel's Stanford freshman, primarily women, in Otero dorm. In high school Jonathan ran cross-country and I still paddle out with him to surf at our favorite spots, Bahia Venado in Panama, Pleasure Point in Santa Cruz, and Sunset Cliffs in San Diego. When it's big, I watch him rip and slice the face of oncoming swells. On overhead waves in Panama last spring I watched and realized he's a better surfer than his dad ever was. Olivia is the Principal at an almost purely Latino elementary charter school in Southeast San Diego. With Linda and Carlos LeGerrette, Olivia helps organize Cesar Chavez Service Clubs in schools throughout the San Diego area.

Just before dawn on my 63rd birthday, Jonathan, my brother Tom's son David, and I left Happy Isle in Yosemite Valley. We crossed the Vernal Falls Bridge just after it grew light and continued hiking up the steep trail, stuttering through five or ten yards of boulders every hundred yards. A little over an hour later we crossed Nevada Falls where Olivia, Jackie, Jonathan, Olivia's niece Miriel, and I had seen a man plunge to his death a few years earlier. We continued climbing up, trying not to trip too often as we traversed about 100 yards of boulders, trudged through the sand the length of Little Yosemite Valley, hiked up the hill to the left climbing through boulder crammed switchbacks for another three miles, and arrived at the giant granite rise Jonathan calls The Wall.

Over my macho protests, after nearly falling to my death, I finally took Jonathan's hand and we climbed the narrow granite stairs etched into the rock, a thousand foot drop to the left, a two thousand foot drop to the right. After we reached the crest of the steep granite rise, we arrived at the base of the parallel cables ascending to the top of Half Dome. In ten foot durations, from pole to pole, over several hundred yards, we muscled our way up a rise that seemed like 85 degrees, but was probably closer to 60. The cables ended and before us was El Capitan and Yosemite Falls across the Valley floor thousands of feet below. A wave.

I know I am not the oldest person to climb Half Dome, but I would be surprised if many other one-eyed hikers have made it after the doctors swore they would be a vegetable if they lived the weekend. I thank God, my family, and my friends for making it possible, through their persistence, hard work, and confidence.

Like my confrontation with tragedy, Kathy too faced trauma. She didn't prevail because she chose not to do everything necessary to survive.

My family and friends, and the thousands of farm workers who struggle as part of the United Farm Workers, have shown me that with a little luck and a lot of faith and persistence you can do what many say is impossible. A long time ago, not long after my wreck, my brother Tom said, "Shit happens." Tom and the rest of our family, and our friends, did not let me lie around and feel sorry for myself. Together, they made sure I had short range goals I could reach and a long range goal, a reason to live. This forced me to remember that if we stay positive, everything has a good side, and with faith, persistence and effort, we can recover from anything. Like my mom taught us as children, If we don't demand things be perfect, but accept what is okay, we can move beyond every trauma that suddenly strikes. In the words of César Chávez and Dolores Huerta, who fought the toughest bullies on the block, we can do anything if we believe. ¡Si se Puede!

Afterword

In the mid 80's, Olivia and I moved to San Diego where I wrote legal opinions for the Court of Appeals. Olivia was a near-perfect mother and taught elementary school in a nearby public school. She is an expert in teaching children English who have a second language such as Spanish. Within 20 years, our daughter Jackie graduated as a history major with a minor in Education at UCLA and was named one of the outstanding teachers as Teacher of the Year in San Diego County. Jonathan graduated as an Economics major at Stanford University. He went to New Mexico to oversee Obama's presidential campaign in the area around Las Vegas, New Mexico. Olivia and I worked with him in the presidential campaign. After President Obama was successful, Jonathan joined his administration with the Interior Department in Washington D.C. Soon Jonathan learned that to get anyone to listen to you, you have to be an attorney. He attended law school in Boulder, Colorado. As a public defender in Durango, Jonathan is a Colorado lawyer representing primarily Navajo and Utes who have been charged with a crime.

With Jackie teaching in San Diego and Jonathan representing Natives in Colorado, Olivia no longer needs to remind me, "I want us to raise our children not in the streets like I was. Mo you were lucky to have your mom guide you in life to be a good person."

Several years later, in 2008, Olivia and I were on holiday in Italy. Staying for a few days in a bed and breakfast near Siena, Italy, we ran through the countryside. It was warm and clear. Suddenly I awoke one night with severe stomach pain. We decided it was time to go home. The flight from Rome to Newark seemed to last forever. About half-way, when I would do anything to sleep, I watched the television monitor and saw a PBS Special on changes in Washington D.C.'s Smithsonian Institute. The new additions to the Museum of American History included the Woolworths, a five-and-dime counter where on February 1,

1960, four African American students at an all-black college sat at the counter and ordered lunch. When the youths were denied service because, like much of the South, the Woolworths did not serve food to African American patrons, the students just sat there. The next day, they were joined by 15 more African American youths. When they too were denied service, they sat. As the days passed the number of youths sitting in continued to rise. They began the Civil Rights sit-ins that moved African Americans a step to equality.

A second new addition was the portable desk Thomas Jefferson used to write the Declaration of Independence.

I almost cried when I saw the third new exhibit. It was the cortito or the short-handled hoe.

"I can't believe that El Cortito case is in the Smithsonian. What a great honor to have banned a harmful tool that crippled farm workers. Now farm workers can stand tall and be proud of the work they do to feed us," commented Olivia.

When we arrived home, I immediately went to Scripps Hospital. A doctor found I had stage four stomach cancer. I began a series of chemotherapy sessions. Within a few months the cancer was gone, thanks to Doctor Banageer at Scripps Hospital and Olivia's care at home. Another Wave of Recovery.

Although the cancer had vanished the effect of my collision with the roiled tanker continued; repeated eye infections, teeth fractures and dead facial bones have kept Olivia and I busy with doctors.

After my cancer recovery, I agreed to go to Los Angeles and meet with Attorney General, Jerry Brown to look into why so many farm workers were dying in California fields from heat exposure. The evening before I left San Diego, Olivia and I talked. "So, what do you want to do about farm workers dying from the heat?" Olivia asked.

"Stop it," I replied. "When you see a problem, you have to stop it. California may need to strengthen standards and enforcement of safety standards,"

"There are public reports of six farm worker death cases in California this year," Olivia responded. "Since May 2008 when a 17-year-old pregnant immigrant from Southern Mexico died of heat exposure near Lodi, other farm workers have died working in 100 plus degrees in Santa Maria, Kern County, the Fresno area and Delano."

I reminded her, "the Labor Code requires all employers to provide employees with a safe and healthful place to work. The Attorney General has a duty to enforce California law and protect the public interest. I anticipate that an expanded investigation will lead to evidence that grower and farm labor contractor are failing to provide farm workers with safe and healthful work and a safe and healthful place to work."

Over the following weeks. Olivia and I learned that the effect of heat on the body is measured by the heat index. The heat index enables one to determine the impact of heat on the person by considering the person's metabolic rate considering the air temperature, humidity, radiation (direct sun) and wind speed. Generally, when the air temperature is one hundred degrees, a person working in the sun with a humidity of around 30% is working in a heat index of around 115 degrees. When the person's activity is at an elevated level, for example when the person is working on piece rate lifting grapes from the field to a truck, the metabolic rate is high and the effect of heat on the person is greater.

Olivia and I met with doctors in the Imperial Valley, San Joaquin Valley and Salinas Valley to discuss how heat causes illness, exhaustion, and stroke. Dr. Robert Harrison, a doctor at the University of California San Francisco agreed that when the heat index gets too high, work must stop to save lives. All the doctors

Olivia and I spoke with agreed that when it gets too hot, lives are in danger.

Olivia and I and the doctors talked primarily about a possible remedy. Dr, Harrison told us that he was on the OSHA standards board that set the 2005 standard. We discussed possible remedies. Doctor Harrison worked with Olivia and I to eliminate the problem. Doctor Harrison provided us with information, written material and testimony. He told us that during consideration of the current heat standard, he unsuccessfully advocated for a simple risk assessment as the trigger for employers allowing rest breaks for farm workers. The remedy he advocated was used by the United States Marine Corp to stop the death of recruits during training. It involved use of a heat index to measure temperature, humidity, and radiant heat or direct sun (the heat index). Under the Marine Corp. program, there is a simple chart that indicates how long and how many rest breaks are recommended. Rather than the recruits needing to ask for a rest break, it is up to the Marine Corp. to ensure that adequate rest breaks are taken.

Olivia and I were convinced that the evidence supported the Attorney General filing a civil lawsuit to compel OSHA to enforce its duty to stop employers from forcing workers to toil long hours, particularly when working at a piece rate that causes an extreme level of activity, in excessive heat.

"Just like we did to stop stoop labor that caused farm workers to suffer disabling back injury can't the attorney general sue and file a suit to stop death of farm workers from excessive heat in violation of Labor Code section 6400? The Attorney General could base the suit on the Marine Corp program that when the heat index is 85 or greater trainees are limited to light work with 15-minute rest an hour; at 85-88 degrees heat index workers must avoid strenuous exercise with breaks for 45-minute breaks. If the heat index is 90 or more degree all outdoor exercise must be suspended." explained Olivia.

Olivia and I recommended that the Attorney General issue a delegation of authority to file a lawsuit against OSHA based on employers' failure to provide employees with adequate rest breaks and cease working in extreme heat.

During the following winter returning home from a family ski trip to Lake Tahoe, I worked regularly at the Attorney General's office in downtown, San Diego. Meanwhile, Olivia shifted her legal and teaching skill to art. She started to call and email hundreds of friends and family to contribute to the making of the El Cortito mural in Chicano Park. The mural honors farm workers and tells the story of the banning of the dangerous tool, the short- handle hoe. In less than two months, she raised half the cost. However, the Chicano Park Steering Committee was not ready to lift their moratorium for not allowing any more murals in Chicano Park. It took over a year of Olivia's effort before the moratorium was lifted.

Since I retired from the courts Olivia and I have dedicated our lives to helping others. We travel up and down the southwest of the country sharing the story of El Cortito through a multimedia speaker series to community organizations, schools, colleges and universities.

Olivia and I encourage students, "When you see a problem get those affected, community activist and leaders involved to help you find a solution. A brave and courageous lawyer with activist at their side always helps justice to prevail." Leaders of the Farm Worker Movement have proven that with patience, when you work hard, love compassionately, and act humbly, you succeed.

Si Se Puede! Yes you can overcome obstacles in life.

The End

About the Author

Maruice "MO" Jourdane

Maurice "MO" Jourdane's journey unfolds as a tale of unwavering commitment and legal prowess. In his youth, Mo's passion and fervent desire for justice while surfing was spurred by encounters with icons like Cesar Chavez and Dolores Huerta in the late 1960s. This catalyzed his decade-long dedication to representing farm workers, first at the California Rural Legal Assistance (CRLA) and later at the Agricultural Labor Relations Board (ALRB). Attempt on his life has left him disfigured and seeking medical assistance since an oil rig shattered his path. Mo withstood to continue and served as legal counsel for Governor Jerry Brown, then donned the robe as a municipal court judge and then as a superior court judge relentlessly pursuing justice.

In San Diego, Mo led his legal crusade, championing causes like juvenile justice and labor rights. His three published books, "The Struggle for the Health and Legal Protection of Farm Workers: El Cortito, "Waves of Recovery" (overcoming horrific accident) and "The Soledad Children, The Fight to End Discriminatory IQ Tests" shed light on critical issues— farmworker protections and discriminatory practice.

Amidst his professional strides, along his side, is his partner Olivia Flores Jourdane, a formidable force who not only has helped maintain Mo's life but has assisted him as a spouse, editor, and author. She, too, has ensured that Mo's legacy will not be forgotten by managing the creation of an El Cortito Mural at Chicano Park in 2023. Their dedication as parents created two wonderful children, Jacquelyn Flores Jourdane, Teacher of the Year in San Diego County, and Jonathan Julio Jourdane, Colorado Attorney of Law, defending the rights of underrepresented people. Mo and Olivia continue their contribution to society living in San Diego.